BROKEN CHORDS

RYDER BROTHERS
BOOK 1

KAT SUMMERS

This book is a work of fiction from the author's imagination. Though inspired by the world around us, all of the characters, places, and events are fictional and not based on any one source. Any resemblance is entirely coincidental.

Broken Chords

Edited by EJL Editing

Cover by Kat Summers

For all the girls who went to a concert and thought, "maybe." May your rock star look your way.

DICKTIONARY

For those of you who want to find or avoid the spice in this book, you can find it here:

- Chapter 16/17
- Chapter 20
- Chapter 23
- Chapter 28/29
- Chapter 39

TW: There is a brief moment of sexual harassment in Chapter 18.

1

Ellie

"YOU HAVE SPENT the last four years thinking about your future post-graduation, but I implore you to be open to opportunities you may have never conceived of. If I stuck to my original plan, who knows where I would be? I certainly wouldn't have auditioned for some singing contest show no one had ever heard of. If I leave you with one thing today, it is this: spare enough room in your plans for dreaming," Cami Graham implores to me and my fellow graduates.

That shouldn't be too hard for me, considering I don't even have a pla, let alone a plan. I don't have any dreams, either, which may cause a problem. But who had time for dreaming and planning when you were getting your bachelor's and master's in only five years. Any time not spent studying was used on extracurriculars, sleeping, and, you know, having a social life.

They—whoever 'they' is—say these are the best years of our lives. And I made the most of them while still being the high achieving oldest daughter everyone expected me to be. That isn't to say I didn't run through the fountain naked after too many peach schnapps shooters sophomore year, but I managed to balance my need for scholarly validation and my FOMO.

As I sit here, half listening to the commencement address from the reality-TV-star-turned-talk-show-host I should be fangirling over, I am struck by an overwhelming sense of dread. It is finally dawning on me that I have to enter the 'real world.' Dun dun dunnnnnn.

The thought makes me shiver in my gown despite the stifling air in this overstuffed auditorium. I prolonged graduation as much as I could without taking a fifth undergrad year, choosing to tack on a master's degree. The idea of needing an extra year to graduate and not being the overachiever my family expected gave me hives.

I don't want to seem cliché, but my parents are a huge reason I worked hard. Partially because I didn't want to disappoint them, but mainly, I didn't want to become them. *Not* being a cheater with a superiority complex like my dad should be easy, but avoiding Mom's flaws is more nuanced.

As much as I love Clara O'Leary Compton, a role model, she is not. I don't blame her for the mess she was after Dad left. But I never wanted to be in her position: a stay-at-home mom with no job history or skills forced to rely on alimony until she remarried. I could have lived without constant complaints about Dad's financial security. He may be an ass, but he is a workaholic ass who worked for that money.

I will *never* need a man to support me. That is another reason I put so much effort into school. No matter what happens to my relationships, I will always be able to support myself thanks to my education.

Not that I have been in many relationships, unless you count the few boys I went out with in high school or the three months I dated Tyler Geiger freshman year of college. I was too busy and too cynical for a long-term relationship. No man could ever live up to the fantasy. That's what happens when you grow up watching a dysfunctional marriage and perfect boys next door. I'll stick to fictional men, thanks.

As much as my education gives me a leg up, I won't be able to support myself at all, if I don't decide what I want to do with my degrees. I've been anxious about what comes next since the time my junior year internship adviser asked me what I wanted to do with my life. The question stressed me out so much I promptly applied for the dual master's program that gave me an extra year to stay in school.

Now my time has run out and I need to pick a direction. I know I want to work in fashion, but I don't know in what lane. I have always loved clothes and helping people gain confidence from their outfits. I thought I would enjoy being a stylist, but I hated my internship working as one. I spent more time catering to clients' emotions than I did picking out clothes.

I enjoy the business side of fashion as much as the styling. Analyzing trends, understanding markets, and audience demographics has always come naturally to me. I think I would make a good buyer, but those jobs are hard to find, especially in Nashville. I'd have better luck in New York or LA.

"Hey," the girl beside me whispers as she elbows me. "Our row is next."

Whoops. In my revelry, half my class got their diplomas. At least I didn't miss seeing my best friend, Lainey. I don't want to miss her walk across the stage. Shoutout to the alphabet gods that her last name isn't Jones or something earlier.

Shooting my seatmate an apologetic grin, I make my way onto the stairs. Sensing eyes on me, I chance a glimpse away from the steps and catch my bestie waving at me frantically. An involuntary smile spreads across my lip. I love that girl. Lainey Ryder is the definition of a ride-or-die. We've been attached at the hip since we met over a decade ago after she and her family moved next door. Together we have faced it all: our first periods, geometry, crushes, and almost getting caught by campus police during the previously peach schnapps-fountain incident.

Lainey is the chaos to my order. The Phoebe to my Monica. The "we'll figure it out as we go" to my minute-by-minute itinerary. Despite our differences, or maybe because of them, we work. She has always been my number one supporter, and I've been hers.

Once the ceremony wraps up, she practically tackles me in the lobby of the performing arts center.

"We did it!" she shouts, startling an elderly man beside us. I offer him a contrite grimace before pulling her closer to the wall and away from the mass of grads and families searching for one another.

"We did it, babe." I echo. "I'm proud of you."

"We both know without you, I wouldn't be here."

"Don't sell yourself short. You did the work. I simply helped you stay on track and motivated."

Lainey is beaming and I understand why. A lot of people didn't think she would make it here. She tends to be indecisive, as demonstrated by her three major changes. I knew when she found her passion, she'd kick it into gear. And I was right. Once she settled on fashion design, she threw herself into her coursework. After a victory lap, she's leaving here with her degree.

Unlike Lainey, I knew what I wanted to study from day one. Thanks to that conversation junior year, I'm walking out with an MBA alongside my fashion merchandising bachelor's. As much as I wanted to follow my passion, I also wanted something that gave me flexibility for my future. Plus, the MBA stopped my dad from constantly harping my ear about getting a 'respectable' degree.

Not that I have any idea what I want to do. But I'm not thinking about that today. Today I am celebrating my accomplishment. What I should do next is future Ellie's problem, and she is not here. Today Ellie is ready to let her hair down and celebrate.

"Are your parents here?" Lainey asks.

"They're around here somewhere."

"Both of them?"

"Mhmm."

"Together?"

I shoot her a disbelieving expression. "Of course not. Mom is here with Todd and Dad is here alone, hopefully. We are all supposed to grab lunch, though. But I have my doubts everyone will be in attendance. I'm surprised your parents haven't hunted you down already."

"Me, too. They have been acting weird today. Even Bryce is being cagey. They were supposed to video me walking to show the superstars. Jack bet Gray $500 bucks I wouldn't make it on time. Jokes on him. Gray said he'd have a surprise for me if I made sure he won and you know I am not above bribery."

Bryce, Jack, and Grayson are three of Lainey's brother's, along with Declan. They're all older except for Bryce. Considering how wealthy her older brothers are and how much they dote on her, there is no telling what that bribe could be.

"I wonder what the surprise is. Maybe they finally got you the teacup pig you always wanted."

"Don't tease, Ellie! You know that would make my life," she pouts. I'm only half-joking. I wouldn't put it past Jack to get her the pig she's been begging for as long as I've known her. I'm not sure he's ever told her 'no' on anything.

"There they are!" she points behind me. I turn around in time to the two of my favorite people walking over.

"There's my baby! I can't believe you graduated! It seems as if you were driving that Barbie Jeep over Bryce just last week." Mama C cries, engulfing her daughter in a hug. She is definitely where Lainey gets her dramatics from.

"I'm not the baby," my bestie mumbles. I hear the smile in

her voice. Bryce may have taken her spot as the youngest Ryder, but you'd never know with how they all treat her.

"You, too, honey," her mother directs to me, ignoring her daughter's protest. "We know how hard you worked."

"Thank you, Mama C." I sink into the warmth of her embrace as she hugs me next. I love my mom, but she was too preoccupied by her rocky marriage and then dating to nurture me the way Lainey's mom did. Our relationship was more of a friendship, forcing me to parent myself far sooner than I should have. Luckily, I had a safe space at the Ryder's house where I could retreat and be a kid.

A heavy hand lands on my shoulder, and I peer up to see Lainey's dad. "You done good, Ellie girl. Your last check is in the mail," he says with a wink. It's been a long-standing joke on his part that he paid me to be friends with his daughter to keep an eye on her. He would take away my imaginary salary if he knew about the schnapps incident, but what he doesn't know won't hurt him.

"I'm going to go find my parents," I say to my second family. Normally, I never want to leave them, but watching the love between them makes me crave a similar moment with my family. "I'll see you tonight, right, Laines?"

"Ten p.m. sharp!"

I fight to hold back my eye roll. The day Lainey is on time for something is the day I play the lottery.

Pushing through the crowd, I stand on my tip toes searching for my mom or dad. When my calves get tired, I pull out my phone to call them. Switching it off 'Do Not Disturb,' I am greeted by several texts.

12:16 PM

Congrats on graduating, E! I'm sorry I couldn't make it. Drinks on me when I get leave to come home.

I snort. My brother turned twenty-one a few months ago. He can barely get himself a drink. My heart sank when I found out he wasn't able to attend. Not because I care if he saw me walk, but because I haven't seen him since Christmas and won't see him again until later this summer. Finn attends the Naval Academy and is taking part in some specialized training this summer.

I send him a 'thank you' back and scroll back through my messages as one from Dad pops up.

Hey, kiddo. You looked great up there with all those chords. I know I said I'd go to lunch, but I've got to hit the road. One of my clients is having a crisis with customs allowing his dogs into the UK. You know how these celebrities can be about their pets. Rain check!

Letting out a sigh that is equally annoyance and relief, I ignore his message and text Mom where to find me. Dad isn't expecting a reply. This is nothing new for us. My father isn't what you would call reliable unless you are one of his clients. He loves me as best he knows how, but he's missed or left early from almost every important event in my life, even before the divorce.

I think being the youngest of five played a role in his inability to care about anyone but himself. When you are catered to your entire life by your family and then your wife, it's easy to see how that could warp your view of the world. It's a wonder he can be responsible for other people when he never had to be responsible for himself. I try not to hold it against him, but I also don't set my expectations high.

I deeply love both my grandparents, but they had their hands full with a house of seven. I can relate to kids raising kids. I tried to ensure Finn didn't end up spoiled like Dad. I think I did a good job even if, like Dad, he left home as soon as he could.

Finn went into the military while my dad left to get a taste of the rock and roll lifestyle. He bounced around until settling in Nashville after meeting my mom and becoming a tour manager for some of the biggest names in country music. Honestly it's a miracle my parents stayed married as long as they did if the stories I've heard about the tours he's been on are true.

That can't be blamed on his parents. I thought my Irish Catholic grandmother was going to have a heart attack when she found out about the divorce. Thankfully, she did not because I want more time with the spitfire. I am envious of all the extra time my cousins have gotten by living close to her. She was supposed to come today, but she broke her foot carrying a garden gnome.

Thoughts of my father and childhood kill the warm fuzzies I got from the Ryders, by the time I finally spot my mom plowing through the crowd, her new husband Todd trailing behind. The silver lining of Dad's departure is lunch will be much less awkward.

DID I say lunch would be less awkward? L-O-L. Mom was in rare form, oohing and aahing over my accomplishments and how hard she worked to get me there. I don't recall a single time she helped me with a project or checked my homework, but I don't point that out. I also say nothing about her sacrificing for my education in the hard times even though Dad is the one who paid for my private school tuition. I learned at a young age that it is easier to let Mom live in her delulu fantasies.

After the longest meal of my life, I am ecstatic to head back to my apartment to get a much needed nap before my night out with the girls. Plugging my phone into the charger, I cue up my favorite ASMR audio and drift off to sleep to the sound of a deep, soothing voice.

2

TIPPING MY HEAD UPWARD, the tension in my muscles slowly loosens as the water cascades down my body. One night in my own bed and a hot shower, I'm a new man. As smooth as our driver is when we're on tour, there is nothing that beats a stationary bed, especially when it costs as much as mine did. One night alone has already corrected months of strain.

Even though I love touring, I can admit it is nice to be home for a few days. Especially when I'll get to fill those days with my sister, Lainey. Despite touring with two of my brothers, Lainey is the sibling I am closest to. Maybe it's because I spend *too much* time with my brothers.

After forming a trio before we hit puberty, Declan, Grayson, and I rode around Texas playing county fairs, rodeos, and anywhere else that Mom could get to take us. At one show, a producer for a kids' TV network was in the audience. A few auditions later, we moved to Nashville to spend the next few years filming *Along for the Ryde* before launching into a music career.

I used to feel guilty about uprooting Lainey's childhood, until I realized she thrives in chaos the same way I do. My love language is stirring the pot and she is my favorite victim. Despite all the shit I give her, I am proud as hell of her for graduating. I know I wouldn't have had it in me to make it through college. Hell, I didn't even have to go to real high school, and I still struggled.

I'd never admit it, but one of the best parts of our show ending was that I didn't have to attend set school anymore. I got my GED to make my mom happy and then called it a day on my education. Don't get me wrong, I still learn things every day, but things like chords to our new song or the difference between whiskey and bourbon.

Atypical childhood aside, my life has been awesome. The Ryder Brothers, as our band has officially known, has been going nonstop since our first album was released almost eight years ago. Three double platinum records, eight CMAs, and one documentary later, the Ryder Brothers are a household name. If I had my way, we'd go straight to the studio after this tour to record the next album. Unfortunately, it isn't up to me.

Declan and Grayson are tired of our two year album write-record-tour cycle. I get the vibe that they're itching for something new. How they aren't fulfilled by a nationwide tour of the country album that won us a Grammy is beyond me. They talk about other goals they have which is great, but where does that leave the band? Where does that leave me?

Shaking my head to clear the heavy thoughts, I wrap a towel around my waist and I step out of the shower. During my extensive mustache maintenance routine—it takes more care than you'd think—I see our brother chat light up.

8:53 AM

DEC

Will you be ready by 10? We're going to stream
the ceremony at the restaurant. That way when
Lainey gets there we'll be in position for the
surprise.

He sent it to the group, but I know he's asking me. Grayson
is chronically punctual. Mom says Grayson has been on time
since the day he was born, coming at midnight on his due date.
The fact that my sister and I rarely run on time drives him crazy.
It drives Dec mad, too, but that's because he's a control freak.

GRAY

Lainey still doesn't know, right?

DEC

As long as Jack didn't spill the beans.

You know I love a good surprise. I want to see
her face when she sees us at lunch. And yes,
I'll be ready at 0100 hours sharp, drill sergeant.

DEC

0100 is not ten o'clock. *sigh*

Call me whatever you want as long as you're
ready.

I'll be at your door at ten. If you aren't outside I
am dragging your ass out no matter what state
it is in and you can explain to the PR team why
you were around town in a towel.

Sir, yes, sir!

GRAY

Don't call him, Sir, J. You know he enjoys that
too much.

DEC

Why do I put up with you two?

See you in an hour.

As much as I joke with my brothers, I love them. We may all have distinct personalities, but it is part of what makes us successful. We each know our roles and stay in our own lane.

Before getting dressed, I know I am going to need caffeine to deal with Declan's grumpy face, and I know for sure he won't stop on the way. Reaching into the back of my bottom cabinet, I pull out my single serve coffee maker. It looks ridiculous sitting next to the overly expensive machine on my countertop Lainey insisted that I get. Something about, 'If you're going to be a rich asshole, I should at least be able to get a premium cup of coffee when I stay at your place.'

I pointed out that I could buy *her* a fancy espresso machine, but she declined. She claimed that it was already hard enough living in the dorms as the 'Girl Ryder.' She didn't need the extra heat of a thousand dollar coffee maker, which is fair, I guess. I also think she uses it as an excuse to drop by more often. It's cute she won't admit she misses me and instead 'drops by for coffee.' I'll carry the secret of my second machine to the grave.

Even though we spend a lot of time away from Lainey and Nashville, when I am home, she and I get together often. And when I'm not in town, I still catch her at my place on my security cameras. I don't mind that she uses it to escape college life occasionally. Plus, I get a kick out of hiding the life-size cut out of Dad we got for his birthday around the house for her to stumble upon. Her reactions are hilarious. Hopefully, surprising her at her graduation lunch will be as good.

SURPRISING LAINEY WAS one of the highlights of my year. She shrieked so loud when she came in that it left my ears ringing.

It's a miracle no other patrons called 9-1-1. The hug she gave me made the potential hearing loss worth it.

She'd never say it, but I know us being there meant a lot to her. She wears a sassy facade, but she has always seemed more relaxed when we're around, even if we tease her. She gives it as good as she gets. She had to, with three older brothers and one younger one.

Growing up as our little sister was hard for her. Lainey never knew if people were her friends because they genuinely liked her or they were trying to get to us. We were all relieved when she found a group of girls to surround herself with in school who didn't care who she was related to. It helped that one of those girls had been her best friend since they were in elementary school.

With our filming schedule, Ellie was at our house more than we were growing up. She and Lainey were attached at the hip from the moment they met. The two attending college together was no surprise. Where there is one, the other is nearby. I take credit for their friendship since I technically met Ellie first.

Because of the girls' friendship, Ellie is in a lot of my memories of early success. I could always count on her to soften Lainey's sass, but they both never let our fame get to our heads. It's hard to get too cocky when your little sister and her friend make you attend tea parties. I used to joke that Ellie was the only girl who'd ever want the real me. And she told me our music was only okay, and we were no Jesse McCartney. I teased her about that for years while also intentionally never introducing the two.

There was always something special about Ellie. She was whip smart, kind, and put together in a way I never was. Even as a sixteen-year-old with a hit TV show, I was intimidated by the twelve-year-old next door who read books bigger than my head for fun. I could barely get through our weekly scripts and child actor math. I was drifting through life happily while Ellie had binders filled with magazine clippings and vision boards.

It must have worked for her since the last I heard she was graduating with an MBA. Due to our touring schedule and the girls no longer living on my parents' cul-de-sac, I haven't seen Ellie in years. She should be at the graduation celebration we are on our way to, and I'm looking forward to razzing her up after all this time. Her pale complexion always turned the brightest pink.

When we enter the bar and I spot her, I am not prepared for what I see. Last time I laid eyes on her, she was a fresh-faced eighteen-year-old and we were riding high off our second CMA win. Lainey brought her along to the awards afterparty and my brothers and I had to warn more than a few guys away from the pair as they enjoyed themselves. Later in the night, Declan tucked them into one of his spare bedrooms and that was the last time I saw her in person.

I've seen a few photos on Lainey's social media, but those pictures don't do justice to the beauty in front of me. With creamy white skin and pale blonde hair, there is something ethereal about Ellie. If you told me she was descended from Gaelic fairies, I wouldn't be surprised. The pale pink dress that seems to float around her only adds to that image.

I have to actively pull my jaw off the floor to stop checking her out. Lusting after Lainey's best friend and my de facto little sister is not cool. If only my body could get on board with that. Maybe it's time to reevaluate our no groupie policy on the tour because being hard up is the only logical reason I am having these thoughts right now.

As if she can feel the weight of my stare on her, Ellie glances up and locks eyes with mine. Falling into her crystal depths, I am transported back to the first time I met her, a lifetime ago when I wasn't Jack Ryder, but simply a boy meeting a girl.

AFTER TELLING *Mom how bored I was with all our stuff still in boxes, she suggested 'get my energy out' walking through the field behind our new house. Trudging through the tall grass, I hear a squeak as I trip over something. Not something, someone I realize.*

"Are you okay?" I ask, when I right myself. Glancing to where the noise originated, big blue eyes stare up at me through a curtain of white blonde hair.

"You're new," her soft voice says when the sound of a buzzing bee breaks our locked gazes.

Without speaking, I grab her outstretched hand in mine pulling her up to her feet from the patch of weeds I knocked her into. She's younger, younger than me, anyway. I'd put her around the same age as my sister, though she is a bit taller and far more angelic than rough and tumble Lainey.

"Who are you?" I ask.

"Who are you? I can't give my name to a stranger," she replies. Fair.

"I'm Jack. I live here."

"Hi Jack, I'm Ellie. I live here, too."

"Here?" I question pointing to the new house my family moved into a few days ago. We've been out of the house a lot meeting with people at the studio, but I think I'd remember a pretty blonde fairy living in our house.

"No, silly. Next door. We used to have a field like this in our yard, but my mom and dad put a pool in the backyard. Mrs. Jonas let me come out here to pick flowers since mine were gone."

I'd rather have a pool than a field, but based on her pout, I don't think she'd agree.

"What do you need flowers for?" I ask. Grayson says I'm nosy, but Mom says I have a curious mind.

"'Cause they're pretty and they make my mommy happy." Thrusting

her hand in my face, I take in the ones she's collected before asking the more interesting question. "Is your mom sad?"

"Sometimes. Usually when she's sad, Dad brings her flowers and presents and she gets happy again. But he's been gone for a while. They were yelling on the phone last night and she's been in her room all day crying."

I nod my head in understanding. Not that I do, really. But at thirteen you think you have life figured out and one thing I know for sure it's that girls crying is bad. For that reason, and to see a smile across her rosy cheeks, I decide to help Ellie.

"C'mon. I see some red flowers on a bush over there. I'll help you reach them."

"You will?" she asks excitedly. I nod my head.

"Thanks, Jack."

"You got it, Wildflower." She blushes at the nickname and I think the color is prettier than all the flowers in the world.

THE TRANCE between Ellie and I is broken when Declan draws her into a conversation. For a brief moment, I wonder if we both drifted back to the same memory. There is no way Ellie's mind is on me tonight, with everything else going on.

Escaping to the bar to grab a much needed drink, I can't stop my gaze from shifting to Ellie all night. I haven't seen her in years, but the thought of going a year, a month, or even a minute without seeing her again stirs something unpleasant inside me. That burning sensation in my gut only grows when I see her laughing and smiling with my brothers. I want to be the one to draw that reaction, any reaction out of her. God, that sounds insane.

Not so insane that I don't follow her when she breaks off from the crowd to go to the bathroom. I thought girl's always did that shit together? Is it safe for her to go alone? Safety. That's why I'm trailing behind her in this bar like a total creep. What kind of big brother would I be if I didn't watch over Lainey's friend? It's a weak argument, but I don't have time to think of a better one when Ellie walks directly into my chest exiting the ladies' room. Unlike my earlier memory, she remains upright this time.

"Whoa there," I grunt, taking the bulk of the impact as my hands wrap around her waist to keep her upright. Which was a mistake because every part of my body touching hers lights up with electricity. Has anyone ever felt this good in my arms? Letting her fall would almost be worth not asking myself that question. But then she could have gotten hurt and I can't have that.

"Oops," her sweet voice lilts as I take a step away, allowing her to stand on her own.

Now that I'm not right on top of her, I can see her in finer detail. The glimpse I got across the bar is nothing compared to this. Of course a fashion major would pick a dress that somehow accentuates all her curves without showing too much skin.

Her outfit is a perfect mix of classy and sensual. The combination is lethal on my nervous system since I haven't managed to say anything after my initial grunt. No greeting, no asking if she is okay, just staring at her as if she's the first woman I've seen in years. And maybe she is.

No. No, she isn't. She's Ellie—Lainey's Ellie. She is not someone for me to lust after no matter how hard I'm having to bit back the groan at the perfect flush of her cheeks that travels down her chest. I wonder how far—no! I have got to get it together.

Darting my eyes up her body, trying to take in as little as possible, I meet her glassy-eyed stare. A mix of shyness and confidence glimmers in her gaze. There is a hint of shyness or apprehension there as well. Though, I'm not sure why.

"Hi rock star," she states when I still haven't said anything else. I usually cringe at that term, but from her lips, it's a call back to the days she and Lainey would tease us for our heart-throb status. "Thanks for catching me."

Clearing my throat, I finally manage to rush out some words. "Yeah, always. I mean, of course. I'll never let you fall."

I'll never let you fall? What am I saying? I take it back. I was better off not talking. I'm supposed to be the smooth Ryder. Jesus Christ.

Thankfully, Ellie either doesn't notice or doesn't care about my weird declaration. She's a couple of drinks in. I'm sure that helps.

"Are you having fun?" I ask, regaining my composure.

"Sure am. It's the last night before life gets real. I'm making the most of every moment."

As I roll her statement over in my mind wondering what it could mean, her hand lands on my arm. "Are you having fun?"

Ellie squeezes my bicep, watching her hand as if it is someone else's. Her eyes widen when I flex under her touch before answering her. If I didn't know better, I'd think she was trying to flirt with me.

"It's nice being able to go out. It's been a minute. We're usually too tired to do much after our shows on tour."

"Tour," she repeats as if it is foreign word. Suddenly, she yanks her hand back and fiddles with her fingers in front of her. She went from bold to uncomfortable. I don't like that. I hate when other people are uneasy around me.

"That dress is gorgeous," I comment in an attempt to distract her from whatever spiral she's going down and it does the trick. Tipsy, smiley Ellie is back.

"Thanks! It's been in my closet for ages but I kept saving it for a special occasion. When I saw it today I decided I deserved to feel pretty."

Ellie twirls around to show off the dress and almost knocks into someone passing through the hall. This time, I grab her arm instead of her waist.

"You're always pretty, Wildflower," slips out before I can stop it. Did my filter break? Ellie and I haven't talked about the night we met ever. In fact, she swore me to secrecy before we parted ways. Her parents didn't allow her to venture into the field alone and she didn't want to get in trouble. I told everyone I met her playing in her front yard and it's never been brought up since.

I used to call her the nickname as a taunt that I had one of her secrets. It was the perfect leverage to get her to keep Lainey in line. As we grew older and drifted our separate ways, I forgot about it until tonight. Now, the desire to have more of her secrets wars in my chest as she peers at me through her lashes, lip worried between her teeth.

My mind is scrambling for something, anything to say when her friend Macy steps into the hall.

"There you are!" she shouts. "Lainey convinced the DJ to play our song next. Let's wobble, baby."

As Ellie edges past me, her floral scent floats in the space she vacated. With a final glance at me over her shoulder and a soft smile she disappears into the mass of bodies on the dance floor. I don't know when I'll see her again, but the prospect of it not being soon sits uncomfortably in my chest.

3

Ellie

"WE ARE SO PROUD OF YOU," Alexis gushes as we dance at Palmetto's. The bar is filled with new grads living our best college lives one final time.

"We?" I raise my eyebrow. I would typically assume she means her and Macy, but she could be referencing her NBA-playing boyfriend. With the Knights out of the playoffs, he was able to party with us, too. He may be a basketball superstar to most, but to us he's the guy who simped over our roommate until she finally relented and went out with him.

Alexis and Aiden are a perfect pair. They make every relationship I've ever been in seem like an elementary school crush. It doesn't help that they are both tall and beautiful. I'm no slouch, but Alexis is model tall. The world is not ready for the D1 babies these two will produce.

"Her and I, obviously," Macy states as she saddles up beside us. "You earned two degrees in the same amount of time most people get one. That is worth celebrating!"

Macy's no nonsense tone tells me she knows my head has been a mess about my next move and she isn't tolerating any self doubt. And I love her for it. As much as I plot and plan, I would have been lost these past few years without my girls. The four of us, Alexis, Macy, Lainey, and I were put in a dorm together freshman year and we've been inseparable ever since.

I offer Macy a smile because I am proud of my accomplishment, even if getting two degrees was a decision I made out of fear. I never told anyone that, and I doubt I ever will.

Macy passes me a vodka pineapple and I happily sip. "Lainey isn't here yet?" I question searching for the fourth member of our group.

"Not yet," Alexis replies. "She said she had a surprise coming with her, though."

The infamous surprise. Before I have time to wonder what it is, the energy of the entire bar shifts. I peer around for the cause and my chest squeezes at the answer. Sauntering into the room is Lainey flanked by four dark-haired, handsome men. I recognize all of them instantly, even little Bryce who is not little anymore.

"Girlies!" Lainey yells, bouncing over to us. "Look who decided to surprise me for graduation."

The resemblance between the siblings is uncanny. Despite the scruff decorating some of the men's faces, they all have dark eyes, strong brows, and Greek noses so perfect they would make a statue jealous. Bryce and Jack break off for the bar while the other two head our way.

"Hi, ladies," Grayson greets. "Long time, no see."

"Hi!" Macy and Alexis shout in unison. It takes me longer to recover as my eyes followed Jack, Lainey's middle brother. The one I spent the most time around as a kid and the one who gave me my first heartbreak, even if he didn't know it.

"Congratulations," a voice says from beside me. Turning, I notice Declan has made his way over to me. He may be the youngest of the trio, but he is the most serious. Grayson and Jack adopted more causal attitudes after their mother while Declan is all Daddy Ryder. He has an air of dominance that somehow makes him instantly comforting.

"Thank you," I reply. "We didn't know y'all were coming."

"It's not every day your little sis graduates from college. We wanted to support Lainey. She'll have to show you the video of us surprising her. It was priceless."

As I speak with Dec, I can't help but notice jealous glares aimed my way from around the room. If only those wearing it knew I'd know the man over half my life and had nothing but platonic feelings toward him. If only I could say the same for his brother.

Risking a glance, I seek out Jack among the crowd. I almost audibly groan once I take him in. Wearing faded jeans, boots, an open short sleeve button up, and his signature ball cap, he is making country boy chic happen. His hair is longer than it used to be and he is rocking a Tom Selleck stache. It's not my usual taste, but it *really* works for him.

Alexis and Aiden are laughing at something he said. He always had that ability. He effortlessly charms everyone in whatever room he is in. It's a skill I've admired. It's not that people dislike me, but the words 'intense' and 'high-strung' have been used to describe me on more than one occasion. It must be nice to be easy going and not focused on a million things at one time.

Even though he gives off a carefree, lovable vibe, I can see the insecurity it masks. I've always seen Jack. Of all the Ryders, he is the one who cares the most about being liked as if his existence is validated by those around him. After years in the spotlight, he thankfully doesn't care what strangers think of him, but it has made the opinions of those he does care about weigh more heavily.

As if he can sense my stare on him, his gaze rises and locks onto mine. Neither of us breaks it for a long moment until he winks and returns to his conversation.

"What are your plans now that you've graduated?" Declan asks, reminding me he is there. If he found my staring contest with his brother odd, he doesn't let on. I pray the lights in the club are dark enough he doesn't see my pinkened cheeks.

"That's the million dollar question," I sigh. "I was so focused on earning the degree, I didn't exactly make plans on what to do with."

"What do you want to do?"

"A million things. Nothing. Everyone keeps telling me I have endless options, but the issue with endless options is how to narrow it down. I have all these expectations on me now and not the faintest plan on how to meet them. It's kind of crippling."

I let out a humorless laugh. "I'm sorry, I don't mean to dump on you. That is probably not what you were expecting when you asked."

"It's alright. I've been told I am easy to talk to. You sound a bit like Lainey before she finally settled on her design major. Do you know what helped her?"

"Jägermeister and a Phi Delta party?"

"I don't think I want to know what that means." He grimaces. "And no, time."

"Unfortunately, I don't have much of that. The longer I am unemployed, the more people will wonder why and the more annoying my dad will become."

Declan ponders this for a moment before he settles something in his mind. "What if you had a job, a temporary one, that bought you time to figure out your next move? Something most people would call you a fool to pass up."

"That would be nice, but I haven't found that on LinkedIn."

"What are we chatting about over here?" Grayson asks as he joins the two of us. "I recognize the look of Declan when a plan has formed."

"I was about to offer Ellie a job on the tour," Declan replies.

"You were?" I question. "Doing what exactly?"

"Merchandising assistant. Shonda is constantly saying she needs more help with the merch."

"You want me to help sell merch on the tour?"

"No, I mean yes, technically. Shonda does oversee all that, but she is also in charge of the set up and styling of the area. Plus, she chooses the items we have available on tour and in our store. The tour goes on for another three months, so you would have plenty of time to get something lined up when it ends."

"Wow. Thank you so much for the offer. I'm not sure I am cut out to be on a tour, though. I know y'all are used to it, but it is kind of intimidating doing it alone."

"Lainey will be there," Grayson supplies.

"She will?"

"That was another part of our surprise. This is probably our last chance to all travel together with Lainey graduating and Bryce starting to do his own thing. And the first chance we have as adults without Mom and Dad over our shoulders. Bryce is going to help the sound engineers, and Lainey is going to work with the stylists."

"That's perfect for her," I state. Lainey has been searching for a way to get her foot in the door as a stylist, and this is a great opportunity for her.

"You don't have to decide right now," Declan informs me. "We have this week off and are playing at a music festival next weekend. We kick the end of the tour off Memorial Day Weekend and that is when Lainey will join us. Talk it over with her and whoever else you want, but the job is yours if you want it."

"I don't know what to say. Thank you."

"Of course, Ellie Bellie," Grayson coos. "You're almost as much of a little sister to us as Lainey. It's going to be a blast getting to know the adult version of you. Put it out of your mind tonight, though. You're supposed to be celebrating!"

"You got it, Gray," I say, giving both brothers a squeeze. "I'll let you know soon."

Rejoining my girls, I spend the rest of the night drinking, dancing, and pretending tomorrow will never come.

4

Jack

FLOPPING into the overstuffed office chair, I snag the freshly opened water bottle in Grayson's hand and take a sip. Sending me a quick glare, he grabs a new one while we wait for the rest of our team to join.

Unlike the first night spent in my bed, I had a fitful night's sleep. I had a few glasses of whiskey, but nothing more than normal. For someone who doesn't usually dream, last night, I was haunted by an implacable floral scent and visions of myself chasing a fairy through the forest. I'll have to ask Lainey to remind me what site she uses to look up dream meanings.

My attention is pinged when a name I have been trying to forget is mentioned between Declan and our tour manager.

"What did you say?" I ask, joining the conversation.

"We offered Ellie a job on the tour," Dec replies.

"You did?"

"Yeah," Declan says, taking a swig of his water.

"She wasn't sure what she wanted her next step to be. I thought working on the tour would buy her some time. Shonda has been asking for help. Plus, the amount of trouble Lainey could get in on her own is downright terrifying. Hopefully, Ellie's presence will even her out."

He's not wrong there. Lainey may be our sweet baby sister, but she is also the queen of mischief. I wouldn't put it past her to run off with one of our openers on a whim and start a new life in Wyoming.

"Smart, those two have always been yin and yang. I was always surprised at how quiet little Ellie got on with Lainey."

"Every introvert needs an emotional support extrovert, I suppose," Grayson muses. "Except Dec."

"I'm not an introvert."

"You hardly ever speak," I note.

"I speak when I have something to say. Excuse me for not jabbering constantly and to fill silence like you two."

"We do not jabber," Grayson gasps in mock offense.

"Everything we say is of pertinent conversational value," I agree. "You just don't want to ruin your rep as the stoic mysterious one. Gray and I both know it's because what's really running through your head is the Twilight fanfic scenarios. Don't worry. Your secret is safe with us. We'll cover your perversion with our 'jabber.'"

"Personally, I would love to hear about your why choose vampire-werewolf romance," Grayson adds.

"You two are exhausting." Declan pinches the bridge of his nose while Gray and I high-five.

He is right, though. My inability to sit in silence is the lie I am telling myself that I swing the conversation back to Ellie. There is no other reason I'm asking about the blonde who hasn't vanished from my thoughts since seeing her again last night.

"Did Ellie say she was going to come on the tour?"

"I don't know yet. She's going to talk it over with Lainey, I think. But based on how stressed she sounded about not having a job lined up, I'd say it's a safe bet. You remember how her dad was. I'm sure he's all over her about it."

I don't remember much about Ellie's dad except that he was a bad husband and a giant kiss ass. He works in the industry, but I've never crossed paths with him. He can't be that bad if his daughter turned out as great as Ellie, but what do I know?

A weight I didn't realize was sitting my chest lifts at the prospect of Ellie coming on tour. I tell myself it's for Lainey's sake. I don't acknowledge the small part of me that was hoping to see her again, soon. She's Lainey's best friend. Nothing could ever happen between us. But I don't hate the idea of getting to know her again as an adult and not the gangly teen I remembered.

"If we are done talking about your pet project, can we begin the meeting?" Eliza, our PR manager, snips in annoyance. She's not my favorite person in the world, but she has done an amazing job keeping our image clean. Not that we have a bunch of skeletons in our closet. But when you reach our level of notoriety, there is constantly someone coming out of the woodwork with some crazy story or request. Eliza's a shark, and that is what we have needed.

Declan and Grayson both bristle at her tone of choice words. When none of us reply, she jumps straight into her agenda. "You have thirty shows left on this tour. I know we've discussed you all taking some time off once it is over, but we need to discuss what that means. We need to be prepared for the breakup rumors when Declan's solo EP is announced."

"We're a family, surely people won't think we ended the band simply because Dec decided to do his own thing for a while. The only reason we aren't doing it together is because it is a different sound and we have our own projects we want to pursue," Gray justifies.

Speak for yourself there, buddy. I can't say I'm not somewhat worried that this time off will end up being more permanent than everyone is saying—intentionally or not. We've been in such a groove since our career started, none of us have considered doing anything alone until now. I haven't at least.

"You'd be surprised," Eliza states. "With two other big groups ending their partnerships this year, there will be talk. Have you officially signed on with the show?"

"The final contract should be sent over this week," my older brother confirms.

"What about you, Jack?" she asks, directing her attention to me.

Shit. That is never good. I try to fly under her radar as much as I can. When she's talking to me it is usually because I've taken a joke too far or I'm in trouble for a stunt I pulled with the press. "What about me?"

"What do you plan to do next?"

That's the million dollar question. I have no clue. We're only *planning* to take a year off before we write the next album. That gives Declan enough time to record his EP and do a mini-tour while Grayson serves as a judge on *Singing Sensation,* a music competition show.

Unlike my ambitious brothers, I have no plans. I have no idea how I will fill the twelve months we take off. Typically even if we aren't recording or touring, I spend most of my time with them. With Declan on tour and Grayson in LA I'm not sure what I'll do. Maybe I can convince Lainey or Bryce to move in.

"Chill?" My answer comes out more question than statement.

"Chill?" Eliza echoes. "We can't tell the press you're 'chilling,' Jack."

"Why not?"

"They'll assume the band isn't together because there is something wrong with *you.* If your brothers both have other projects, people will think *you* had some issues and wanted to stop working. I suppose we could say you are working on your-self, but that will make people think you have a drinking or mental health problem."

Yeah, I don't want that. Neither are true, but I'm not sure telling the world I'm aimless is much better. The thing is, I am already doing what I love. Being in a band with my brother's is all I've ever wanted and all I've ever known.

I don't have any songs eating away at me for release and I have no desire to judge a reality show. I don't have many hobbies, either. We've had a grueling recording schedule or been on tour since our show ended eight years ago. There wasn't time to explore many interests outside of that.

Eliza ponders the possibilities for another moment before asking, "How do you feel about a fake girlfriend?"

"Not great."

"Wouldn't people think we got Yoko'd?" Declan chimes in.

The idea of pretending to be with someone has never sat right with me. I might have agreed to PR dates in my younger days, but never full-fledged relationships. I've matured a lot over the years. I'm not interested in doing things solely for optics anymore.

As much as the press would eat up seeing me in a relation-ship, my recent experiences with dating haven't been great. Getting famous as young as we did, it has always been hard to know when people are seeking a genuine connection or want to use you for clout, money, connections, etc. After making a few misjudgments in my teens and early 20s, I haven't found it worth it to invest in someone whose intentions aren't crystal clear.

Eliza takes a moment to ponder Declan's assertion before agreeing. "If we said you wanted to spend time focusing on your relationship, they would think that. For anyone else, I would say you're spending time with your family, but that won't work here either."

She lets out a frustrated huff as she swipes through what I assume are her ideas on how I can appear to be a functional member of society. "Can't you find something to work on? I'm sure I could get you a guest star role on some TV or find a charity you can work as an ambassador for. You could produce?"

"That's more Bryce's forte," I reply in response to her last suggestion. Our younger brother has been trying to make a name for himself in the production world. I don't want to step on his toes. I also have no desire to work on someone else's album. It's hard enough working on my own.

No closer to resolution, Eliza sighs. "We have a few weeks before we need to discuss things publicly. They won't announce Gray is a judge until the current cycle ends. Try to come up with a believable story on how you're going to spend your time. I don't care if you do it or not. I simply need to feed the press something."

"Got it," I reply tersely. I love our fans, but I hate the expectation of the press. What's wrong with the way my life is now? I know my brothers have other dreams, but I'm living mine. There are people who would kill to be in my shoes. Despite that, I do feel the weight of others' expectations. I have never been a high achiever.

The only thing I hate more than being the least ambitious Ryder is having to lie about being the least ambitious Ryder. At least when Lainey was in college I could hide behind her indecisive ass, but now she's graduated and getting her life together putting all the pressure on me. I guess being the overlooked middle child doesn't count for much when you're famous. People are always looking.

The rest of the meeting is spent with Declan and Grayson nailing down their post-tour plans and me racking my brain for something that doesn't make me seem like a loser with nothing in his life but his brothers. There is a pressure to pick something meaningful, especially since I'm not convinced my brothers won't want to extend our time off if they love what they're doing.

The charity idea isn't bad, but I don't know of any specific nonprofits I want to throw my weight behind at the moment. I haven't had much of an opportunity to explore any causes I might be passionate about.

I could always say I'm using the break to explore other interests, but I don't know what those would be. The only things I enjoy are making music, my family, and whiskey. Maybe I could go to Ireland? I doubt traveling is an Eliza-approved reason considering we've spent the last eight months driving across the country.

So much for getting rest and relaxation on my year off. Maybe I'll check myself into a silent retreat for a few months. Who am I kidding? I could never go that long without talking. Blowing out a raspberry, I will myself to chill. I have time to think up something. I'm sure it will come to me as we get closer to the end of the tour. A lot can happen in twelve weeks.

5

Ellie

"WAIT, WAIT, WAIT," Macy laughs. "Can you repeat that?"

"They asked if I would be comfortable having semi-monthly meetings with the owner's psychic and functional healing coach."

"You're kidding?! I thought G&K had some wild practices, but we're a stuffy corporation in comparison to that."

I groan and lay my head on the table at our favorite restaurant near campus. I am glad she suggested we meet here. I didn't realize how hungry I would be after that disastrous interview. I forgot to eat dinner last night and breakfast this morning, stressed from preparing to meet with Virgo, the start-up apparel brand whose offices I could not get out of fast enough. The company was founded by a couple who relocated here from California and let's just say they are still operating as if they are in the southern California desert. It's one of the many interviews my dad set up for me.

"I want a job," I say. "But not that badly. Surely there is a better fit out there."

"Have you given any more thought to the Ryders' offer?"

Lifting my head, I eye her appreciatively. "I never told you about that."

"You didn't? Are you sure? I mean how else would I know." Avoiding my gaze, Macy plays with the straw of her Dirty Diet Dr Pepper. Humming when she takes a sip. I have no idea how she drinks that. It gives me flashbacks to drinking too much Malibu freshman year. I'm not letting that distract me, though.

"Macy . . . "

"What?"

"Macy Anita Martin!"

"Fine! Lainey may have texted me about it and asked me to pressure you a tiny bit. But I wasn't planning to push. I only wanted to see if you were considering it. It's a great option for you."

"Et tu, Mace? Lainey has been blowing me up about it."

"She's excited. You can't blame her for wanting you to join her on tour. She may be the extrovert but making new friends isn't all that fun when they're all you have. Trust me."

"Aw, do you miss us, Macy?" I tease. She rolls her eyes, but the way she avoids eye contact is telling.

"Maybe a little. I know it's part of growing up, but everything has changed. You and Lainey got to avoid it for a bit, but with the hours I work and Alexis moving in with Aiden, I miss the days when we didn't have to plan lunch weeks in advance."

"I know, babe. I hate it, too. It wasn't the same without the two of you this past year. I promise once I get this job thing settled I will get into a groove and you'll see me all the time."

"Don't worry about me. Worry about you. Lainey's needs aside, I think you should consider the job. It's a great opportunity for you. Eliza, the guy's PR manager is kind of a bitch, but the tour manager is cool and I have only heard nice things about the merchandising manager. It will be great on your resume."

"I don't know." It's good to hear the team is nice. Macy works at G&K, the same agency the guys are signed to. She's on the sports management side, but it's a small enough company that everyone is friendly.

"What's holding you back?"

Taking a sip of my own drink, I consider how much to tell Macy. The four of us are all incredibly close, but push comes to shove, it's me and Lainey and her and Alexis. I trust her to keep my secret, but I don't want to put her in an uncomfortable position. This secret has been weighing on me for years, though. It would be nice to share it with someone.

Taking a deep breath, I decide to reveal my truth. "What I'm about to tell you does not leave this café. Don't tell Lainey. Don't tell Alexis. Don't even tell your diary."

"Got it," she nods enthusiastically.

"I'm worried about Jack."

"Worried about Jack, how?"

This is harder to admit than expected. I may as well rip off the Band-Aid. "I kinda sorta used to have a crush on him and maybe had a moment with him at the bar the other night."

"You have a crush on Jack?!" she yells. When I widen my eyes at her volume. With a sheepish grin, she repeats more quietly, "You have a crush on Jack."

"Had," I emphasize. "When we were younger, I had a crush on him. Can you blame me? He has that charming golden retriever energy. he has the ability to make you feel like the most important person in the world when he shifts his attention your way. You've heard their songs. Who wouldn't swoon over the men who can write those lyrics?"

"You say 'men' but you only had a crush on one of them, right? This isn't a why choose situation?"

"Oh my god, no! Only Jack. The other brothers are safe."

"And what moment did you have the other night?"

My cheeks heat simply thinking about it. When I saw Jack at Palmetto's, I was surprised that all the attraction I thought I'd let go of years ago came rushing back. I'm embarrassed to say that in a moment of weakness I even thought about hitting on him when we were alone.

"I ran into him when I was leaving the bathroom and I may have felt up his biceps. Until he mentioned the tour, I was even considering flirting with him. I thought I was over my old crush, but seeing him reignited some of those buried emotions. Which is annoying because I know better than anyone how men in the music industry are. And Lainey would go mental if I ever hooked up with one of her brothers."

"First, who says it would just be a hookup? Lainey would love it if you became her actual sister."

I shoot her an expression that says I'm not convinced. It would be cool to be my bestie's sister-in-law and an official Ryder, but that is not in the cards for me. There is no way Jack and I could be together.

"Second, not all men are like your dad. The way they treat Lainey, I doubt any of them are hardcore players and you know their mom wouldn't stand for them treating a woman badly. Remember her reaction when Jack 'dumped' that popstar in a voicemail?"

"I forgot about that!" I gasp before laughing. "It took years for me to be able to listen to her music. The jealousy I held toward her was unreal. That should have been enough to convince my teenage self to give up on the man. If only I'd been that smart. I wouldn't have gotten my feelings hurt later."

"That sounds juicy. Spill!" she demands, shoving homemade chips in her mouth as if she's snacking on popcorn at a movie. I'm glad she's enjoying this confession. Reliving my embarrassing interactions with the middle Ryder brother has me in knots. One memory sticks out that was particularly embarrassing.

"You know when you're sixteen and think you can land any guy with the right outfit and prearranged scenario?"

"Absolutely." She nods in agreement, motioning me to continue.

"When the guys' show had came to an end, they spent a lot of time at their parents' house while they decided on their next move. I was doing my best to seem as grown up as all the girls I saw Jack with in the tabloids, I even convinced my mom to highlight my hair. I thought I was cute.

"One day, I was hanging out with Lainey by the pool when we wanted some snacks. I volunteered to get some, hoping to run into Jack which I did. He and his cousin Rhett were hanging out on the patio. In the tiniest bikini I could confidently wear, I batted my eyelashes and lamely asked him if he'd been working out because he was 'extra buff' lately."

"You did not!" She gasps before her face washes with sympathy. "Oh, sweetie."

"I know. I know. Anyway, when I went inside to grab the snacks, I realized the window was open and I could eavesdrop on their conversation. I missed the beginning but what I did hear was them talking about me. Rhett said it was cute how I kept trying to flirt with Jack and that if he were him, he'd go for it. Jack brushed him off saying I was just a kid, which in retrospect, I can see. He was twenty and fresh off dating a model. I was a high schooler he'd known since she was nine."

"Fair. We stan a non-predatory man," Macy agrees.

"He didn't leave it at that, though. Jack took it a step further and said I was his little sister's nerdy friend who spent more time in the fictional world than the real one.

"Ouch."

"Yeah. It was especially hurtful since for my birthday he had given me a limited edition set of my favorite series. It was signed by the author and everything. I was sure it meant something, especially with the heartfelt card gave me with a wildflower crushed inside it."

"A wildflower?"

"When we first met, I was picking them in the field behind our houses. I was touched that he remembered that. It's a core memory for me but to think it was for him, too. . . You can guess how my imagination blew it way out of proportion. Turns out he thought of me as the weird girl who had forced her way into his family by befriending his sister."

Telling Macy the story of how we met feels like spilling a lifelong secret. I wasn't supposed to be outside of my yard alone. I don't think he told Lainey because it wasn't mentioned when we met or ever since. He would teasingly call me 'Wildflower' from time to time, but never in front of anyone else.

"The last thing I heard was Rhett saying he liked smart girls. I was so embarrassed I ran straight home and told Lainey I got my period."

Macy's shoulders shake as she tries to hold in her laughter and maintain a sympathetic expression. Obviously, I'm over it, but a girl never forgets her first rejection.

"Not his finest moment," she finally replies. "I can see how that would sting. But that was seven years ago, El. You've both changed a lot since then. You're a gorgeous college graduate and he's almost thirty and probably thinking about settling down."

That's true. The change from sixteen to twenty-three is huge, physically and mentally. I have to imagine despite his playful mask he is more mature now than he was at twenty. I know I am different and it's only been three years for me.

"It's whatever. I'm sure he doesn't remember the conversation. But every time I saw him after that, all I could think about was him saying he saw me as a sister while I was doodling hearts around our names."

That isn't what I was thinking the other night though. The

other night when he wrapped his arms around my waist, the only thought in my head was how to keep them there. He seemed flustered at our interaction, but that was probably me projecting.

"You two weren't giving off sibling vibes when I found you in that hallway," Macy states with a smirk. "The sexual tension was thiccccc."

"Yeah, right. He'll always see me as the good little girl next door."

"There is nothing wrong with a well placed good girl."

I jaw drops at her mumbled admission. Macy is a total badass. I wouldn't expect her to be into praise. In fact, I'd expect her to be the one giving it. She has a 'fuck with me, I'll fuck you right back' vibe that I do not.

Amused by my silence she continues. "You know what would shake your good girl image and save you from anymore interviews with your dad's friends?"

"What's that?" I ask.

"Going on tour with a band of rock stars."

I groan knowing she's right as Macy smiles victoriously. "Tell Lainey I accept commission in the form of cash, check, or Sonic gift cards."

AFTER LUNCH, I decide to take a walk through Hillsboro, one of my favorite areas in Nashville. As I stroll, I weigh the pros and cons of accepting Declan's offer. Tonight when I get home, I'll pull out all my colored pens and make a proper list. But this will do for now.

Pro: Time to find the right direction and not settling for the first job I'm offered.

Pro: Extended sleepover with Lainey.

Con: Excess time around Jack and more potential embarrassment.

Pro: Traveling to cities I've never been to.

Con: Living out of a suitcase on a tour bus.

Pro: Experience working with an industry pro I could never get elsewhere.

Pro: A once and lifetime experience.

Dammit, the pros seem to be winning out. Can I do this? Can I leave my life for three months to travel around with the Ryder Brothers? I'm tempted but is it another attempt at putting off the inevitable?

Lost in thought, I realize I've stumbled onto a block I've never explored before and ended up in front of a women's boutique. Noticing a suede fringe skirt in the window, I pop in to check it out. Once inside, I am delighted by a selection of western chic clothing that would all be perfect if you were attending a country concert or twenty.

"Hello. Can I help you find anything?" the middle-aged woman behind the counter asks.

"The skirt in the window, do you have any more?"

"We surely do. What size do you need?"

After telling her my size, she scoots to the opposite corner of the store and grabs it.

"Buying this for something in particular?"

"Maybe."

"Maybe?" Her eyebrows raise in question.

"I've been invited to work on a country tour. I'm not sure if I'm going to accept, though."

"Why on earth not? If I was as young and as cute as you, I'd take that offer in a minute! Heck, I'd take it today if I wasn't planning to sell my shop and move closer to my grandkids."

"You're selling this place?" I ask. The store itself is a little outdated and cluttered but it has a great location and size. This place will be snapped up quickly.

"I've been haunting these halls since the 80s. It's time to give someone else a shot. I'm in no hurry, though. I want to make sure I sell to someone who will appreciate it and not a developer who will put up another townhouse or stuff office building."

We chat for a few minutes before I head into the dressing room to slide into the skirt and a distressed tee Misty insists I try on with it. She wasn't kidding when she said they would match perfectly. I thought the outfit would make me appear as if I was trying too hard, but instead it's effortlessly chic.

"Oh honey," she coos when I step out. "You need to get this outfit and wear it around the first country heartthrob you can."

"You think?"

"Absolutely. I'll even give you the friends and family discount."

"You don't need to do that," I argue.

"Nonsense. That skirt deserves this to be worn as much as you deserve to wear it. Don't deprive the skirt of its destiny."

Shaking my head at her theatrics, I purchase the skirt and top along with a few other items to help round out my tour wardrobe. I guess Misty and my new fringe skirt made the choice for me. I shoot Lainey a text telling her the good news.

1:47 PM

[picture of the outfit] Does this outfit make me look like I'm on tour with the Ryders?

LAINEY

You're in?

I'm in. I need to let your brothers know.

I'm with them now. They said they'll have Teri reach out with the details. When I get home tonight, we can plan out all the things we're going to do.

I'm so excited you're going on this adventure with me!

Me too.

And I mean it. I don't know what the next few months are going to bring, but having a temporary plan takes a weight off my shoulders. I've got three months to get my shit together and I'm determined to make the most of it.

6

Ellie

BEING LAINEY'S BEST FRIEND, I have been to my fair share of Ryder Brothers concerts. But usually we arrive shortly before the show starts and are in a private box away from the mayhem. That cannot be said today. Today we arrive hours before the show and are thrown straight into the gauntlet.

The moment our car pulls up at the arena in New Orleans, we and I are split up and ushered to our respective jobs. Lainey is sent to the wardrobe department while I am left to wander until I find my new boss, Shonda. After walking the length of the concourse, I finally stumble upon the merch area.

I'm greeted by the sight of a tiny blonde woman barking orders at a group of sweaty men as they unload boxes and set up tables.

"Excuse me," I interrupt, in a soft voice. When no one acknowledges, me, I try louder.

Ponytail whipping around, Shonda appears shocked to see

someone there. When she sees the lanyard around my neck, she asks, "You Ellie?"

"Yes, ma'am."

"Ew, no. We're not doing that. I am not old enough to be a ma'am. Call me Shonda or Boss Lady like these schmoes. You ready to work?"

Damn. This woman is a force. I don't think I've ever been this intimated and in awe at the same time. For such a small woman, she has a commanding aura. The 'schmoes' are all big guys who have a good thirty plus pounds on her. I need her to teach me her ways.

"As ready as I'll ever be, I suppose."

"Great! You can start by unboxing anything marked 'L.O.' and 'N.O. 1' and stocking it into the wire cubbies the roadies have built. That is all the product left over from previous shows and what is allotted for today. Each style and size gets its own cubby. Smalls on the bottom. 3XL on the top. Got it?"

"Yes, ma—Boss Lady."

She narrows her eyes at my almost slip before nodding and leaving me to my task.

Working diligently, I unload the boxes she mentioned and organize them as best I can. The system is easy to understand, but I'm not sure it is the most effective. I keep those thoughts to myself, though. Shonda has been doing this way longer than I have.

As I make it to the end of the shirts and get to hats and accessories, a badly tatted hand rests on the box I need to open. As my eyes trail up the arm it's attached to, a cocky grin waits for me.

"Well hello there. I didn't know we had a new girl helping out. What's your name, beautiful?"

I hold in my eye roll at the come on and take the compliment. I get my share of male attention, but the men who usually hit on me are not quite this forward. Shifting my gaze up, I take in my new companion. The man in front of me is a mix of good ole boy and indie rocker with a hint of 'my dad has money but I'm a rebel.' He is far from the type that usually approaches me, but cute nonetheless. He must be one of the 'schmoes' Shonda spoke of.

"Hi, I'm Ellie."

"Donny," he replies, extending his hand to mine. He lets go after holding it a beat too long while he scans my body. The lick of his lips before he meets my gaze again tells me he appreciates what he sees. "You Boss Lady's new lackey?"

"I guess. I'm here to help with merch for the rest of the tour." I almost mention that Lainey and I came together, but I'd hate to rob her of her own introduction. She loves guys who are too cocky for their own good. The thicker they lay it on the more fun she has squashing their egos.

"Donny! The other merch stands aren't going to put themselves together," Shonda barks across the open air space from a similar set up.

"On my way," he replies. Turning back to me he gives me one final once over. "See ya around, beautiful. Find me if you need anything."

I barely manage not to laugh as he saunters away. That guy has peacock energy if I've ever seen it. Despite his attempts to hit on me, he seems fun. I'm sure Lainey will prefer partying with roadies over her brothers. It doesn't hurt to make friends early.

As I pull out the first set of hats, I hear my name muffled.

"Ellie?" I glance around for the source, but there isn't anyone around me.

"Ellie, do you copy?" The sound grows as I get closer to the table. When I shuffle the cloth around, I find a walkie-talkie buried under discarded packaging.

"Hello?" I question into it.

"Finally. I need you to take a hat to the dressing room."

"A hat?"

"Yeah, the new vintage rope hats. The black one. Wardrobe needs one for Jack. It's a new item for this leg of the tour and they want him to showcase it during the concert. I need you to take it since you apparently have full access to all the dressing rooms. A fact we will definitely be discussing later," Shonda says.

"Where are the dressing rooms? They sent me straight to you when I got here."

"Go through the tunnel on the floor. Take the first hall on the right. The dressing rooms will be labeled."

"I'm on it."

Grabbing the hat Shonda mentioned, I head off on my mission. It only takes a few minutes of wandering to reach my destination. Knocking on the door, I release a tense breath when no one replies. Jack isn't there. Thank God. I know seeing him around is inevitable, but I am not mentally prepared only hours after my arrival. I'm a sweaty mess after unloading all those boxes in a warm concourse. Not the impression I want to make, even if I know he sees me as a little sister. A girl has some pride.

I peek inside the space to ensure it is empty before stepping inside. Peering around my mouth waters when I see a basket of snacks. The grumble of my stomach reminds me I haven't had anything except crappy airport coffee and a minuscule bag of pretzels. Flying makes me too nervous to eat before and I have been too busy since we got here to grab something.

Placing the hat on the coffee table, I sift through the snacks, squealing to myself when I see Zapp's voodoo chips. These are my absolute favorite and are getting harder and harder to find. It makes sense they have them here in NOLA, though. Snagging the bag, I tear it open and moan as the sweet and tangy flavor with the perfect amount of spice explodes on my taste buds.

"While this isn't the first time I've had a girl moaning in my dressing room, it is the first time I wasn't the cause."

Letting out a gasp, I drop my treat and chips cover the ugly grey carpet. I momentarily consider putting them back into the bag, but I'm not sure I'm ready for Jack to see me that low. I almost want to cry at the loss of them. RIP my dinner.

I swing my gaze up to him to complain about the loss of my beloved snack. The words die in my throat when I see he's standing there wrapped only in a towel as water drips from his hair down his ripped torso.

How on earth does he stay in such great shape while traveling? I got a glimpse of those strong biceps when I saw him in Nashville, but I was not prepared for Jack Ryder to have abs. It is truly unfair for him to be both an amazing musician and have the body of a professional athlete. How are mere mortals supposed to compete?

Watching as a droplet trails down his obliques, all I can think of is how much I want to chase it with my tongue. Almost as much as I want to explore the tattoos that trail from his shoulder to his left wrist. The blood in my veins heats at the idea.

The sound of him clearing his throat rips me out of my thoughts and draws my attention back to him. The smirk on his face tells me he caught my perusal and I flush hotter with embarrassment.

"You're not supposed to be in here!" I stammer.

He glances around as if to confirm his surroundings. "I'm not supposed to be in my own dressing room? I'm pretty sure of the two of us, I am *the most* supposed to be in here."

"I-no one answered when I knocked."

"Ah, so you thought you'd be able to steal my chips without an audience?"

"I didn't come in here to steal your chips," I protest, even though I did technically do that. Something about the glint in his eye has me unwilling to concede to that fact out loud, though.

"Why did you come in here then, Wildflower?"

My heart hammers at the nickname. The endearment reminds me of simpler times when I didn't have the weight of the world on my shoulders or expectations I set for myself. A time when hearing his voice would cause butterflies to erupt in my stomach. Much like I am pretending they aren't right now.

Lainey's brother. Lainey's brother. Lainey's brother. I repeat in my head as I scramble for something to say. Jack watches me expectantly.

"I brought you a hat," I eventually reply, lamely pointing to the coffee table before wringing my hands together.

Sauntering past, he leans behind me, close enough that the heat from his shower radiating off his skin warms me. How much better would it be against my skin instead of through fabric? Bad Ellie! No more thoughts about him or all the sexy skin he's displaying.

"This hat?"

I nod.

"I gotta say, Ellie, giving me a hat with my own band name on it is a lame present."

His familiar teasing takes some of the tension away from the moment and for that I am grateful. "It's not a present. Wardrobe asked us to drop it off. They want you to wear it tonight to entice people to buy it."

"That's a shame," he muses. "I might have been willing to trade you my other bag of voodoo chips for it. Guess all that salty goodness will remain with me."

"There are more?" Whipping around, I rake my gaze through the basket and spot more under some red vines. My stomach grumbles again, causing me to blush for the second time in this conversation.

Jack laughs, reaching into the basket to pull out both the chips and candy, handing them over to me. "Sounds like you need these more than I do. Make sure you grab real food before the show, though. I'd hate to have you passing out on your first night."

"Thank you," I murmur, pressing my bounty to my chest. "I'll, uh, let you get dressed. Sorry about all this. I really did think the room was empty."

"Don't worry about it. You've seen me in a towel plenty of times by the pool. You're not the first girl to see me post-shower and won't be the last. Plus, my parents would kill me if I let their 'Ellie girl' starve."

"I appreciate your dedication to your parents' wishes and will happily accept it in the form of my favorite chips. Good luck tonight."

"Since you're manning the merch tables, you may need luck more than me. Fans can be feral. Stay safe out there."

The reminder that he's concerned about me out of obligation is the reminder I need to douse the last tendrils of lust pulsing through me. I'm his sister's friend, his pseudo-family member, and nothing else. If I could just get my body to get back on board with that.

Waving goodbye, I make my way slowly back to the concourse, savoring my snacks as I try to brush off our interaction. The further away I get from his dressing room, the more I realize this would be harder than I anticipated.

When out of sight, I can forget the way being near Jack causes my body to react. In person, with his flirty charm directed my way? Not so much. Even though he acts this way with everyone, my inner teenager laps up the attention every time.

7

Jack

AS WE WALK off the stage, a familiar buzz pulses through my veins. The cheers of the crowd fuel my adrenaline even after setting my custom Gibson down. It's been less than two weeks since we performed together, but I missed it. The heat from the lights, the thrill from the screams, it's a high I've never been able to replicate.

The satisfied grins on my brother's faces say they agree. We are never more in sync than when we perform. Grayson keeps our tempo with his drums as Dec and I play off each other with our guitars. The rest of the band backing us up has been with us for years and together we put on a show our fans pay top dollar for.

"You played good out there," Tim, the sound guy says as he takes my ear piece. He hands it over to Bryce and I wonder how the youngest Ryder is enjoying his crash course in sound engineering. He can put together a DJ set well enough on his own, but if he wants to produce, Tim has a lot to teach him.

"Thanks, man. I felt good." And I did. Better than usual. I want to say it was the excitement of the crowd, but there was something different about this show—this night. Maybe it was knowing Lainey was in the crowd, but I don't find myself wondering what she thought of the performance. My mind goes straight to Ellie and wondering if she enjoyed it. I know she was busy at the merch table, but I'm sure she caught bits and pieces.

When was the last time she attended a show? It's been years, I'm sure. Does she dig our new stuff? Was she impressed by my solo? Some needy part of me hopes she is.

After the way her eyes ate me up in my towel earlier, I find myself craving those baby blues on me more. Something tells me flustered isn't a normal reaction for her, and I soak that up. My family would call me a shit disturber, but I can't help it if I love getting a reaction out of people.

And I would love to catalog all of hers. It took all my self-restraint not to pull her into my arms and kiss that shocked expression right off her pretty mouth. I bet she makes the sweetest noises. I don't think kissing the daylights out of her would not be well received, though—not by Ellie, not by my brothers, and especially not by Lainey.

I'm glad she was too busy checking me out to notice I was doing the same or take in the semi under my towel. Show me an unattached man who can resist a long-legged blonde surprising him in his dressing room, and I will show you a man with restraint of steel. It's not the first time a woman surprised me in my dressing room before a show, but it was the first time they weren't there for me.

Ellie wasn't there to get ravaged. She was there to do her job, which is a shame for both of us. If she wasn't my little sister's best friend, I one hundred percent would have turned up the charm. It was hard not to, as it were. The forbidden aspect makes me want it that much more. Call it the middle child in me, but I love to buck the rules. I wouldn't call myself a rebel, but I do seem to find myself in trouble more than my brothers. I may not be the middle child anymore, but it felt like it growing up with all the attention on me, Grayson, and Declan. Lainey and Bryce were a separate entity outside the spotlight.

I bring my mischievous energy to the greenroom after the show as I lift my hat off to pour water on my head and shake it around the room.

"Damn, Jack. You're worse than a dog," Grayson gripes, wiping the droplets off his face.

"Aww, are you saying I'm friendly and lovable, Gray?"

"More like a menace," Declan answers for him. "Do you have to do that every time?"

"I think the better question is why you guys always stand in the splash zone knowing I'm going to do it. I think you secretly enjoy it."

"No," they say in unison. I simply shrug, downing the rest of the bottle and catching my breath before our post-show meet and greet. I know they love it.

"YOU WERE ON FIRE TONIGHT," Paris, a reporter for a popular country channel, says as her partner points a phone toward us, capturing footage for social media. "What made this show better than others?"

"I wouldn't say this show was better than any others," Declan says.

"All the credit goes to the crowd. We feed off their energy and tonight the vibes were chef's kiss," I add, making the motion with my hand.

"It didn't have anything to do with your time off? Sources say you guys enjoyed some time out in Nashville. Any special ladies fueling you, or are the three of you still on the market?"

"Who's asking?" I wink. Paris pretends to blush, but I see the sultry gleam in her eye. I may be hamming it up, but it's exactly what she wants. Flatter her and give her a nice clip for social media. We're all single but we try to keep our private lives out of the spotlight. That way, whenever we do have someone in our lives, we can keep it on the low.

I dated around in my early twenties and it blew up spectacularly. And that is nothing compared to Gray's only public relationship. We learned that vague is the best way to keep people guessing. Never confirm, never deny.

"With the tour closing out and exciting projects on the horizon, a relationship is the last thing that is on any of our minds. That said, we did spend some time with a special," I say. "Our baby sister Lainey graduated from college and we went to celebrate with her. It's no secret family is important to us and we try to be around for all the big events."

I swear Paris's eyes get hearts in them at my response. Chicks love the good big brother act. Not that it is one for us, but we've been told on more than one occasion that it 'markets well.'

"Isn't that the sweetest! I'm sure she was thrilled to have her big brothers there to cheer her on. It's too bad you couldn't take her on a graduation trip. I know we would all have loved some Ryder Brothers take Hawaii content," she laughs.

"It is, but duty called. And we wouldn't trade this for anything. We may not have taken her to Hawaii, but we did bring her on tour with us. I think it's a nice consolation," Gray jokes.

"Did you now? And where is this mystery sister? I'd love some shots of the four of you together."

"She should be around here somewhere . . . " My eyes

search the space. The meet and greet takes place in a backstage area to keep fans from sneaking into our dressing rooms. It takes a few moments, but my eyes eventually land on Lainey. And Ellie. They're in a corner near some merch bins chatting with a few of the roadies. My jaw clenches when I see the smirks on the guys' faces, as if they're lions about to catch a gazelle. Nope, not happening. Not my baby sister and not Ellie either.

Any other time I would question why my outrage at them being hit on is equal. I shouldn't care who hits on Ellie. She is a smart, capable woman who can date whoever she wants. Not that Ronny—or whatever the fuck he's named—wants to date her. I'm sure he has something very different in mind.

I elbow Declan to ensure he sees what I am. I may be the closest with Lainey, but he's the most protective. I remember when Lainey was eighteen and one of the guys at our label asked about her. I don't know what Declan said to him, but he never looked her way again. Declan isn't a big dude, but his energy is intimidating if you're not part of his inner circle.

When he spots the girls, he quickly but politely ends the interview. As soon as the press leaves the room, the three of us walk straight to the girls. Ellie sports a pleasant, friendly expression, while Lainey exudes mischief.

"Laines," Declan greets, sliding an arm over the younger Ryder. "You girls ready to see the bus?"

The three roadies that surround them all take a small step back. That's right fellas. Not for you.

"You're with the band?" One of them asks, voice laced in disappointment.

"No," Lainey says as the three of us say, "Yes."

The brat rolls her eyes. "These goofs are my brothers." Her face morphs in annoyance as the men wince, lips tipping down. Men afraid of her brothers aren't going to do it for Lainey. If they can't handle us, they sure as hell can't take her attitude.

"What about you, beautiful?" the roadie—Ron? Jon?—asks Ellie.

"Also, with the band," I answer for her as she shoots me a confused glance. I don't have the authority to make that claim, but it's for her own good. I know what our staff gets into on tour, and Ellie and Lainey don't need to be anywhere near that. It's brotherly concern, and nothing else.

I don't know what Ellie's type is, but I can't imagine it's these wannabe rock stars. She's too smart to end up tangled up with them. Hell, she's too smart to wind up tangled with someone like me. She has the kind of intelligence that intimidates weak men. She tends to hide it, but when it comes out even I can't help the inferiority complex it triggers. I am evolved enough to see it as a turn on, but I doubt these guys are. They're here for a good time, not a long time and Ellie is no good time girl.

Throwing an arm around both girls' shoulders, I lead them away from the men and toward the exit. "Sorry, Sis. You're gonna have to search for trouble further from home. Though, I'd love to watch Dec kick a roadie off the tour."

"You three are ridiculous," Lainey huffs. She's right, but she isn't going to win this argument. That's life with three big brothers.

"Get used to it," Grayson quips. "Now, let's go check out your home for the next twelve weeks."

8

Ellie

AS LAINEY and I are unceremoniously dragged away from the new friends we were making, I try to ignore the weight of Jack's arm on my shoulders. I should be annoyed at their show of alpha male BS, but I have always found it endearing how protective they are of Lainey. It's cute seeing these megastars growl any time a boy flirts with their sister. I don't know if it's luckier for them or Lainey that their career kept them too busy during our years of college to check on her much.

The brothers lead us out the back door of the venue to the lot where the buses are parked. We give Bryce a big hug before we ascend up the stairs.

"Welcome to our humble abode," Jack drawls.

Glancing around, I can't help but think 'humble' is not the right word for where we are. This bus is incredible. Decorated in navy blues and wood accents, it is both masculine and cozy. The five of us stand comfortably in the front lounge area. On one side sit two recliners with a sofa on the other.

Past the seating area is a kitchen with a fridge and cooktop. I know the Ryders aren't hurting for cash, but this bus is way nicer than I anticipated. I tell them as much. "I'm impressed."

"Did you think we were slumming it, Ellie Bellie?" Grayson asks, ruffling my hair.

"Of course not. I honestly hadn't given it much thought. But I never knew buses could be this nice."

"This is nothing—you should see some of the pop stars' buses. How about a grand tour?"

I nod, excited to see the space, but Lainey pulls out her phone and mumbles something about 'seen one, seen them all.' Humble brag harder, Laines.

Ignoring her pouting over the loss of her potential boy toys, Grayson shows me around. "Right now, you are standing in the living area. We use this for relaxing, getting creative, and beating each other's asses in Mario Kart."

"I'm pretty sure I'm undefeated," Declan chimes in.

"That's because your main competition wasn't here but that's all about to change," my best friend taunts.

Continuing on with his tour, Grayson walks into the kitchen to show off the extensive drink collection in the fridge, coffee maker, and sparse pantry.

"We don't make a lot of meals on the bus since the tour has catering, but we have the capability if we wanted to. And behind this curtain is where all the magic happens."

"Ew. I don't need to hear about all the groupies you've brought on to the bus, thank you," Lainey quips with an exaggerated gagging noise.

"We haven't fucked on the bus in years. This is strictly for family and friends," Declan states. Lainey eyes him skeptically, but holds her tongue as we watch Grayson pull back the curtain with a flourish. Behind it are four bunks and three doors.

"Uh, I only see four bunks here." Lainey comments as she turns to her brothers. "I thought your bus had more?"

"Our old bus had nine bunks when we shared it with the band. For this tour, we splurged on something that gave us more room. The band has the old one. We thought you would be more comfortable in a space that wasn't filled with stinky, cursing men."

"We would be more comfortable away from the band, or *you* would be more comfortable with us away from the band?" Lainey questions.

"Both," Jack replies with a smirk. "Plus, between you girls and Bryce, we wouldn't have fit."

I can't help but smile at their banter. As much as I love my little brother and as close as we are, we don't have the easy rapport the Ryders do—especially Lainey and Jack. I think I spent so much time parenting him that our sibling bond got lost in translation. Mom was easily wrapped up in new boyfriends or mourning her latest break up. Not only did I have to make sure Finn was fed, I also helped with his homework, ironed his uniforms, and took him to extracurriculars.

I love my little brother and would do anything for him, but knowing he is safe and productive at the Naval Academy is a weight off my shoulders.

"How are six of us going to fit in four bunks?" I question, still unsure where I will be laying my head tonight. Something that I hope is soon. Running the merch table is no joke. People lined up the second the doors opened, an hour before the show, and continued long after Shonda dismissed me during the encore.

Jack points to one of the unopened doors. "There is a bedroom through there we thought the two of you could share. It has a king size bed. We figured you wouldn't mind sharing a bed since you've done it approximately ten thousand times before."

"It's a mobile sleepover!" Lainey squeals, bounding into the bedroom.

Following behind her, I am in awe of the space. The bed is way larger than I would have imagined fitting on a bus and even had a cubby on each side and a dresser with a TV across from it.

While taking in the room, I try not to notice how close the guys' bunks are. I've slept at their house dozens, if not hundreds of times, but never this close to them. The idea that Jack will be sleeping only feet away from me has me tingling inside. Not that anything could or would happen, especially surrounded by his family, but the scenarios flashing through my mind after seeing him half-naked this afternoon don't seem to take that into account.

"I take it, you find the accommodations suitable?" Declan asks half-sarcastically.

"Hell yeah," Lainey answers for both of us. "It's way better than the van we had to use when you guys first started out."

Before landing their show, Lainey's parents drove her and her brothers all across Texas to perform at county fairs, rodeos, and anywhere else that would give them a chance. It was at one of those festivals they were discovered by a big wig exec. and signed to a label. One thing led to another and now they have a tour bus that is fancier than my apartment.

"The bathroom is right outside the door to your room and a storage area is on the other side. Most of our stuff is stored underneath, but we keep some things up here. There are two small closets in this room the two of you can use."

"Thank you, this is great," I say as a yawn escapes me.

"I think that is our cue, boys," Grayson laughs. "We'll let you girls settle in. Since we're in New Orleans tomorrow, too,, you don't have to worry about the bus jostling you awake. Though, the ride is smooth most of the time."

After the guys leave, I make quick work of my nighttime routine and slide into bed while Lainey does the same. She nods off almost immediately in a way I envy. It has always taken me a long time to fall asleep, even more so in a new place with unfamiliar noises. I know who is on the other side of the door, but my fight-or-flight reaction is close to the surface.

Popping in my headphones, I turn to my favorite ASMR creator and hope his voice will distract me enough to drift off. Tomorrow is our first full day of the tour and I don't know yet what that means for me. Closing my eyes, I focus on the deep voice lulling me to sleep and push out all thoughts of another voice I'd rather be listening to instead.

THE BROTHERS ARE BLESSEDLY GONE DOING press for a local radio station when we wake up. Since Lainey and I don't have to report until later in the afternoon, we explore the city.

In typical touristy fashion, we enjoy beignets and shop in the market. After I pick up a notebook featuring a cover design by a local artist, Lainey convinces me that we need to commemorate our time on the tour. Her idea was to get matching tattoos, but I talked her down to necklaces instead. The delicate gold chains feature alternating aquamarines and citrines—our birthstones.

After the stress of finals and graduation, spending time bumming around New Orleans with Lainey was exactly what the doctor ordered and helped me forget about our current 'living' situation. I knew I would be close to Jack during this tour, but I didn't consider the logistics. I should've asked more questions.

The bedroom Lainey and I are in is super nice and cozy. But being in a confided space with her brothers is asking for embarrassing moments. On show days it will be fine, but what about when we're traveling? I can't hide in the bedroom the entire time. They'll think something is wrong. I definitely can't say being around one of them turns me into a bumbling, blushing idiot.

I have no desire to tell Lainey that, like every other girl we knew growing up, I have a crush on her brother. Had! I *had* a crush on her brother. I am a twenty-three-year-old college graduate. Crushes are for middle school girls.

I *had* a crush on Jack Ryder because he was cute and playful and how could I not? But it wasn't a real crush. It was the same way every other girl did. Or similar to my crush on Aladdin. A silly celebrity crush . . . except it feels different. It feels more like the crush I had on the surfer boy I met the summer I turned thirteen when I went on a trip to California with my mom. Or the crush I had on Brad Swift, my 'boyfriend' in high school.

As soon as we are back at the arena, my thoughts turn back to the man I've been trying not to think about all day. I hope I don't have to take anything to his dressing room again. I can't live through the mortification of seeing him freshly showered again, a knowing glint in his eye. No thank you.

The merch booths were a mess when I arrived. Even though we stayed in the same city, the products are still locked up on the trailer to prevent things from going missing. It makes sense based on the number of people coming and out of the arena, but it creates more work for us. However they were put away must have been disorganized because I walked up to a cursing Shonda.

"Everything okay?" I ask hesitantly.

"Thank God you're here," she answers. "It is chaos. The roadies loaded things up last night in the dumbest way conceivable. They didn't mark what products came from which booths and put things up in a snake pattern. I have some XXL vintage tees mixed with XS silhouette tees. It's madness."

"Yikes. Don't worry. I am here to help. And I'll be sure to

stick around for clean up tonight to make sure things go into the trailer more orderly."

"That would be amazing, thank you." Gratitude shines on Shonda's face. From what I gathered, the merchandising assistant isn't a position they've had before. She's never had anyone to help her aside from venue staff and the roadies.

As we unload the crates and divvy them up between the booths, my mind spins with the best way to pack for easy set up at our next stop. This position may have been created for me as a stopgap for my future, but that doesn't mean I'm going to slack off. I want to prove I deserve to be here and am not free-loading on a free tour experience.

It doesn't hurt that this is the kind of problem my brain enjoys. Merch storage reminds me of a mix of a logic puzzle and Tetris—two things I love to solve. My thoughts focused on the task at hand and then on working the booth that the show passes by in a blur. Before I know it, Donny and Trent are there to help me load up what we didn't sell.

Before they start loading, I grab the duct tape we use to help hold the shelves together and walk them through my new plan for packing.

"That's actually a good idea," Trent says once I finish explaining the plan. I bristle at his use of 'actually.' Did he think I wasn't capable of having good ideas?

"Thanks. I aced my logistics course," I quip. I normally find it rude when people point out their accomplishments, but I don't want these men assuming I'm some dumb blonde brought to pal around with the band. I can be an asset here.

"Oh, we got a college girl on our hands," Donny coos. "Pretty and smart. You're the total package. It's no wonder you've been swooped up by a famous musician."

"What?" I question, then remember the night before when Jack claimed I was 'with them.'

"I'm not dating one of the Ryders. They were being overprotective of Lainey last night, and I got caught in the crossfire. Although, they should be protecting you guys from her, not the other way around."

Trent perks up at that. "Is that so? I love a strong woman." Hmm, earlier comment forgiven, then.

"She might eat you up and spit you out," I joke.

"I'd love every moment."

Poor guy has no idea what he's in for. Before I can tell him that, Donny chimes in. "I thought it was weird they had their girl slumming it with us. Figured she'd be backstage enjoying the VIP access. How did a smart cookie like you end up on tour with bums like us?"

"I grew up next door to them. I guess they think of me as their honorary sister. When Lainey and I graduated, they offered me a spot on the tour and with nothing else lined up, I thought 'what the heck?' When would I ever get a chance for an adventure like this?"

A mischievous smirk takes over Donny's face at my declaration. "Don't you worry, beautiful. We'll make sure you get the full tour experience."

The way he sizes me up and licks his lips, tells me everything I need to know about what he has in mind. I'm no prude, but I don't think hooking up with someone I have to spend time with every day for the next twelve weeks is a good idea. I'm about to tell him as much when Lainey finds us.

"Ellie! You need some help? The sooner you finish, the sooner we can catch up on our show. Mace and Alexis are waiting."

Lainey and I are obsessed with *Singing Sensation*, a reality show where contestants are coached by superstars as they compete for a record deal. The first episode premiered last week, but Alexis and Macy couldn't catch it. We agreed to wait until we could all watch it at the same time. We used to watch it together when we all lived in the dorms and then our apartment. It's kind of our *thing*.

Now we settle for watching it at the same time when we can and texting each other about it. We even have a group chat specifically for the show to avoid spoilers in our main chat.

"Hi, Lainey," Trent greets before I can say anything.

I fight in to hold in my laughter as Lainey eyes the roadie. Lainey doesn't have a type that I've been able to pin down. She tends to go for quiet men who balance out her big personality. And who have no problem giving in to all her whims. She may lust after dominant book boyfriends, but in real life, she enjoys running the show. At least until she is ready to move on to the next guy.

"Hey, Trent. How's it going?"

"Better now that you're here. I gotta say, it's lucky for your brothers that you're a girl because you'd outshine the three of them combined if you were a dude."

"Is that right?" she asks, giving me a 'can you believe this guy' expression. I'm getting the vibe Trent does not have a way with words. It's cute that he tries, though.

"For sure. I understand why they're protective of you. I'd never let a guy near my sister if she was as gorgeous as you. I'd lock her away and throw away the key."

I can tell by her expression that whatever she's about to say is either going to crush Trent's spirit or make his day.

"Maybe if you're a very good boy, I'll let you lock me up," she drawls, running the tip of her finger down his chest.

Poor Trent's jaw hits the floor. He reminds me of a glitching computer as he tries to come up with a retort. Luckily, Donny saves his friend.

"We're good here, girls. We'd hate to keep you from your show. Maybe the four of us can hang out at the next stop?"

"Sounds like a plan to me," Lainey replies, grabbing my hand. Once we are far enough away, we both bust out laughing.

"This is going to be fun," she says. "Come on. The boys are still at their meet and greet. I grabbed some food from catering to take back to the bus since I'm guessing you forgot to eat."

On cue, my stomach grumbles.

"Thought so. What would you do without me to take care of you El?"

"Surely perish," I reply seriously before we break out into another fit of giggles. We make it back to the bus without running into her brothers. Maybe avoiding them won't be as hard as I expect.

9

BY THE TIME we got back to the bus last night, I was wiped. As nice as it is to have shows in the same city, it can sometimes be more stressful. The PR team loves to pack our schedules with in town events. At least on travel days we get to rest.

I half expected the girls to be causing chaos, as is Lainey's nature, but they were already in their bedroom watching something on TV. We were all grateful we didn't have to go track them down. Since I showered in the dressing room, I passed out almost immediately after laying down in my bed.

I woke up this morning to the sound of quiet chatter. Declan and Grayson are both earlier risers, but I was surprised to see Ellie sitting with them in the lounge.

"Y'all are up early," I mumble as I walk into the room in search of coffee. Thankfully, the bus is too small to house anything more than a standard single serve coffee machine, much to Lainey's chagrin.

"It's ten o'clock," Declan deadpans as if I slept the day away.

"Don't you mean 0100 hours?"

"I really, *really* don't."

"Isn't that one a.m.?" Ellie questions.

"Don't try to reason with him, Ellie Bellie," Grayson replies. "At this point we assume it is willful ignorance that he refuses to understand military time."

He's not wrong. I enjoy fucking with Declan about his rigidity. My jovial mood plummets as I watch Ellie smile at my brother. A smile he returns. He's making her smile and calling her a cute nickname? Does he have a thing for her?

We all decided a long ago that any of Lainey's friends were off limits. Being a teenage girl is hard enough without having to worry about your brothers ruining your friendships. It helps that we were older than them but teenage girls don't tend to consider things like age, especially when we played younger on TV. The age gap certainly never stopped Lainey's David Beckham crush.

Grayson isn't going anywhere near Ellie if I can help it. The man is still pining over his first love. No chance am I letting him mess around with Ellie. He'd end up breaking her heart and could fuck up the dynamic between her and Lainey. Which is why we all need to keep Ellie in the sister zone.

Is that a thing? Similar to the friend zone but for people you think of as family? The friend zone is total BS, but the sibling zone has merit. Despite my thoughts of staying away, I can't help the buzz that runs through me when I catch her staring at my chest. I wonder if she's remembering seeing me in a towel. Just because we can't act on it doesn't mean we can't enjoy the view. That's a dangerous line to toe.

I'm shaking out my shoulders trying to relieve the sudden tensions from watching the exchange between Ellie and Gray when Lainey joins the mix. It's perfect timing. If I clutched my mug any harder I think the handle would have snapped off.

"Sleeping Beauty has finally risen," Grayson taunts.

"Hop off it, you ogre," she retorts with a yawn. Walking past me, she grabs the coffee out of my hand and takes a sip.

"Bleck! What is this sludge?"

"Sorry princess, you're going to have to get used to instant coffee for the next few weeks," I reply.

"No thank you. I brought cold brew. Only uncultured swine can drink that shit."

Stealing my cup back from her, I take a big gulp, making an exaggerated "ah" sound once I swallow. Lainey rolls her eyes before walking away, and I catch Ellie watching the exchange. I don't miss her adorable blush when I wink her way.

"Alright, loser. How are you planning to keep me from dying of boredom today?" Lainey asks once she gets her caffeine fix.

"I didn't realize we were responsible for entertaining you," Declan says.

"An oversight on your part," she quips. "You've been responsible for occupying my attention and keeping me out of trouble since day one, brother dearest."

"If that's the case, how did you manage while in college?"

"That would be me," Ellie interjects. "And I would only give myself a C for that project."

"Hey! I didn't end up in jail or naked in a viral video. I'd call that a win," Lainey asserts.

Ellie snorts. "What a high bar to meet. Shall we tell them about what we got up to in PCB spring break of sophomore year?"

"We shall not." Lainey cringes.

"I'd love to know," I state as both girls shake their heads. "Come on, you can tell me. I'm the fun brother!"

"I thought I was the fun brother!" Grayson shouts.

"Sorry, Gray. Jackie is right. He's the fun brother, and Declan is the protective one. You're the reliable one."

"Reliable? That's fucking bull. You don't think I'm reliable do you, Ellie?"

She purses her lip to ponder it. It's so cute that all I want to do is pull her into my lap and kiss her plump lips. Instead I stay rooted in place as I listen to her response.

"Once when you were sixteen, you drove us to the video rental place at 11:45 p.m. to return a DVD before the midnight deadline," she recalls.

"If I remember correctly, you were panicking about it, Little Miss. I was trying to get you to calm dow—oh my God. I am reliable!" Grayson's crestfallen expression causes me to bust out laughing as I cross the space to the couch he vacated to process this revelation.

"You also picked us up from that party senior year when we were too shi—never mind. Got any games?" Lainey asks, taking in Declan's chastising expression..

"I think Mark kept the new gaming system on the band bus, but we still have the Nintendo." I waggle my eyebrows at her.

"No way, you guys always team up on me at Mario Kart or cheat."

"We do not!" Grayson says, clutching his chest in mock offense, even though we do. Lainey may be the most competitive out of all of us. Seeing her lose is worth forming an alliance.

"I saw Uno in one of the kitchen drawers," Bryce adds, as he ambles up from the back.

"Sold."

"YOU CAN'T STACK up draw +4s!" Lainey complains after Declan and I gang up on her.

"Of course you can," he argues.

"Tell them, El!"

"Why are you appealing to her? She didn't invent the game," I say.

"No, but she always plays by the rules. She'll know." When we all turn to Ellie, I notice a hint of sadness in her eyes. Does she not want to be thought of as a rule follower? It's sweet that she is, but I always remember her as the little girl who picked flowers in the field. Or the one who threw a stick in Timmy Carlson's bike wheel after he pushed her little brother down. That girl had a little wild in her. I wonder if it's still buried there and what we can do to bring it out during this tour.

"Technically, Uno did come out and say you're supposed to lose your turn after a draw and that you couldn't combine them."

Declan scoffs. "They're wrong and we make our own rules. And Ryder rules say we can rack up the draws."

"Living in a world where Ryders make the rules is dangerous," Lainey warns.

"Nah, you've been living in it for twenty-three years and you've been fine." When he boops her nose, chaos erupts as she bats his hand away. He catches both of hers in one and she launches at him. I fall off my chair laughing and Ellie lets out a sigh that says this isn't the first time she been put out by our family's antics.

Once Declan has Lainey secured in a headlock, she calls for mercy and returns to her seat. She may have lost the battle, but her eyes tell me she is already calculating her revenge.

"Am I at least the pretty one?" Grayson asks, mind still clearly on our earlier conversation and not even phased by our siblings.

"Sure, buddy," Lainey answers, blowing hair out of her face before slamming a card down on the pile. "But you're also the one who has to draw twelve."

AS MUCH AS I thrive being around people, bus life gets overwhelming for even me. It's part of the reason the three of us get separate dressing rooms when possible. It gives us a chance to center ourselves and go through our pre-show rituals.

My new favorite pre-show ritual is the visit from Ellie. It's probably too soon to officially call it part of my routine, but twice is the start of a pattern. At least that's what I tell myself when I hear a soft knock on my door. None of my family members would knock and Eliza's always bangs as if the world is on fire. No, that sweet sound can only be Ellie. I don't know if she's here to pilfer more chips or drop something off, but I am eager to find out.

"Come in!"

Walking in with her hand over her eyes, Ellie enters the room. "Are you decent?"

"Depends. Do you consider a banana hammock decent?"

"A what?"

"A nut hut, marble sack, Daytona dong sarong, grape smuggler, manberry pud—"

"Are you in a speedo?!" she asks, sounding scandalized.

"What a pedestrian way to put it."

I revel in the way her cheeks are flushed. She's frozen in place as if she doesn't know what to do next.

"I, uh, can come back?"

"I'm kidding, Ellie. I am fully clothed. No free show today."

She huffs at the reminder of the last time she was in my dressing room and peeks through her fingers before fully uncovering her face.

"It's not nice to tease," she states.

"On the contrary, teasing can be very nice when done right."

I shouldn't be pushing her, but the boost I get from her reactions almost rivals the one from performing. Knowing I can knock her off kilter gets me.

Her eyes widen when she takes in my meaning. She glances away quickly, but not before I catch the heat in her eyes. Interesting. Is this turning her on? Because it sure as fuck is doing something for me.

"Did you bring me another present?" I ask to get the conversation into safer waters. Waters that will keep my dick from getting any harder in my joggers. I may have been joking about wearing a boner suit but these pants won't be anymore decent if little Jack decides to make an appearance.

"New hat," she replies. Her eyes search my room and I clock the moment they land on what she's after. "I'll trade you a bag of chips for it."

"You'll trade me my own merch that you were asked to bring me for a bag of *my* chips?"

"Yes."

"You drive a hard bargain. Let's see what they want me in tonight."

Reaching behind her, she pulls a white ball cap out of her pocket. It's emblazoned with the name of our current album. Instead of taking it from her, I bend my head down.

"What are you doing?" she asks.

"Put it on me."

"Put it on you."

"If I'm going to part with my precious chips, I think I deserve some personalized service, don't you?"

She appears skeptical but steps forward anyway. Ellie isn't a short girl so with my head bent we are practically eye to eye. This close, I'm able to see light freckles that decorate the bridge of her nose and the way her pupils are blown.

She gingerly places the hat on my head and toys with the bill, positioning it the way she wants. When she's happy with it, her baby blues lock into mine and she sucks in a quick breath. The electricity between us seems to swell as we stand there for a long moment.

Taking a risk, I reach up and tuck a loose strand of blonde hair behind her ear. Staring into her glittering gaze this way, it's hard to remember all the reasons I shouldn't kiss her. She must be thinking the same thing when her tongue darts out to lick her lips. I'm about to say 'fuck it' and lean into to take her sensual mouth when I hear a noise outside the door.

At the sound of a knock, Ellie jolts backward and away from my grasp.

"Jack!" Eliza calls. "We need you for a phone interview in ten."

Initially, I don't respond as my brain scrambles to process the moment I shared with Ellie. All the reasons we shouldn't kiss slam back into me as I finally break our eye contact.

"Jack!"

"Got it! I'll meet you in Gray's room in a few."

Eliza says something about not being late, but it is muffled by all the blood rushing between my ears. Ellie stares up at me with lust and confusion on her pretty face. As much as I enjoy her annoyed expressions, I think this one might be my favorite.

Putting my back to her, I grab the voodoo chips we both love. Handing her the bag, I crack a joke to ease the sexual tension that surrounds us.

"I guess you'll have to wait until next time to see my pickle pincher."

That breaks her out of her trance and she scrunches her nose. "You don't actually wear those do you?"

"You asking me about my undies, Ellie? I'm not sure that is workplace appropriate."

"I'm n-you-are you messing with me?"

"Always, Wildflower," I say, plastering a fake smile on my face. Because that's all it can ever be. Jokes, pretend, messing around. Ellie is off limits and I need to stop letting my attraction to her make me forget that.

"I better go. I don't want to incur Eliza's wrath by making you late for an interview."

"She's more bark than bite."

Ellie shrugs before taking her leave. Tilting my head back, I blow out a raspberry. The buzzing in my pocket tells me it's time to go. With one more centering breath, I make my way down the hall to join Grayson and Declan.

10

Ellie

THE GUYS PLAY a single show in Little Rock, before we hit the road for another double header in Dallas. After staying late to help Donny and Trent pack the trailer with my new method, I'm beat. Unfortunately, any hope of sleeping in was dashed when my mom called at 8 a.m. to chat.

What she really wanted to do was to complain that she was lonely because Todd is on a business trip. His new promotion means he is on the road more visiting hospitals across the country trying to sell whatever fancy machine his company came up with. She doesn't understand why they can't 'sell on the phone like they used to.' I kindly don't point out that the archetype of traveling salesman has been around longer than commercial air travel.

She is not pleased I am not in town this summer. She spends twenty minutes naming all the things we could be doing if I would have stayed home with her instead of joining the tour.

She apparently forgets that if I was home, I'd have a job and wouldn't be able to play pickleball with her on a random Thursday. But sure, the tour is what's holding us back.

I planned to go back to sleep after that, but I was bombarded by texts from my dad also harping on my decision to come on the tour. He's worried it's 'no place for a girl like me' which is ironic considering his history with tours. He also thinks I am wasting my time and employers will be concerned I didn't get hired right away.

He contrasts that concern by asking me a myriad of questions about the tour. Apparently he has been trying to get an 'in' as their tour manager for years but never made much headway. I can't imagine why after seeing the way he treated his wife and kids they'd be reluctant to hire him . . .

The conversation ends with me fulfilling my password child duties by explaining to him that Netflix isn't 'messing with him' and that he clicked on Finn's profile by accident. Which reminds me that I need to text my brother to ask about his questionable viewing choices. The kid is watching way too many high school rom-coms for a Midshipman.

Between the conversations with my parents and replaying the moment with Jack from the day before, I need a distraction. The pendulum of emotions is too much for my system. I typically have them on a tight leash, but being this close to his playful energy is wreaking havoc on my ability to self-regulate. I am constantly keyed up.

I can almost convince myself he is similarly affected based on the moment we shared in his dressing room. But the logical side of my brain knows that isn't true. No way is Jack Ryder thinking of me as anything other than his sister's best friend, but the way he looked at me . . .

Too discombobulated to go back to sleep, I decide now is as good a time as any to formulate a plan for what to do with my life post-tour. I know it's only the second week, but the interview process can take months, especially in such a niche industry. I pull out my handy dandy notebook and pen collection and inventory my favorite classes and projects during school. I'm hoping I can find a common thread that may give me a direction to move.

Unfortunately, I don't find one. Aside from not enjoying the designing side of things, I love all the rest. I enjoy helping style an outfit that gives people confidence as much as I enjoy marketing products. Defeated, I pull up a job board on my iPad and apply to the first three jobs that appear remotely interesting. If I can't figure out what I want to do, maybe I should let fate decide. I promise myself to do this once a week for the rest of the tour. At the very least, applying will be good practice.

After submitting my last application, I'm debating the merits of going back to sleep when the door to the bus opens and I hear heavy footsteps coming up the stairs. Glancing up from my tablet, I find the wide eyes of Jack. He appears surprised to see me. I wouldn't call 9:30 a.m. early, but in tour world it kind of is.

I'm shocked he's up as well. I didn't check the bunks because I'm not a creeper, but I did notice all the curtains were closed when I snuck out of the bedroom to answer Mom's call.

"I didn't think anyone would be up yet," he says, breaking our silent standoff. I didn't realize I was staring at him until now. That's embarrassing.

"My parents have never been one to observe quiet hours," I joke.

"Even your dad?"

I laugh because, fair. "Mr. Rock and Roll hated mornings as much as Lainey until he dated a yogi. That had him up at 6 a.m. drinking chai and meditating."

Jack grimaces. "Couldn't be me. Are they still together?"

"Nah. She bailed once she realized he was serious about never marrying again. For a hippie, she was surprisingly focused on commitment. But the habit stuck. He can't sleep past nine no matter how hard he tries. Mom was the one who woke me though."

"Everything okay?"

I warm at his concern. And then I remember our exchange from yesterday and heat for an entirely different reason. I could have sworn Jack almost kissed me before Eliza knocked on the door. That shouldn't make me as happy as it does. Not only would it be a betrayal of Lainey, but it would make things hella awkward for everyone. There is no future for Jack and I. And yet, knowing he cares enough to ask how I'm feeling makes me swoon like a school girl.

"Aside from the fact that my mom thinks I abandoned her and my dad is worried about my virtue on this tour? Peachy. I don't have the heart to tell him I left my 'virtue' at Craig Steven's lake house."

"Lainey's ex-boyfriend?"

"He wishes," I snort. That boy was down bad for our girl. She let him take her to prom and a few other important events senior year, but she wasn't about to commit to anyone before college.

"He wishes he took your virtue or that he was Lainey's boyfriend?"

"Both, probably. He was a horndog. And can we stop calling it my virtue? It's freaking me out."

"You started it."

"And I deeply regret it," I deadpan.

"Fine," he huffs. "So Craig Stevens did not take Wildflower's wildflower at his lake house."

"Ew. That is so much worse. And no, he didn't but his hot cousin did."

Jack makes a motion as if he is clutching his pearls. "I am shocked our little Ellie would do such a thing. I hope he made it good at least."

I shake my hand in a so-so motion and Jack gives me a

sympathetic smile. This is the first time we have been alone—dressing room run-in aside—in years. A large part of me is cringing that we're talking about me losing my virginity, but I guess there are worse topics.

"Is everything else okay? You looked stressed when I walked in. If your parents are harping on you that much, we can sic my mom on them. She'll straighten them out."

"I bet she would, but I don't want to subject Mama C to my mom's pity party. She might keep her prisoner until her husband gets back in town." The visage of my mom locking Crystal Ryder in her house and forcing her to watch the Home Renovation Network brings a smile to my face. I'd pay to see that.

"It's not my parents that are stressing me out, not exclusively," I confess. "I'm still not any closer to figuring out what I want to do next."

"Do you need to have it figured out?"

"What?"

"Do you need to have the rest of your life figured out by the time this tour is over?"

"I guess not, but it would be nice to have a plan?"

"Plans are overrated."

"That's easy for you to say. You're already living your dream."

Jack pauses as if to think over what he wants to say next. He may be the jokester of the group, but I appreciate him taking our conversation seriously.

"You're right in that I am living my dream, but that is almost scarier. I think you're lucky to be in a place where you can embark on any dream you set your mind to. The ball got rolling on our career so young, I sometimes feel we missed the excitement of the journey itself."

Hmm. I hadn't considered that perspective. It puts me

slightly more at ease, but I am still crushed by the weight of expectations—both mine and other people's.

"That's a fair point," I reply. "I wish I was one of those kids who knew what they wanted to be when they grew up. Stable is not a job title, unfortunately. If I don't have a plan A, then I won't be able to have a plan B or plan C to fall back on."

"Some people would say you only succeed when you don't have a safety net to back you up."

"Tell that to the nepo babies."

"You want to know what I think?"

"What's that?"

"I think that you're afraid to fail. You've overachieved at everything thus far, but none of it was what you truly wanted. If you choose a path now and fail, it will be at something you genuinely want, and that is scary."

"I wanted my achievements," I argue.

"*You* wanted to win the eighth grade science fair?"

"Of course!"

"Why? Not because you love science. Because if that were true then you wouldn't have gone to school for fashion. You enjoyed the feeling of pleasing your teachers and parents, but you didn't have a passion for solar power or alternative energy."

"I might!" The tilt of his head and raise of his brows tell me he doesn't believe me, and he's right. I don't care about science. In fact, I hate science. But I quickly learned that when my parents were both praising me, they weren't bickering with each other and having tangible proof of my work warmed something inside of me.

Jack takes my deep exhale as a concession and continues on his observation of me.

"I bet if you dig down deep, there is an idea niggling at the back of your mind. Something that you think would be fun 'in another life.' We only get this one, Wildflower. We gotta make it count."

"Who would have thought the Ryder who never takes anything seriously would be spitting epiphanies at 10 a.m.," I joke, trying to take the attention off me. A flash of something—hurt maybe—flashes through Jack's features before he pats my shoulder and walks into the kitchen.

As I sit and process Jack's words, he rifles through the cabinets. Finding what he wanted, he plops down on the chair across from me and flips on the TV.

My tumultuous thoughts turn to desire when I see what he has. Catching my hopeful expression, he laughs and tilts the bag of yumminess my way. Doing a happy dance in my seat, I ask, "How do you keep getting these? Do I have to be a rock star to get the hook up?"

"I'm hardly a rock star," he chides. "But yes."

"Disagree. But seriously, teach me your ways. Is there a secret website I don't know about? These are my favorite and I thought they were discontinued until I saw them in your dressing room the other day."

His lips tip at the mention of our dressing room run-in as heat spreads across my cheeks. "They're in my rider."

"In . . . your last name?"

"No." He laughs. "My rider. The list of things I like to have in my dressing room. Most musicians have them. The label sends them to venues so we have the things we need to get ready. In my case, it's honey lemon tea, these chips, and four mini bottles of local whiskey if they have a distillery nearby."

"Why mini bottles? Surely they can afford a fifth?"

"Probably, but this leg of the tour is twenty cities alone. As big as my house is, I fear adding dozens of bottles of whiskey will give it more of a frat house vibe than I would prefer. I usually drink one mini bottle in my tea, do a shot right before we go on stage and save two for my collection."

"We'll revisit your secret mini bottle collection after we

discuss the more pressing question: You're telling me at every stop, you're doing to have voodoo chips?"

"I should." He nods. This is a revelation. Crunching on another chip, I try to think up a plan to convince him to share his spoils.

"I don't know what that look means, but I'm a bit worried for *my* virtue if you plan to sneak into my dressing room before every show. To keep you from becoming the next great chip burglar, we can ask whoever stocks the bus to double the amount of chips they get."

"We can? That would be amazing! And I wasn't planning my next B&E. Besides, I could have Donny or Trent go in while performing. They're no stranger to sneaking around backstage. No one would suspect a thing. Trent would do just about anything to get on Lainey's good side."

"Is that so? And would Donny do the same to get on yours?" There is a distinct shift in mood from our friendly banter to something more tense, but I'm not sure why. Maybe Jack doesn't like the idea of Lainey and Trent? He doesn't need to worry. She can take care of herself, especially against a sweetheart like Trent.

Glancing away, I shrug in response with no concrete answer. I don't know if Donny would steal chips for me, but I would never ask him to so we'll never know.

Jack places his knuckle under my chin and drags my eyes back to his. "If you need chips, you come to me. Got it?"

There is heat in his tone that I can't decipher. If I didn't know better, I would say it's desire and . . . jealousy. But that can't be. He's never seen me as an object to lust after.

I want to laugh at the silliness of the statement, but the intensity of his gaze tells me he is being serious. Even though I don't understand the subtext, I nod.

"Good girl. Now, want to hear about the crazy shit in Gray's rider?"

11

Ellie

I AM PRACTICALLY SKIPPING my way through the arena to deliver a new hat to Jack. Since Declan and Grayson don't perform in any headwear, it is apparently up to Jack to showcase all the options for sale at the merch booths, one show at a time.

Unlike my first night, I am not dreading visiting him before the show. Butterflies fill my stomach as I get closer to the guys' green room, and it isn't because I'm that much closer to my favorite snack.

Jack and I had a moment yesterday when we chatted on the bus. He may come off as playful, but he validated my feelings while challenging my beliefs. And most importantly, didn't tell me to suck it up and make a decision. As much as I didn't enjoy his sentiments in the moment, I can see the truth in his words upon reflection. Also, upon reflection, I think the heat in his eyes might have been for me. That combined with the maybe almost kiss we had in Little Rock has a seed of hope sprouting in my chest.

Thinking that makes me want to smack myself. I'm not better than the girls in the crowd convinced that if they can make eye contact with him, he'll fall in love with them. But maybe . . . there is something there?

Not that I want there to be anything there because I absolutely do not. There is no future for us, but tell that to the sixteen-year-old inside me. She's already been crushed once. What's the harm in giving her a little hope? And if I have to flirt with a sexy country music star, that is a cross I will bear. It's not as if Jack would ever want anything serious, but maybe I could be down for some fun. Smoothing out the merch tee I style over a shirtdress, I knock on the dressing room door.

"Come in!" a muffled voice yells from the other side.

I come to a halt when I walk in. I knew the guys were sharing a room on this stop, but I didn't expect it to be packed. Declan is in the corner arguing with Lainey over what appears to be a pair of ripped jeans, while Grayson sits closest to me scrolling on his phone.

"Hey, Ellie Bellie," he greets.

"Hi."

Scanning the room, I spot Jack on the opposite side of the room, getting his hair zhuzhed by the makeup artist.

"Do you want a comb to brush your mustache?" she asks, running her fingers through his collar length locks.

"Nah, I like it unruly. Keep people guessing if it was mussed by pulling on my shirt or a pair of tan thighs."

I fight the urge to roll my eyes at the line while she giggles like a schoolgirl. She doesn't even fake blush to match her faux innocence act.

"Why can't it be both?" she coyly replies.

"Naughty girl," he chides playfully.

Watching them banter back and forth, something tightens in

my chest. Something that feels all too familiar when it comes to Jack Ryder.

"Is that the hat?" Lainey yells across the room, causing everyone's attention to come to me.

"Y-yeah," I stammer out.

"Give it here so I can stop watching Julie fawn over Jack's hair."

"He's got good flow," the woman in question admits unashamedly checking Jack out. He winks at her in response.

Releasing the hat to Lainey, I cringe at the indentions from clutching it too tightly. In my defense, I didn't expect to be surprised by not only a full dressing room, but also Jack flirting with someone else. So much for feeling special these past few days.

Things are made even worse when the guys' publicist, Eliza, walks in the room. She barely spares a glance at Lainey and me before stomping over to Declan.

"Uh oh, Mommy is mad," I hear Jack mutter.

"What are you doing here, Eliza? We usually don't see you until after the show?" Declan asks, seemingly annoyed by her presence. Me too, Dec. Me too.

"Trust me, I don't want to be here anymore than you want me here," she huffs. "This is my Zen time. Unfortunately, it was interrupted by potentially breaking news."

"Jack, is there something you need to tell me?"

"No?" the man in question replies, face full of confusion.

"So you didn't have a late night rendezvous with Kacey Klass when she opened for you in San Antonio last month."

My heart seizes in my chest. Kacey is gorgeous. Her latest album is one of my favorites. I could understand why Jack would want to hook up with her, but my stomach still sours all the same. Everyone waits frozen in time for Jack's answer.

"Jesus, no. Is she even eighteen?"

"She's twenty," Grayson supplies.

Jack cringes. "No, I one hundred percent did not have a rendezvous or a hookup or even a private conversation with the girl. She's practically a baby. Is she saying we did?"

"Someone from her camp is telling anyone that will listen that the two of you are quietly dating and on the fast track for an engagement."

Instead of a plain denial, Jack barks out a laugh. "You know that's a lie. No one in their right mind would think I'm boyfriend material. Tell whoever asked you that question it's a crock of shit and that I am very much single."

"What about you, Mr. Knew Her Age?" Eliza asks as she turns her attention to Grayson. I tune out the chatter as I focus on what Jack said. I guess I was right about him not being interested in anything serious. Despite our moment, I always knew we could never be anything more than a fling. Though, after watching him flirt with Julie, I doubt the moment more and more.

"Are you listening to me?" Lainey asks, interrupting my thoughts.

"Um, yes . . . "

The roll of her eyes tells me that she doesn't believe that for a second. "Have you eaten today?"

"Ye—" I pause to consider the answer because no, I don't think I have. The hesitation is enough to have Lainey reaching into Jack's basket of snacks and throwing a bag of chips my way.

"Here. I need you to have energy later."

"What's happening later?"

"I knew you weren't listening. Trent, Donny, and a few of the other guys are going two-stepping. I told them we'd join."

"Won't it be late by the time we all finish up?"

"Yeah, And? We haven't gone out since we joined the tour. The point was to enjoy a last hurrah before entering the real world. The time to live is now El! You're going."

"Fine," I acquiesce. "You know I'm not the best two-stepper, though. I haven't done it since the Delta Mu party junior year."

"Don't worry." She beams at me. "It's like riding a bike. Plus, the guy does most of the work, anyway."

"I'M glad you made me do this," I say to Lainey as we saddle up to the bar. My feet are going to be sore tomorrow, but I can't find it myself to care. I haven't had this much fun in a long time. After watching Jack flirt with Julie and then hearing him say he has no interest in a relationship, I needed this distraction. I may have overindulged on the tequila, but that's future Ellie's problem. It sucks to be that girl.

"I told you!" Lainey yells over the band.

"You and Trent are getting pretty cozy," I tease.

"He's sweet. Too much of a pushover for the long-term, but perfect for a fling."

"Does he know that?"

"He is aware of the situation. He isn't in a position for anything permanent either, considering he spends most of his time on tour with one band or another. After this ends, he's heading out with another band for six months. And it's not as if I'll be around."

That's ominous. Lainey hasn't talked to me about any post-tour plans. To my knowledge, we'll both be going home and searching for full-time employment. "What does that mean?"

"Nothing," she answers quickly. "Forget I said anything."

I'm going to need more than that, but before I can pry, she lets out a deep groan. "What are they doing here? Did you tell them where we were?"

"Who?" Turning to face the dance floor, I see two figures

walking toward us. They both have on cowboy hats that hide their faces but fit in perfectly to the setting. Since we don't know anyone in Dallas, I have no idea who 'they' could be until they get closer and two pairs of identical brown eyes narrow in on us. They're the same ones Lainey has.

"Look what we have here," Declan says to Jack. "Two runaway coeds enjoying a night out on the town in a strange city without telling anyone where they went. Don't they know how dangerous that is?"

"We weren't keeping it a—" I start but am interrupted by Lainey.

"I don't have to tell you where I go. I'm an adult."

"An adult wouldn't go traipsing around an unfamiliar city without letting anyone know."

"As if you guys tell me everywhere we go," she counters. "And I didn't tell *no one*. I told Jeffrey."

"The geriatric bus driver who goes to bed at 9 p.m. and sleeps like the dead? Not helping your case, Laines," Jack scoffs.

"He's sixty, not eighty-five. And if that's true, then how did you find us?"

"Tim posted a story on social media and we spotted you two in the background."

"Stupid, Tim," she mumbles. "We aren't leaving. We're having fun. And I'd like to point out, we didn't come here alone. We came with your team."

"Lucky you did, or you'd be in even deeper shit," Declan warns.

As the three siblings volley back and forth, I take the opportunity to examine Jack. Wearing the same faded jeans he performed in and a black tee that stretches deliciously across his chest, he appears a mix of relieved and annoyed. Does he care that much that Lainey and I went out? I'm used to Declan being overprotective, not Jack. His eyes lack their normal mischievous gleam and his shoulders are tense by his ears.

The raised voices of Lainey and Declan halt my perusal.

"Alright, I think that's enough arguing." I break in. "You two are here now, meaning we're no longer 'alone in a strange city.' You are more than welcome to watch us dance, but we aren't leaving."

"Let's get back out there and make the most of our night before the band calls it quits," I direct to my best friend.

"We'll be over there," Dec says, pointing to a table by the dance floor where their security guy Martin and Bryce are already posted up.

"Great," Lainey grits.

As they walk over to their table, we down a shot and head back to the group we came with, though some of them have moved to chat with the brothers.

"Everything okay?" Donny asks, arm slung over a woman he met earlier. Not that her presence has kept his eyes from lingering on me.

"Yes," Lainey huffs. "Just my brothers being overprotective dill holes, but we aren't going to let them ruin our night. It's dancing time."

Grabbing my hand, she pulls me with her as we join in on the current line dance. It takes me a minute to catch on, but when I do, I let the music flow through me. Dancing is one of the few times I feel free. Absorbed in the moment, I don't realize the song changed until I bump into a hard chest.

"Oh my gosh! I am so sorry," I rush out.

"Not a problem, darlin'. A man shouldn't complain when a pretty lady gives him an excuse to talk to her."

Holy shit. If his accent wasn't sexy enough, the man attached to it is as hot as my cheeks feel right now. Letting my gaze drift up from his chest into his ocean blue eyes, I wonder if I am drooling. In a short sleeve button down, jeans, and boots that are clearly used for work and play, the man in front of me is a sight to behold.

"I'm Garrett. And who should I file my insurance claim against?"

"Insurance claim?"

"For the hit and run you're about to perpetrate."

Is this sexy as sin man flirting with me? Me? It wouldn't surprise me to find out he's a model hired to play a cowboy, and he's spending his time flirting with me? Taking a quick glance around, Lainey gives me the universal look for 'OMG he is so hot' and 'don't mess this up.' Right. Time to flirt back.

"It's Ellie, and what makes you think I'm going to run for it?"

"Aside from the fact that women as beautiful as you are hard to catch? Must be the doe eyes that remind me of all the deer that scamper off at the first crunch of boots in the woods."

"Hmm, you called me beautiful and compared me to an animal in the same sentence. I'm not sure if I should be flattered or offended."

He lets out a deep laugh before replying, "I must be off my game if you're anything but flattered."

"We can blame it on your near death collision," I tease.

"Very kind of you. How about I make it up to you with a dance?"

"Sure you can handle it? I didn't hurt you, did I?" I know I didn't. The man has a good fifty pounds and six inches on me. He has the kind of muscles earned working hard and not at the gym. Farm strong.

"I'm up for the challenge. How about I show you how much?"

Something in the back of my mind tells me I should say no. That I should be dancing with Jack. But he didn't ask me and he isn't interested. The hunk in front of me is.

"Lead the way."

NURSING A BEER, Declan and I stay rooted at our table as we watch the girls dance. I thought my brother's head was going to explode when he realized Lainey went out without telling him. She may be an adult, but she's still our little sister. We'll always feel responsible for her, especially Mr. Overprotective.

Thankfully, our sound guy, Tim, is addicted to social media and chronicles his life. Grayson was checking to see if he had any good pics from the show when we came across Lainey and Ellie out dancing. Dec and I threw on hats, hoping it would be enough to hide our identities and hightailed it here with Martin and Bryce before the sneaky sneaks could relocate.

When we spotted the girls, I almost tripped over my own feet seeing Ellie. Out of her usual leggings and in a suede fringe skirt and milkmaid top, she was a vision. A vision far too many men were checking out for my taste. If my mind was wondering how her long, boot clad legs would feel wrapped around my back, I'm sure theirs were, too.

While she may currently look like a country boy's dream girl, Ellie has the kind of classic beauty that transcends style. Whether she was in an old Hollywood gown or '70s muumuu, she would shine through. She also has this doe-eyed air of innocence that makes it almost impossible to be stern with her. Which we're supposed to be right now.

Using the last few steps to collect myself, I put on my game face. I zoned out as Declan lectured Lainey on the dangers of running off with people she hardly knows. Instead, I focused on Ellie's perusal of me from peripheral vision. Get your fill, pretty girl. I love knowing the attraction is mutual even if we can't act on it.

Now, sitting at our table, I can't help but keep my eyes glued to the blonde beauty. She channels a freeness as dances to "Boot Scootin' Boogie." I can't help but smile as she twirls around, completely unaware that the song changed. That's the wild girl I knew.

That smile is quickly wiped off my face when a blond himbo lets her bump into him. He could have moved out of the way, but he allowed her to make contact to give himself a reason to chat with her. I have to admit, it's a good move. One I probably would have done if I'd been in his shoes.

Which I should be. In his shoes, I mean. I should be out there talking to Ellie, making her eyes sparkling as she laughs. Fuck. It's getting harder and harder to put a lid on the emotions I'm having for his girl, especially the jealousy overwhelming my logical side. Tearing my eyes away from the flirting pair, I toy with the label of my beer, tearing it into pieces. The more I watch her, the more I examine my feelings, and that isn't going to lead us anywhere good.

"Can you believe this shit?" Declan grouses.

"Are you surprised? Lainey has always been a rebel."

"She can rebel all she wants, but she still needs to be safe about it."

"I mean, she did come out with our guys," Bryce comments. "They wouldn't be dumb enough to pull anything with her. Plus, I'm pretty sure she'd eat them alive."

"That's beside the point. I know the label background checks the roadies and crew, but backgrounds don't check for douchebag or creep. And they all seem too preoccupied with the local talent to be watching our girls. Even the one who has a hard-on for Ellie is letting someone else swoop in."

"One of the roadies wants Ellie?" I ask. I've seen the way Donny watches her, because I'm watching her, too. I didn't realize anyone else noticed. Does that mean they noticed me? "I knew about the one practically in love with Lainey, but I thought we'd scared the rest of them off both of them that first night. Clearly, we aren't scary enough."

Declan hums in agreement while Bryce seems amused. "He's practically a cartoon character with smoke coming out of his ears watching that other guy move in on his girl. "

"She isn't his girl," I snap. No way. Ellie belongs to no one. And if she is going to belong to someone, it isn't going to be some roadie who hookups with a different woman in every city. She's spectacular. She's smart, sweet, and sinfully sensual without even realizing it. The kind of book that you can't put down. She deserves someone dedicated to her and her alone.

"I'm inclined to agree with you with the way she's letting that Eastwood look alike swing her around the dance floor."

Eyes darting up in the direction he's staring, I spot Ellie and the blond cowboy. He's spinning her around, bodies in tune to each other's moves as if they've been dance partners for years. I don't care for it one bit. When he dips her over his knee, my jaw clenches so hard, I'm surprised my teeth don't shatter.

Shooting up from my stool, I stomp across the dance floor toward them. I'm moving so fast, I almost miss the way Bryce and Declan laugh at me. Dec won't be laughing long when he spots Lainey sucking face with—Brent?—in the corner. He can deal with that problem. I have my own couple to bust up.

I reach the pair as the song transitions into a new, slower one. "Mind if I cut in?"

My question startles Ellie, but not Cowboy Casanova. He clocked me as I made my way over. Whatever he sees on my face is enough for him to decide to bow out, but he still glances at Ellie for her confirmation.

To her credit, she appears conflicted. Biting her lip, she shifts her gaze between the two of us. With a smile, he makes the decision for her. "It was a pleasure, Ellie. Come find me if you need a partner again later."

"She won't." He gives me a knowing nod and heads to the bar. Smart man.

Slipping my arms around her waist, I pull the confused blonde to me and move us to the beat of the slow '90s ballad.

"What are you doing?" she finally asks.

"Dancing. You may have heard of it. You've been doing it all night. I believe you did it at your graduation party as well."

And by believe, I mean I watched you all night.

"Wow, that was lame," she deadpans. "I know what it is. Why are you doing it with me?"

Leaning back, I scan her face. Her cheeks are pink from exertion, but I can still see the light freckles that dot her nose and cheeks. The urge to trace them with my fingers hits hard, but I push it away. Her blue eyes glisten in the neon lights, and I'm surprised when I see a small amount of insecurity in them.

"Who else would I dance with?"

Ellie shrugs. Her gaze darts down to my lips for a brief moment and I swear she contemplates pushing her mouth to mine, but she doesn't. The movement distracts me from questioning her further.

Instead of kissing me, she lays her head on my shoulder and

I soak in the sensation. She feels perfect in my arms. Better than she has any right to consider who she is to me and my family. Her gaze darts down to my lips for a brief moment and I swear she contemplates pushing her mouth to mine, but she doesn't.

When she nuzzles into my neck, I let myself forget all the reasons it should feel wrong and enjoy the rightness. Every time I have had Ellie in my arms it has felt this way. It's been a long time since I had this—maybe I never have. All my past relationships have been surface level. It's nice to be able to relax with someone who doesn't have any nefarious motives.

Breathing her in, I try to think of something, anything, to say, but I can verbalize these emotions. The scent of her rose shampoo overwhelms me. Of course she smells like flowers. The fragrance unlocks memories of sitting in our backyard as the wind blew through the field that surrounded us. It smells like peace and it makes me realize that is how it feels to be around Ellie.

My entire world is tilting on its axis from this epiphany and I don't know how to process it. To my relief and annoyance, Declan lets out a whistle that is so distinctly him, I immediately know its meaning. Pulling back from Ellie, I peer into eyes whose confusion mirrors mine. "Time to roll out, Wildflower."

Before she can voice any of the questions rattling around her head, Lainey loops her arms through hers and leads our group toward the front of the bar. Loading the girls up in our SUV, they both fall asleep on the drive back to the arena. We manage to rouse them enough that they can crawl into bed.

As I slide into my bunk, my mind replays the entire night, attempting to make sense of it all. Somewhere between seeing that social media post and now, Ellie went from my sister's friend to the object of my desire and fuck if I know what to do about that.

13

Ellie

THE NEXT MORNING I am greeted with a pounding headache. Rolling away from the light sneaking in through the shades, I groan at how criminal it is that my legs and feet are this sore considering I wasn't even in heels.

"Stop being so loud," Lainey grumbles beside me.

Using the little strength I have, I roll over and face the orchestrator of the night that has been feeling like death. Lainey looks rough this morning. After falling asleep in the car on the way home from the bar, we managed to make it inside the bus and into the bed. We may have taken our boots off, but not much else was done.

I'm pleased to see that I changed into an oversized tee. But based on how dry my mouth is, I don't think I brushed my teeth or washed off my makeup. Not that I was wearing much. Lainey, on the other hand, could pass for a zombie bride in her white dress, disheveled hair, and makeup smeared all over her face.

"You look hot, but isn't Tim Burton missing you?" I rasp.

"Shut up, Casper."

"Rude! Casper is a boy. And a blob." Picking up my pillow, I smack her in the face with it.

"It's too early for violence," she whines.

"I have a sneaking suspicion it's not that early and the guys let us sleep in."

"Early is a state of mind. I'm going to go wash my face and brush my teeth. You can shower first. I'm not going to be able to stand up for more than two minutes without coffee."

"Sounds good," I reply, plopping back on the bed as I wait my turn.

While she takes care of business, I reflect on last night. I wasn't drunk enough to black out. I remember that way Jack interrupted my dance with Garrett vividly. I'd like to attribute the sensation in my stomach to the hangover, but I think it may be butterflies.

Jack seemed as jealous as I was seeing him flirt with Julie, and it gave me a thrill to know I could affect him that way. He is one of the most chill men I've ever met. Knowing I can get under his skin even a small amount is heady. Even if he doesn't want a relationship, he still wants me at least a little.

My thoughts continue to swirl as I shower. By the time I emerge from the bathroom, I don't have an explanation for what happened between Jack and me, but I do have some color back in my face. Casper wasn't a far off description of my appearance.

I hear Lainey slip in while I'm changing. She makes quick work of the shower and by the time I'm sitting on the bed enjoying the coffee she left me, she is back in the room. She glances in my direction several times as she dresses and combs her long brown waves.

After the tenth time, I can't take it anymore. "What?"

"What *what?*" she asks.

"Why do you keep staring at me as if you're going to tell me my dog died?"

"You haven't had a dog since Bleaker died in seventh grade."

"I know, and this is what your face looked like then. Spill it!"

"Okay, but you have to promise to not get mad."

"Not off to a great start. What did you do?"

"I didn't *do* anything. Not anything bad anyway." God, she is the queen of semantics. I am never going to get it out of her if we go down this road.

"Oh my God. Just tell me."

With a face of resignation, she paces the room in front of me before sitting down on the edge of the bed. "Do you remember the fellowship program Professor Stovall convinced me to apply to with Marcia Tabers?"

"The one Kelly Klieman got?" She nods. Marcia Tabers is the 'It' stylist right now. She got her break in the couture houses in Italy before moving to New York and then LA to work with the hottest stars. One of Professor Stovall's former TAs worked her way up from assistant to fellowship program coordinator. She encouraged anyone interested in being a stylist to apply.

I was surprised Kelly was chosen over Lainey. Their grades were similar, but Lainey's portfolio was far better. I wondered if Kelly's East Coast pedigree played a role, but never had proof other than intuition.

"What about it?"

"Turns out Kelly can't hang and quit after a week because she missed her boyfriend."

"And that would make me mad, why?"

"Because they called me yesterday and offered it to me."

Jumping up, I pull her into a tight embrace. "Laines, that is amazing news! You're going to kill that position."

"Thank you," she sighs. "I think so, too. It's the opportunity of a lifetime to even see her styles, let alone be involved in the process."

"I still don't understand why you think I'd be upset about

that."

"Because it's in LA." Shit. I forgot about that. Even though Alexis and Macy graduated before us, they stayed in town. The four of us haven't been separated for more than a few weeks since freshman year. This tour was going to be the longest we'd gone without seeing each other, but at least we paired off. I'll be sad to see Lainey go when the tour is over. Unless . . .

Studying my friend, I watch her chew on her lip and fiddle with the ends of her hair, a telltale sign she's uncomfortable. It dawns on me then that the fellowship has already started. If Kelly bailed, they would need someone ASAP to fill her spot.

"When?" I whisper.

"I'm taking a flight out as soon as we get to Tulsa."

That is in two days. Not only is my bestie leaving me, but she's doing it in forty-eight hours. That gives me no time to figure out my next move.

What am I going to do? I know I have a role on this tour, but the main reason I was invited was Lainey. If she's not here, do I have a place here? Do I want one without her?

"Should I go home?"

"Of course not!" she asserts. "The guys love having you here and Shonda has said what a godsend you are."

"Are you sure? I don't want to make them uncomfortable. It's one thing when you're here. It's another to have their sister's best friend freeloading when you aren't here as a buffer."

"You don't need a buffer. It's my brothers. You've been around them more than half your life. It will be fine."

She may be right about me being around them for most of my life, but she isn't right about not needing a buffer. If the energy that cropped up between me and Jack yesterday was any indication, we very much need a buffer. Not for the first time, I am hit with guilt for never telling her about my crush on him. She wouldn't have loved to hear about it, but I think she could respect it. Probably. Maybe. I need to know what Jack thinks about all this and if I'm the only one who noticed our increased tension.

"What did the guys say?"

"I haven't told them yet," she confesses.

"Lainey!"

She lets out a big exhale before pursing her lips. "I know. I know. I'm going to tell them, but I wanted you to know first to make sure you were okay with it. If you needed me to, I would stay. They could find someone else."

"Absolutely not! This is a great opportunity. I am so proud."

"Thank you," she says sincerely.

She grimaces when we hear the sound of laughter through the bedroom door. "I guess it's time to face the music."

"It will be great. They're going to be excited for you, babe."

"I know. I hate letting them down and they were excited to have this last tour together before we split off for a while."

"They'll get over it. If anyone is going to be upset, it'll be Trent. I wouldn't be surprised if he tries to sneak into your carryon."

That idea brings a smile back to her face. "I'm sure he'll survive."

"Wish me luck telling the Bossy Bros."

"You don't need it," I quip, slapping her ample ass. "Go get 'em, Tiger!"

Once she exits the room, I sit back on the bed. I can't believe Lainey is leaving with nine weeks left on the tour. Can I handle this alone for two months?

I'm not worried about the work. Even though it isn't my life-long dream, I have been enjoying it. I just hate that I'm not any closer to a plan. Pulling out my laptop, I decide now is as good a time as any for my weekly job applications. If Lainey is moving forward, then I need to, too. Scary is it might be, I can't get left behind.

14

WHEN LAINEY TOLD us about the internship, we were happy for her. Working with Marcia Tabers in any capacity is career making for a stylist, but especially one trying to break into the industry. We would never deny Lainey the opportunity to pursue her dreams. As bummed as we are that she's leaving, we know she is going to kill it in LA.

That said, driving my baby sister to the airport was hard. It's weird being on this end of the spectrum. We've left for tours, specials, and photoshoots countless times. But dropping Lainey off at the airport was one of the hardest goodbyes we've had as siblings. It didn't help to watch the tearful exchange between her and Ellie.

When it was my turn, Lainey made me promise to watch out for her best friend and make sure she was taken care of. I was given explicit instructions to make sure she doesn't forget to eat when she gets busy working or stressed. I have noticed she tends to be hungry after shows but I didn't think anything of it since I am, too. Ellie doesn't perform for an hour and a half on stage, though.

She also told me in no uncertain terms to remind Ellie that she doesn't owe her dad anything and that she should tell him to screw off. I have no idea what that is about, but my curiosity is piqued. I give Lainey my word Ellie is in safe hands.

With all those emotions swelling inside me, it took all my restraint to not pull a sniffling Ellie in my arms on the way home. The urge to comfort her was overwhelming. I'm glad I was in the front seat, otherwise, I might have given in. I hated seeing her sad, so I made it my mission to keep her mind off it.

As much as I wish it could have been with the rush of endorphins that comes from an orgasm, I went a different direction. With Lainey gone, I need to be even more careful about my contact with Ellie. Dec and Gray are around, but they are nowhere near as good of a buffer as Lainey was.

I've spent the last week teasing Ellie any chance I can get. It's giving 'pulling her hair on the playground,' but luckily my natural joke-y personality is masking the deeper motives. I know I shouldn't push her buttons, but it's hard not to when she gives me the reactions I want. Her cheeks turn the prettiest pink when she's embarrassed. I'm addicted to the color. I'm desperate to see how far down the flush goes.

My favorite prank to date was laying on the bottom bunk and grabbing her ankle when she passed by. She wasn't impressed. Her reaction wasn't nearly as funny as Grayson's. He screamed so loud security came to check on him.

Since Ellie seemed particularly sad as we headed out of St. Louis, I decide she needs something to turn her frown upside down. She's napping now, and I just so happen to have picked up a fake spider at our last stop. I call that fate.

As quietly as I can I approach her door. Turning the handle, I slowly pull it open when the timber of a male voice rings in my ear. There is no reason anyone aside from Ellie, but especially a man should be in her room. She could be on the phone, but I know she talked to her dad last night because she was in a foul mood after. Leaning against the door to hear better, I know it isn't him based on the soft tone.

Shhh. It's okay, baby girl. It was just a nightmare. You're okay.

Ellie's having nightmares? Does she normally? And who the fuck did she call to talk about it?

I know it feels real, but none of that would ever happen. It's just some terrible scenario your brain cooked up. Sometimes when we are super stressed, it bleeds into our dreams and manifests in weird ways.

A stress dream? It's only been a week and I'm already failing at keeping Ellie from stressing out. Damnit. I had one job. I didn't check on her eating once this week. I'm failing at this whole 'take care of Ellie' thing. Lainey would be disappointed.

We can look up what those things meant. Maybe it will help you understand what your subconscious is thinking. Nuh uh. Not now. You can look tomorrow. Now we're going back to sleep. Yes. Yes we are. You need sleep, baby. You have a big day tomorrow.

What's happening tomorrow? We will arrive in Iowa, but we don't have a show for two days. Tomorrow is a rest day. They should have plenty of time to get merch set up.

Don't worry. I got you. I won't fall asleep until I know you're out. Of course, sweetheart. You should never feel bad about waking me up. I always want you to wake me up when you have a bad dream. That's what I'm here for. Come on. Lay on top of me and—

Nope, fuck that. She is not fake laying on what every asshat she called to comfort her. Abandoning my prank, I fling open the door, ready to face the intruder, but instead I only see a now gaping Ellie clutching her chest.

"What the fuck are you doing?"

"Who is he?" I ask, still hearing his voice but seeing no one.

"Who is who?"

Her eyes widen when she registers the noise. Scrambling

onto her knees, she digs through the covers until she finds her phone. Pressing a few buttons she pushes it under her pillow.

"Why are you in here, Jack?"

"Answer my question first."

"There is nothing to answer."

She won't meet my eyes and I hate it. If she's going to lie to me, she can at least do it to my face. Putting a knuckle under her chin, I tip it up until her eyes meet mine. "Who?" I growl.

"I don't know."

"You're calling strangers? That isn't safe, Ellie."

"No, he's not a stranger. I mean, he is, but it wasn't a call." Her expression pleads with me to drop it, but now I'm more confused than angry. I won't be able to let this go until I know what the hell is going on.

Sensing that, she lets out a resigned huff. "Have you heard of ASMR?"

"Like typing or crinkling paper into a microphone?"

"Yes. I was listening to an ASMR recording."

"That wasn't some random noise, that was a full on conversation."

She narrows her eyes at my continued inquisition. "You are insufferable, you know that right? I don't pry into your business and critique your sleeping routine."

"Ellie, just tell me. The faster you spit it out the sooner we can move on."

"There is a subset of ASMR called boyfriend ASMR where it's a one sided conversation or situation with the male speaker. They have girlfriend ASMR, too, but I've never tried that."

"Like a spicy situation?" I ask, interest piqued.

"Sometimes, but that isn't what I usually listen to." The pretty flush of her cheeks says it sometimes is, though.

"What do you usually listen to?" I am totally curious now and back to being a little jealous that she spends time listening to a man that isn't me. I mean, I have dozens of songs she could choose from.

"Day in the life stuff. Sometimes it's similar to the one you heard where it's a conversation about going to sleep or having anxiety. Mostly I listen to ones where the person is doing mundane things such as reading or playing a video game while the listener is napping beside them."

"Why do you like it?"

"I don't know," she hedges.

"Come on. You've already come this far," I needle.

"It's soothing. There is something about falling asleep next to someone who is awake that makes me—and other women based on how much content is out there—feel safe and cared for. It's easier to sleep when someone is watching over you, real or imagined."

"So you give this strange dude from the internet money to get access to non-personalized recordings to help you fall asleep?"

"I knew you wouldn't get it," she grouses. "What are you even doing in here? There is no reason for you to be in my room."

"I heard a voice, and I was checking on you."

She glares at me skeptically. "You didn't have a reason to be close enough to hea—What the hell is in your hand?!"

Shit. I forgot all about the giant fake spider in my hand. I attempt to hide it behind my back, but it's too late for that now. I'm busted.

"Ugh! Stop pranking me. The fact that real life men act like this is why these ASMR boyfriends make so much money."

"Well, that is a gross generalization," I argue.

"Get out!" she shouts loud enough that the other guys might have heard it.

When I make it back to the lounge, Grayson and Declan glance up from the video game they're planning.

"You're so lame, man," Gray comments while Declan shakes his head. Bryce is zoned out making beats on his laptop.

Whatever. Sinking down on the sofa, I pull out headphones and start searching YouTube for 'boyfriend ASMR' videos. With so many to choose from, I realize Ellie is right. It is popular.

The idea that she's going to an anonymous man on the internet to help her sleep doesn't sit right with me regardless of how many people do it, too. It doesn't take long for me to come with an idea that I hope will make Ellie happy. With a little help from my youngest brother, I think I can make it happen.

15

Jack

"YOU WANT TO DO WHAT?" Bryce asks, confusion evident in his tone.

"I want to record myself doing some mundane tasks and maybe some audios where I'm talking,"

"Is this for social media?"

"No."

"Is it for some press thing?"

"No," I grit. I thought I was the nosy brother but Bryce is giving me a run for my money. I haven't been able to the ASMR incident earlier this week out of my head. I hate the idea that Ellie is turning to a stranger for comfort. I hate the idea that she needs comfort at all, but especially the turning to a stranger part.

If she's on tour with us, we should be the ones comforting her. That's the lie I told myself when I asked Bryce to help. He has all the gadgets and software I need to record audios for Ellie to listen to. So far, I have a handful of ideas.

"You're not recording something for Only Fans are you?"

"Jesus Christ," I mutter. "No. I want to record some ASMR videos for a friend. Can you drop the third degree?"

"Is that friend a leggy blonde who you can't help but stare at every time you're in the same room?"

Shit. Do I stare at her? I know I *look* at her, but I wouldn't have classified it as staring. When my jaw tenses Bryce's face lifts into a shit eating grin. Not dignifying his question with a response, I ask, "Are you going to help me or not?"

"I'll help. Don't get your panties in a wad."

"You're a real pain in the ass, you know that?"

"A pain in the ass you can't do this without."

Damn it. He's right. I could record them as voice notes on my phone but the quality will be much higher and more AMSR-y with his equipment.

Bryce helps me set up in my dressing room a few hours before soundcheck. Once I finish recording, he is going to edit out any interruptions and convert the files before putting them in a cloud folder I can send Ellie.

After recording a couple of sleep aids, I get the idea to record something to help with anxiety. Ellie seems to live in a constant state of stress and pressure. Whether it's from her parents or self-inflicted, I'd love for her to be able to bask in her accomplishments and positive traits without the need to do more.

She has no idea how impressive she is. I am constantly in awe of her. She may not think she has her life together, but I am low-key intimidated by all her plans and lists. As a go with the flow kind of guy, Ellie is my exact opposite. She thinks everything through before making a decision. I do most things off the cuff.

Her sharp wit always has me on my toes. She's beyond beautiful and sweet as hell. Ellie is the total package, and I have no idea how she doesn't see that. It's a wonder no one has snapped her up. I guess I have her father to thank for making her skeptical of men. Lainey's let it slip through the years about what an ass he is. I wouldn't call him a sleaze ball, but he tends to take on clients that lean that direction. I can see why Ellie enjoys listening to emotionally mature, considerate men.

Whatever guy ends up with her is one lucky bastard. Not that anyone deserves her. I sure as hell don't, but that hasn't stopped me from wanting her. I swallow down the lump that forms in my throat at the prospect of anyone else being with Ellie. Aside from the few almost-kisses we've shared, nothing has happened between us and it needs to stay that way. But that doesn't mean I have to like the idea of anyone else getting to kiss her or hold her or soothe her.

Ever since we danced together, I haven't been able to get the idea out of my head. Every day without her, my need grows tenfold. With Lainey gone, it's been even harder to hold back. Lainey is the reason I am making these recordings. If it wasn't for her, I'd be demanding Ellie get her comfort straight from the source: me. But I have yet to figure out how to pursue Ellie without hurting Lainey or jeopardizing their friendship.

EVEN THOUGH I am naturally a yapper, I decide to drink an extra cup of tea after recording audios this morning. Unfortunately, I almost choke on that tea when Ellie stops by sound-check in the tiniest neon biker shorts I've ever seen. She paired them with a tour shirt cut up the sides. Seeing my name across her body does something for me on a primal level.

Wiping tea from my mouth, I glance around to see if anyone noticed my jaw hitting the floor. No one is looking my way, but

Declan is smirking to himself. I don't know if it is from me or something he conjured up in his own mind.

While there are no eyes on me, there are plenty on Ellie. Half the men in the room are shooting her lecherous glances. Glaring at those I can, I call her name across the room to draw her to me.

Somewhat cautiously, she walks over the edge of the raised platform where I can tuning my guitar. "Can I help you with something?"

"Still mad at me, Wildflower?" I coo. She narrows her eyes at me but her cheeks pinken. I guess she is still embarrassed. I hate that she feels that way, but it is also adorable to see her shy. She's so strong and badass most of the time that seeing her out of her element lights me up. I don't want her upset though.

"What if I told you I had a way to make it up to you?" She purses her lips fully intrigued and waits for me to continue. "I have a present for you in my dressing room."

"Last night you had a fake spider. What is it today? Snake hiding in your pocket?" At her words, she sucks her lips into her mouth as her gaze drops to my legs where there is most certainly a snake waiting for her. God she's cute when she blushes. I want to trace the color all the way down her body. It'd be like a rainbow with the pot of gold at the end except the gold is—not something I need to think about right now surrounded by our entire band and sound crew.

"If this is another prank, I'm going to be pissed," she replies. "I will call Lainey to help exact revenge."

"No need to call in the big guns, you'll like it, I promise."

"Tell me what it is."

"Nope."

She pouts at my answer and that expression on her face combined with the way she peers up at me from the stage below makes my knees weak. Which is ironic because all the blood in my body is heading south. Ellie is gorgeous from every angle but sinful from this one. Thank God my guitar is here to hide my boner. I think the only thing more embarrassing than getting a hard-on from a pair of shorts and a little attention would be anyone else knowing about it.

Reaching for my tea, I take a large gulp to combat the sudden dryness of my throat.

"Little early to start drinking," she teases.

"No whiskey in this one."

"Is that my present, because I have to say, it's not my favorite taste."

"What's your favorite taste?"

"Voodoo chips," she says, 'duh' implied in her tone. "What's yours?"

Pride envelopes my chest knowing she's going to love her present. That change of emotion is enough to regain a minuscule amount of my composure. Although thinking about my favorite taste doesn't take me too far out of my current headspace. I'm pretty sure even without trying it that my favorite taste is her.

She must catch the direction my thoughts are in because she turns even redder than before. So Goddamn cute.

"Go enjoy your treat, Wildflower."

With a dubious expression and single nod, she heads that direction, waving to everyone on her way out. Glancing up, I catch Bryce's eye. I flip of his smug face before slyly readjusting my dick behind my guitar.

16

Ellie

"I CAN'T BELIEVE that they kicked Misha off!" Alexis gripes, outraged. Her favorite contestant was kicked off *Singing Sensation* this week, and she is less than pleased.

"Well who else could they have gotten rid of?" Macy questions. "Josiah has the voice of an angel and Amy has the entire state of Arkansas calling in to back her up. He shouldn't have chosen such a hard song. I know he wanted to impress the judges, but he flew too close to the sun and got burned."

I laugh at my friends as they volley back and forth on the merits of a classically trained opera singer choosing *All About That Bass* by Meghan Trainor as his song of the week. The pair are watched together at Macy's apartment before calling me to discuss the results. Lainey was supposed to join us but got called to assist at a last-minute photoshoot. I wanted to question why it was happening at night, but fashion is weird.

Since we're in a new city for a set of weekend shows, I have the night off. The guys are off practicing a change to their set list or doing an interview with local press. I'm not totally sure. All I know is that I was told I'd get the bus to myself most of the evening.

Talking to my girls, I am the most relaxed I have been in days, if not longer. We text every day, but it isn't the same as when we can hear each other's tone and get an immediate response. I've spent that past couple of days holed up in my room applying for jobs, researching career paths, and doing pretty much anything that keeps me out of Jack's orbit since the ASMR incident. I still blush thinking about it. I can't believe he overheard that. He did try to make up for it with a giant haul of voodoo chips, but I am still mortified.

It isn't until I notice silence on the other end of the line that I realize the girls must have seen my embarrassed expression.

"What was that expression about?" Alexis questions.

"What expression? I didn't have an expression. I was thinking about poor Misha being sent home." I rush out too quickly even for my own ears.

"We aren't buying that. Spill. Lainey is not here. You can say anything you want, your secret is safe with us."

Groaning, I decide I need to tell someone what is going on and where my head is at. "There may have been an incident with Jack."

"What do you mean by incident?" Macy asks. "Like a sexy incident?"

"I wouldn't call the most embarrassing moment of my life sexy."

"More embarrassing than the first time you drank Perrier and barely made it to the bathroom before pooping your pants?"

"First and last," I say. I have sworn off the beverage since the incident. "And we swore to never talk about that again, lest I bring up the stuck diva cup of sophomore year or the Bryan Griswell incident."

They both hold up their hands in surrender. "And yes, more embarrassing than that."

After giving them the run down, Alexis is fighting to hold back her giggle while Macy smiles at me sympathetically. "Is that the only thing that has happened?"

"I guess? Things have been weird since Lainey left. At first he was extra annoying trying to keep my mind off it, but since the incident he has been super sweet. And then there was the moment we had at the honky tonk in Dallas and another once in his dressing room . . . I don't know." I pull a pillow onto my face and release a mini scream into it.

"When was the last time you got laid?" Alexis asks.

"Excuse me, ma'am!" I exclaim at the same time Macy answers, "A while."

I let out a huff. "I don't exactly have ample opportunities when living on a bus with three protective older brothers."

"Only two of those boys think of you as a sister, girl. But I see your point. What about *self-care*? Are you doing any of that?"

"When would I have managed that between a bus full of men and sharing a bed with Lainey? The shower isn't exactly roomy."

"You're alone now," she suggests, eyebrows waggling.

"I don't know."

"I think she's right," Macy agrees. Shit. It's never good when they both agree. Their whole opposites attract thing is what balances out the group. As much as I hate to admit it, they may be on to something. My sexual frustration is through the roof. The rare times I can't avoid Jack, everything he does turns me on.

Strumming his guitar, hot. The way he swallows down his crappy coffee first thing in the morning? Tantalizing. Wondering if he's thinking about me when he's lying in his bunk feet away? Full body tingles.

"She's thinking about it right now," Alexis teases.

I shoot her a glare. "You may have a point."

"Of course, I do. You're not the only smart one in the bunch," she tuts. "How long until they get back?"

"I'm not sure, but it shouldn't matter if I'm in my room."

"We'll leave you to it," Macy says with a smirk.

"Let me know if you need a clip of that fight Aiden's team got in during the playoffs," Alexis adds.

"I am not touching myself to videos of your boyfriend, Lex. That's weird as hell."

"Oh my God, no! Not of him, of Xavier Dillon. He plays for the other team and is the bad boy of the league. If I didn't have my gentle giant at home, Mama would be interested in a piece of that."

"I think I'll manage on my own, thanks. Maybe you should find that gentle giant and take care of yourself."

"Maybe I will," she retorts.

Closing out our conversation, I move from the lounge to my bedroom. It's only 8 p.m. I doubt the brothers will think I went to bed this early, but I plan to be long done before they get back.

Learning from the last ASMR incident, I opt to use my imagination and not listen or watch anything. Already dressed for bed, I slide between the sheets and get comfortable. Once I'm there, I queue up one of my favorite scenarios. Me, a sexy mountain man, and a blizzard that leaves me stranded at his cabin. Unfortunately, no matter how hard I concentrate, that one is not doing it for me.

Trying again, I aim for more realistic and think about a past sexy encounter. Last year, I was partnered with the lacrosse captain for a project in my communication studies class. We were supposed to be creating a PSA to preach the importance of safe sex to high school students. Research got away from us and we decided to engage in some safe sex of our own.

Running my hands down my torso, I circle my nipples over my thin shirt. They instantly harden under my attention. I leave one hand on my breasts as the other travels down under the band of my sleep shorts.

Rubbing slow strokes over my mound, I envision Nick kissing my neck as he did that night. I shiver as I remember the way he nibbled the spot where my neck meets my shoulder. Fantasy me reaches her hand up to grab his long dark hair. Wait. Nick had a blond buzz cut. And he certainly didn't have the mustache I sensed tickling my shoulder.

Lifting his head, I see dream Nick has morphed into Jack. I pause my efforts. I am not going to get off to Jack. I do not need to associate orgasm emotions with him. In all the years of my longtime crush, I have never crossed that line. But I've never been as tempted as I am right now.

Attempting to focus back to Nick, I don't immediately stop when he once again turns into Jack. Their voices even sound the same. The 'fuck' that left fantasy Nick sounded exactly like Jack. As amped up as my body has gotten, I fear I'm not going to get where I need. I let out a disgruntled noise.

"If you're having trouble, I am more than happy to lend a hand," Jack's voice says again. It sounded so real. Too real. Opening my eyes, I'm met by Jack's intense gaze. He's watching me as if he's ready to fall at my feet to help me with this problem and I'm tempted to let him.

Frozen, I lay watching him. All he has to do is lift my blanket and he'll see one hand shoved down my pants and the other palming my breast.

When I don't say anything, he steps further into the room, closing the door behind him. When I shoot him a worried glance, he answers as if he read my mind. "It's just me. The guys are in a meeting. I brought dinner in case you hadn't had anything yet. It seems you're preoccupied with something much more fun than eating, though."

"Jack-I-it's not—"

"It's not what it looks like?"

I nod.

"Hmm," he hums. "It looks like you're in here making yourself feel good but you can't quite get there. It looks like you could use a hand to push you over the edge. And I just so happen to have two very capable hands. Can I help you, Ellie? Can I make you feel so good you'll never be able to watch me play again without thinking about the wicked things my fingers did to your hot little pussy?"

I shiver at his question and under the intensity of the way he watches me. I want that. I want to feel his hands on me more than I ever wanted anything. Forgetting what a bad idea it is, I say the two words I thought I'd never say to Jack Ryder.

"Touch me."

17

ARRIVING IN MADISON, WI this morning, the guys and I had a full day of press and filming content for our social team. It was go-go-go until we sat down for dinner. I immediately chowed down on the dairy-filled spread, happy for a few moments when I didn't have to be 'on.' If I was overstimulated, then I know my brothers were even more.

While eating in a comfortable silence, my mind finally has time to drift. And it goes straight to the leggy blonde who has no doubt been avoiding me since I saw her at soundcheck. As bad as I feel about the incident, I appreciate the opportunity it gave me to learn more about her. Plus, she already accepted my chip apology. I hope the audios I have in the works will be even more well received.

Once I've shoveled enough food into my stomach to more than make up for missing lunch, I decide to make good on my promise to Lainey to ensure Ellie eats. It will make me feel marginally better about the way I can't keep her off my mind. Grabbing a plate of food, I tell Grayson and Declan I'm going back to the bus. They nod, letting me know they have a meeting with Eliza and our agency team to talk about their next projects. That's a punch in the gut. I'm still unsure of what my next move is. I'm glad I have feeding Ellie to distract me.

When I first get to the bus, she's nowhere to be seen. I wonder if she's gone out. It's only a little after eight. I can't imagine she's asleep yet. I don't think she'd go out without telling any of us, but after Dallas, I'm not sure. Her silent bedroom points to sleep. I need to know for sure or I'll worry. It won't hurt to peek into her room. If she's there, I'll know not to worry and if she isn't, I'll rally the troops, a.k.a. Declan, to find her.

Edging the door open, I let out a sign of relief when I see her lying in bed. At first, I think she's actually sleeping, but then I notice something moving underneath the covers and the way her chest rises quicker than normal. Is she doing what I think she's doing? I open the door wider to get a better view.

"Fuck." The curse slips out of me before I can stop it and I freeze in place. Waiting a beat to see if my cover is blown, I consider backing out. I wanted to know if she was here and now I do. I have no reason to be standing here watching her like a creep. But I can't seem to get my feet to move.

Ellie is mesmerizing. Even though I can only see her from the shoulders up, she is practically ethereal surrounded by the white bedding. Her face contorts in frustration and I wonder what—or rather, who—she's envisioning. There is no sound in the room, so I know she isn't using a video or audio to get off. It's just her and her imagination. The idea of her getting off to thoughts of me has me stiffening in my pants. I was already sporting a semi, but I'm about to have a full-fledged problem on my hand if I don't get the hell out of here.

Instead of leaving, I do something stupid. Really stupid.

When Ellie makes a sound of discontentment. "If you're having trouble, I am more than happy to lend a hand."

It takes a beat, but then her eyes shoot open, pinning me where I stand. I consider apologizing, but the mix of lust and longing in her expression is too much to turn down.

Stepping further into the room, I let her know that we'll have the bus all to ourselves for a while and reiterate my willingness to help her get off. And holy fuck am I willing. I would give almost anything right now to see her come. And to be a part of it . . . I'd give even more.

Ellie pulls her bottom lip into her mouth as she considers my proposition. She has no reason to accept it, but when she tells me to touch her, I almost come in my pants right then. I take one deep inhale to compose myself and decide on my next move.

"Move the blanket," I command. Her hand moves to clutch the side. She hesitates. As much as I want to rip the blanket off her, this needs to be her decision. If she wants me to help her, it will be my fucking honor, but I won't do it without her enthusiastic consent.

As the second she takes to make her decision drags on, I wait on bated breath. When she finally shucks off the comforter, I want to drop to my knees in gratitude. Placing one knee on the bed, I catch her gaze as I slowly crawl up toward her.

Allowing my fingers to ghost up her legs, my hand lands on top of hers over the tiny sleep shorts that have been tempting me all tour. They aren't lingerie by any means, but with her long legs, they leave miles of creamy real estate to lust after.

"The thought of you in here playing with this pussy is enough to bring a man to his knees, Wildflower. Tell me you haven't been in this room every night making yourself come when I was on the other side of that door dreaming of a moment exactly like this."

"I wasn't," she confesses. "This is the first time."

"So many weeks without relief. No wonder you're pent up. You need to come, Ellie?"

She nods, shivering at the question as I gently tug on her wrist, pulling it out of her shorts. Her pretty blue eyes bore into mine, pleading for relief. Relief I'll give her, but I want something first.

"Give me a taste. Give me a taste and I'll make you come all over my fingers until you're seeing stars."

"You want to taste me?" She looks nervous and excited by the proposition. She reaches to tug down her shorts, but I stop her, causing her to wrinkle her brow.

"I would love nothing more than to bury my face in what I know is a perfect pussy, but if I do, we won't be leaving this room until morning, and I'm not sure you're ready for that."

"Then how?" she asks.

Instead of answering, I pull her hand to my lips and slowly suck the fingers she was using to please herself into my mouth. I moan as the taste of her desire coats my tongue, willing it to imprint in my brain so I never forget it.

As my tongue licks her essence off her fingers, I slip mine under the band of her shorts. She's already wet from her early ministrations as I tentatively flick her bud to see how sensitive she is. She immediately bucks against my hand.

Letting her hand fall away, I move my lips to kiss up her arm to her shoulder. I nip at the creamy skin there, humming in satisfaction as it pinks under my attention. As my lips reach the delicate skin behind her ear, she pushes her hips into my circling fingers.

I slide one finger down her folds and slip it into her entrance with little resistance. When it comes out coated, I add a second. She mewls at the contact of my thumb against her clit as my digits work inside her.

One of her hands shoots to the back of my neck where she pulls me further into her and the other grips my forearm. Her nails are blunt but part of me is desperate for her to leave an indention behind. I'd happily tattoo her nail marks on my skin and wear them with pride.

I touch a spot inside her that changes her tiny keens to a loud, breathy moan. I can tell she is getting close by the way she grips me harder and grinds into me.

"You're so close. Are you going to come for me, baby? Are you going to come all over my fingers?"

"Jack, fuck. Yes. Don't stop."

I suck harder on her neck as I maintain the speed and pressure. I give my wrist a slight twist and she trembles against me, core clenching. As she shudders through her orgasm, I whisper what a good girl she is and how hot having her come on my fingers is.

When she comes down from her orgasm, she releases her hold on me and watches, stupefied, as I slide the parts of me that were inside her into my mouth. As if I'd waste any of her taste. I am going to get myself off later with her taste on my tongue.

Panting below me, uncertainty swirls in her eyes as she reaches for my painfully neglected cock. Grabbing her hands, I shake my head. "Not tonight. Tonight was about you. You feel good?"

"Yes," she laughs. "I don't remember the last time I felt this incredible. That was—wow."

"Glad to be of service. I'm happy to help anytime you need assistance," I croon coyly. I should probably say something more substantial, but all the blood has rushed to my dick and I can't ignore it any longer.

Kissing her swiftly, I push off the bed and walk to the door. Glancing back at her dreamy expression one last time, I make my way into the shower to take care of myself. Using my clean hand to grip my cock, I press my forehead against the wall, inhaling the scent of her on my other hand mixed with the smell of her shampoo in the small cubicle.

It takes shockingly few strokes remembering the sounds she made and the sensation of her falling apart beneath me until I'm finding my own release.

Catching my breath, my thoughts stay on the beauty in the bed in the next room. Tonight we didn't just cross a line. We went so far past it that I can't even see it anymore. And I can't seem to care.

I don't want to fight my feelings for Ellie anymore. The situation is complicated, but to go back to how we were before would be impossible. I want her to be mine. I need to find out if she wants the same and how we can make this work, for me, for her, and for Lainey.

UNSURPRISINGLY, Ellie is back to avoiding me the next morning. We had to leave earning to do some press and by the time I got back, she was nowhere to be found. Part of me is glad because I'm not sure what to say yet. The other part is desperate to see her and know what she's thinking.

My head is full of conflicting emotions. I'm filled with guilt, nerves, and self-doubt. Things I don't normally experience. That would normally worry me, but all those emotions are overshadowed by longing.

I know Lainey won't be happy if something develops between me and Ellie. I also know that I have never felt this way toward another woman before and I would be foolish to let it pass me by. Sure of my intentions, I think we can all be mature enough to handle this situation in a way where no one has to get hurt, except maybe me if Ellie isn't on the same page.

Though, I'm less unsure about that after the way she came on my hand last night.

I'm not so much nervous that she doesn't want me now, but that she won't want me later. Ellie is smart and put together in a way I'll never be. She has a master's degree and I am essentially a high school dropout. If I couldn't play the guitar and hadn't had a few lucky breaks, who knows where I would be.

I know Ellie isn't after my money or clout, but I doubt she would look my way without them. I have no idea what I could offer her, but the way she looks at me sometimes gives me hope that she thinks something. I'd give her the world, but I have no doubt she can get that on her own. The best I can offer is staying back and watching her shine. I can be the safe place she returns to after taking on the world. The place where she recharges for her next adventure.

After searching for her for twenty minutes, I decide to give her the space she clearly wants. She knows where to find me. And if she doesn't soon, let's just say it is a good thing that I know where she sleeps.

18

Ellie

HIDING in my room the next morning, I am reeling from my encounter with Jack. Seeing his eyes close as he sucked my taste off his fingers is one of the hottest things I have ever witnessed. He played my body like a finely tuned instrument. Years of honing his craft paid off. I clench my thighs, remembering the way the callous on his thumb felt against my clit.

Last night was a fantasy come true. If it wasn't for the hickey he left behind my ear, I would honestly wonder if it was a dream or not. I guess Jack wanted to leave no question about what we did. Except I have a lot of questions. Namely, why did he want to help me and what does it mean?

I was shocked when he didn't want me to do anything for him. Was he not as turned on as I was? That fear was mostly remedied a few minutes later when I heard him moan my name from the shower. It still doesn't tell me if he wants to do it—or more—again.

With no desire to be the girl who asks a guy 'what they are' after one sexual encounter, I busy myself getting ready for tonight's show. Getting shoved in and out of tubs a dozen times is rough on t-shirts, so I decide today is as good a day as any to refold them. It's too early for volunteers to be here yet, which means I'm basically alone in the empty concourse. It's both cool and eerie.

Unluckily, I have texts from my father to keep me company.

11:14 AM

DAD

I'm hearing from sources that the boys' tour is a mess. Sounds as if they may need a new tour manager.

How do you do to you, too, Dad. I guess he is jumping straight to the point today. I don't know who his source is, but Teri, the tour manager, is both amazing and beloved. He's been with the Ryders for years. I can't imagine them wanting to replace him. Eliza on the other hand . . .

I haven't heard of any issues.

I doubt you'd know what they looked like if you saw them.

Let them know I would be happy to help them out.

I love that he calls it 'helping them out' when we both know the premium he would be paid to work with a name as big as theirs. He's been trying to get in with this label for years but hasn't had any bites. There are no favors here. I hate that he's trying to exploit my closeness to the guys further his own career. So much for his faux concern with mine. Since it is easier to pacify him than try to reason. I tell him I will mention his

127

'willingness to jump onboard' if needed. A sentiment I whisper out loud into the empty concourse as I finish folding t-shirts. Guess no one was here to see that. Oh well.

"You know, if you're so lonely you need to talk to yourself, I know someone who would happily spend time with you," a voice says from behind me.

I let out a shriek at the sound. Whipping around, I mentally chastise myself for being jumpy and greet the visitor. "Donny, you scared me."

"Sorry, beautiful." He smirks. "What has you working so hard? You know people will buy this shit even if it's wrinkled. Hell, it could have 'Ryder Concert' hand written on it and they would still pay top dollar."

I bristle at his assessment. Designers put in hours creating these shirts and the tour spent a ton of money printing them. I don't know how much of the revenue comes from merch sales, but I know it isn't an insignificant amount.

"What can I say? I take my job seriously."

Donny steps closer until he has me almost pressed against the merch trailer. "All work and no play makes Ellie a dull girl," he singsongs. His breath fans against the side of my face. Uncomfortable, I turn until we're face to face. The movement causes my hair to fall behind my back, exposing the hickey Jack left last night. Donny's gaze immediately catches it.

"I guess Ellie is having plenty of fun," he snorts restively, fingers running over the mark. "I didn't take you as the groupie type. I thought you had more class than that."

"I'm not a groupie," I counter, pushing my hand between us, trying to make space, but he doesn't budge.

"Sure," he laughs darkly. "Tell me, is it only Jack you're screwing or do all three brothers get a turn?"

I rear back at the accusation, but that causes my head to smack into the metal trailer. I don't know what has gotten into Donny, but I don't like his aggressive attitude. Glancing around,

I curse myself for leaving the walkie-talkie on the table and not clipping it to my shorts. I don't see anyone else around to help defuse the situation. It's up to me.

"It's a straightener burn. It's not from Jack or anyone else," I lie. "You need to back up."

"I bet. I gave a lot of girls 'straightener burns' in high school. You're not fooling me. I saw the way he watched you in Dallas. Those boys keep you on a tight leash. Makes sense why now. They don't wanna share their toy."

What the fuck? Even if I was screwing the Ryders and their entire band, it would be none of his business and would not give him the right to corner me.

Not heeding my request for space, he pushes even closer until his mouth is practically touching my ear. "I'll let you in on secret: I've never been good with FOMO. I may need to see what all the fuss is about."

A cold dread washes over me at his insinuation. I'm about to scream for help when my new favorite person comes to my rescue. "Ellie," Bryce calls from the other side of the trailer, "you're going to miss lunch."

Donny backs up before Bryce rounds it, leaving me unbalanced in his wake. He appraises us curiously before nodding his head at me to follow him. Scurrying away from the roadie as fast as I can, I risk a glimpse back at him. His jaw is tense and his demeanor says this is far from over.

What do I do about this? Do tours have HR? It's his word against mine, but I need to get it on someone's radar, at least. I'm sure if I ask, they can reassign him somewhere else. I'm even more thankful now that my dad isn't the tour manager.

I could always tell one of the Ryders. That is a conversation I do not want to have. But if Donny's going to be throwing around accusations that could hurt their reputations, they need to know. I could tell Eliza, she's a pit bull. She's a bitch, but that could work in my favor in this scenario.

When we make it to catering, Bryce gives me a nod and disappears into the masses, too cool to eat with me, apparently. I don't mind this time, though. I'm not especially hungry after what just happened, but I can't stand around aimlessly. Sat at an empty table longer than I should, I'm pushing food around my plate when Declan storms into the room. Sensing tension, the room quiets noticeably as his gaze lands on me. He gives me the universal sign for 'come with me' and I quickly get up to follow behind him.

Instead of going to the bus or dressing room, Declan leads me to an unused office. As soon as the door closes, he faces me and grits, "What happened?"

19

Jack

DECLAN WAS on fire during tonight's show. I don't know what got into him, but he channeled it all into his performance. Once we get into the green room, I can't help but call it out. "You were on another level tonight, bro. What was up with that?"

I can sense the passion still radiating off him as our post-show adrenaline surges.

"Not being allowed to beat the shit out of a deserving roadie will do that to you," he says as he downs a bottle of water.

Grayson and I shoot each other befuddled expressions before shifting our attention back to our brother. "Care to elaborate?"

"I fired Donny before the show tonight."

"Do we have the power to fire crew members?"

Declan shrugs as if that fact is irrelevant to the situation.

"Are you going to tell us why?" I push. "The guy is annoying, but I don't think that's a fireable offense."

"No, but sexual harassment is."

"Shit. Who did he harass?" Grayson asks.

When he answers, I understand for the first time what seeing red means.

"Tell. Me. Everything," I demand as soon as Ellie's name slips from his lips.

"Bryce came to me earlier and said he found Donny cornering Ellie by the merch booth and she did not appear to be enjoying his attention. He wasn't sure, but he interrupted the moment anyway. SinceEllie seemed shaken up, he came to me about it. I asked security for the footage from that area and her body language screamed 'back off.'"

Damn it. I knew that guy was going to be trouble. From the first time I saw him eyeing the girls, I knew his intentions were bad, but to try to hurt someone close to us? Is he stupid? Did he think it wouldn't get back to us or that we wouldn't care? And why the fuck did Bryce go to Declan and not me? I never confirmed it but I know he knows there is something between us.

"So you fired him instead of kicking his ass?" Grayson asks, keeping the conversation on track.

"First, I asked Ellie what happened. She gave me what I imagine is a watered-down version of the encounter."

I am fuming. If this is the lite version, I know I am going to be pissed to hear the full thing. And I will hear the full thing. My brothers don't know what went down last night. Ellie and I haven't had the chance to talk about it. I went back after my shower, but she was already asleep. I didn't want to let my brother's in on what she could potentially label as a mistake.

"You said Bryce told you. Was Ellie planning to tell any of us?"

"She said she was still deciding when I approached her. To be honest, I'm not sure she was."

"That's bullshit," Grayson growls. "She should never have to deal with something like this on her own. No member of our tour should, but especially not her."

I couldn't agree more. I know she was avoiding me after what happened last night, but I can't believe she wouldn't have come to me about this.

"Where is she now?" I ask, itching to check that she's okay on my own and to know what the hell she was thinking.

"I gave her the night off. She should be on the bus."

Without another word, I storm out of the room. I don't acknowledge anyone, not Eliza, not security, not even my screaming fans. I say nothing to no one until I step foot on the bus and see Ellie huddled up in a blanket in the lounge. Heading straight toward her, I pick her up and place her back down on my lap.

Placing my forehead against her temple, wet hair cools my temper as her sweet floral scent surrounds me. "Are you okay?" I ask.

"Declan told you?" is her reply.

"Yeah, he did. And I'm pissed I didn't hear it from you, but right now all I care about is that you're okay."

"I'm fine. Why would I tell you?" she asks, genuine confusion in her voice.

"Why would you tell me that some douchebag is harassing you? Are you seriously asking me that?"

"Yes. I mean, what could you have really done about it without any proof? Plus, if you did do anything, you would be confirming what he said. I wasn't sure you'd care. I was probably going to tell Eliza, but Bryce told Declan first."

"Fuck that," I huff indignantly. I lean back and twist until she's underneath me on the couch. I know she sees me as the good time guy who doesn't take things seriously, but when it comes to her, I find I can be rather possessive and unreasonable. I plan to tell her as much.

"First, I could have done a hell of a lot. Kicked him off the tour at minimum—which is the least he deserved. Second, if you think I wouldn't care, you weren't in the same room as me last night. I may be the 'chill one,' but I am anything but laid back when it comes to you. I don't care if you confirmed his suspicions about us. I don't care if you told him we're secretly fucking married. You are mine and if he had a problem with that, he should have taken it up with me."

"I'm yours?" she questions, hope and nerves evident in her pretty features.

"Yeah, Wildflower. You're mine."

20

Ellie

THE KISS JACK pulls me into is nothing like the reverent way he touched me last night or even the gentle way he held me when he first came on to the bus. No, this kiss is a claim, no ifs, ands, or buts about it.

When he finally pulls away, both our chests are heaving and the gravity of the situation sinks in. Jack called me his. *His.* Sixteen-year-old me would be dancing around her room right now, squealing for joy. Never in a million years did I expect to be claimed by this larger-than-life man.

"You are mine, Ellie. Something bad happens, you tell me. Something good happens, you tell. Something sad, something funny, something boring—"

"I tell you?" I cut him off, teasingly.

"Yes, smart ass. You tell me. I never want to hear something important about you from someone else again."

"Does that mean you're mine, too?"

"I think I've been yours way longer than either of us realizes. But yes, I'm yours."

I want to melt into his confession, but my anxious brain can't let any uncertainty lie. "For how long?"

As he answers, Jack's eyes meet mine. "I'm not going to lie and say I've got our picket fence life planned out and ready to go. The truth is, I don't know what's next for me, for you, for anything. But I know I want you. This thing between us feels right, and I want to see where it goes."

"Okay," I whisper. I want to tell him that it feels like there is an expiration date on this. That once the tour is over and I get a job and he'll get bored. I saw it with my dad when he was between tours. When you're used to the rock star lifestyle, normal gets old fast.

I push those thoughts aside, not wanting to face that reality right now. Leave that to the ill-fated future Ellie. I want to stay in our tour bubble for as long as I can. No real jobs, no best friends, no paps camped outside his front door. Just the two of us enjoying each other holed up on the bus. Speaking of, "your brothers could come on at any moment," I tell him as he kisses over the hickey left me yesterday, humming in approval at its existence.

When I think he isn't going to respond, he stands, lifting me with him as he trudges toward my room. Hands on my ass as my legs wrap around his waist, he kneads my cheeks as he walks. Once inside the room, he drops me on the bed with a bounce and locks the door behind him.

Staring at me from across the room, Jack yanks his shirt over his head before his fingers fumbled with his belt.

"Baby, this isn't going to be as soft as last night. My reign on my control is tenuous at best. If you don't want your clothes ripped, I suggest you take them off, quickly."

His comment breaks my perusal of the tattoos that decorate his chest. I've seen them in pictures and caught a glimpse in his dressing room, but this is my first time seeing them up close. I want to trace the lines of ink that decorate his body, but there will be time for that later. As he steps out of his jeans and boxers, I pull off my tank and shorts.

As soon as the fabric leaves my body, Jack is on me. He takes my lips in another punishing kiss as his calloused hands run down my body. When he tweaks my nipples, I let out a squeak of surprise that morphs into a moan as the pain mingles with pleasure.

My hand travels the expanse of his chest, relishing in each of his strong muscles. I want more time to explore him, but right now the thread of need between us is so taut, it could snap at any moment.

He groans when I reach between us and grip his impressive member. I pant at the thought of his girth stretching me as I pump up and down. He only lets me play for a few moments until he distracts me with ministrations of his own.

When his fingers slide against my wet center, he curses. "Fuck, you're so wet for me already. Tell me you want this. I don't think I can hold off much longer. Tell me I can have you. Tell me I can claim this body as mine."

"Yesssss," I hiss as he toys with my clit.

He uses the wetness he gathered to coat his cock before tapping it against me. He's about to slip the tip in when he stops abruptly. "Condom."

"In the nightstand," I answer.

"I don't know if I hate the thought that you are prepared for spontaneous sex or that Lainey is."

I laugh because yes, the stash is Lainey's. Now is not the time to discuss that, though.

"We don't have to use them. I'm clean," I confess. "It's been a while since I was with anyone, but I'm on the pill."

Jack appears tempted by the proposition of taking me bare, but grabs a condom from the drawer, anyway. He kisses me deeply as he slides it on. "I trust you. And I'm clean, too. But I'd sleep better if you saw my results for yourself. Plus, I'm so turned on, I could use the help to not come the moment I get inside you."

A thrill runs through me at his admission. He takes my nod as confirmation to continue. Lining up with my center, he again rubs his length against my folds before positioning his tip at my entrance. He said he wasn't going to be soft, but the way he teases me to ensure I'm ready for him says differently.

When I'm writhing underneath him near begging for relief, he slowly pushes inside inch by inch. The stretch is glorious. Once he is fully seated, he presses our foreheads together and sucks in a deep breath, pausing to give me time to adjust.

"So fucking tight," he grits. Groaning when my walls clench around him. "Don't do that, baby. I'll never last."

"Who says that's a bad thing?" I whisper, doing it again. The way is body tenses above me turning me on as much as everything else. I'm desperate to make him feel good. "You made me come yesterday. And truthfully, it won't take me long to get there again."

"Oh, sweetheart. Yesterday was a warm up compared to the orgasms I plan to pull out of you." As if to punctuate his statement, he pulls out and glides back into me faster than before. My entire body lights with the motion.

"Yes. More."

With my encouragement, he gradually picks up his pace. Beside my head, his arms are taut, holding him above me as I squirm below.

"You feel so good, Ellie. You sweet cunt keeps trying to pull me in deeper. You're taking me so well." One of his hands reaches behind us and hikes my leg higher, changing the angle of his thrusts. From this new position, he's hitting a spot that sets my nerve endings on fire.

"Jack," I pant, breath knocked out of me from the force of him.

"I know, baby," he coos. "Let go. Let the pleasure overwhelm you. Your pussy was made to come on this cock."

I watch the strain of his features as he staves off his own orgasm. Every slide of his cock against my walls brings me closer to my peak. Leaning down, Jack nips at my ear, begging me to come for him as the hand holding up my ass grasps me tighter. It only takes a few more thrusts before I'm coming apart around him.

My orgasm unlocking his own, Jack fucks me through it before finding his release. Collapsing on top of me, I revel in the weight of him above me as we catch our breath. His warm skin covers mine and I sink into the feel of him. He's like a living weighted blanket.

When his heart rate slows, Jack rolls off me, kissing my temple. After disposing of the condom, he slides into bed beside me and pulls me into him. We lay in contented silence for several minutes before he breaks it. "It's never felt like that."

I can't help but smile into his chest. "Same," I murmur against his skin.

His deft fingers stroke my hair as he hums in contentment. "I meant everything I said. You're mine, Wildflower. I'm not letting you go. Not after that."

"Okay," I whisper, causing him to chuckle.

"Go to sleep, baby." And I do to the sound of his heartbeat, pacified by the motion of his hands running through my hair. It's the most peaceful sleep I've ever had.

21

SNEAKING out of bed without rousing Ellie was a task all by itself. Last night was more than I could have ever dreamed of. All the anger festering under my skin died the moment I kissed her. The second our lips touched, I was a goner. There are a lot of questions still in the air, but whether or not Ellie and I are together is not one of them. I'll do whatever it takes to keep her safe, happy, and mine.

Making use of the bathroom, I'm about to creep back into Ellie's bed when a throat clears behind me. Turning, two pairs of eyes identical to mine stare back at me. Right. One of those questions still lingering is how my brother's are going to take it.

"What's up?" I ask feigning nonchalance. We all know what happened last night. If they didn't come in while Ellie and I were in the middle of solidifying our relationship, they would have at least noticed I wasn't in my bunk.

"A word," Declan says, jaw tight. He tilts his head to motion

140

to the lounge and I sigh before following. It is too early to have this conversation with them, but I doubt I can get out of it now.

Declan leans against the counter while Grayson plops down beside a ruffled Bryce. He juts his chin up at me before returning his gaze to his phone.

I know they want me to explain, but ever the shit disturber, I'm going to make them come out and ask. After several beats of silence, Gray finally breaks. "What are you doing, man?"

"About what?" Holding back my smirk is physically painful, but I'm internally delighted by the bit. Honestly, after last night, not much could get to me.

"Cut the shit, Jack. We heard. You know we heard. We know you know we heard. And now we want to know what the fuck is going on and if we need to beat your ass."

"Testy," I chide.

"What the fuck is going on is that Ellie is mine."

"Since when?" Grayson asks.

I ponder that for a moment. We didn't solidify things until yesterday, but this thing between us has been lingering for a while. "Officially, last night. Unofficially, since the night we night we followed them to the bar? Since the first day of the tour? Since forever? Fuck if I know."

My older brother seems surprised by the admission, while Declan simply nods his head, asking, "And it's serious? This isn't a way to pass the time for the next few weeks? I don't want to be a dick, but you haven't dated in years, and even back then it was passing infatuations. I don't want to see Ellie get hurt."

I should be annoyed at the insinuation, but I can't blame him. And I certainly can't be mad he's looking after my girl. "It couldn't be more serious."

"Damn," Gray mutters. Agreed.

"I think she's it for me," I confess. We don't get touchy feely often, but if I can't talk to them about this, then who can I?

"Is she on the same page?"

"That's the million dollar question." Running my hands through my sleep mussed hair, I wonder the same thing. She seemed to be in agreement last night, but morning light could give her a different perspective. I hope she doesn't change her mind.

Ever the emotionally intelligent one, Declan picks up on my hesitancy. "What are you worried about?"

"I don't know. I guess I'm a little worried she'll change her mind. She'll realize she wants someone more on her level."

"Jack," Grayson murmurs. "You're an awesome guy. If you're all in, she's lucky to have you."

I take in his words, but they don't have much impact. "She's just so smart. And gorgeous. The woman has a colored-coded TBR for Chrissake."

"What's a TBR?"

"It's a book thing you illiterate boob," Grayson says to Declan. We all stare at him, shocked he knew. "Hey, I know things. I'm on Booktok."

"I don't even know how to respond to that," I reply.

"Don't" Declan asserts. "And don't let your self-doubt keep you from giving a relationship a chance. Gray is right that you're a catch. We've kept you around for a reason."

"I think that reason is called the sibling bond."

"Nah, it's because Mom wouldn't let us leave you in Waco," he teases. "But seriously, you are kind and thoughtful, and always willing to do whatever it takes to make those around you happy. Don't sell yourself short."

"Thanks, man." I almost tear up listening to my brother's compliment me. Is this what having a praise kink is? Sign me up.

"You know who might be unhappy about this?" Grayson adds. "Lainey. Does she know?"

We all sober at that. While I don't *care* what my sister thinks, I totally care. One because I know I will matter to Ellie and two because I don't want to hurt her. I know she is going to have opinions about it, but I'd like to think if two people she cares about are happy she will be happy for us.

"Let me know when you're going to tell her so I can be somewhere else," Bryce adds, finally contributing to the conversation. Little shit.

"I'll be sure to tell her you knew the whole time," I taunt, laughing at his stricken expression. While the rest of us were off filming, Bryce had plenty of one-on-one big sister time. She has enough embarrassing photos and anecdotes of him to own him forever.

"Not cool," he replies.

"Why did Bryce know before us?" Grayson questions, offense in his tone.

"Relax," Bryce says, patting his knee. "I knew before Jack did, too. He may have been lying to himself, but I saw the way he looked at her. I'm the Heimdall of this tour. I see all. I know all."

"More like Lady Whistledown, ya nerd. You keeping a secret blog of all the gossip?"

Bryce scowls at the comment as the rest of us chuckle. Breaking away, I make coffee for myself and a still sleeping Ellie.

"You got this," Declan says, clapping me on the shoulder as he heads to shower.

I sure as fuck hope he's right.

22

Ellie

I WAKE up the next morning more rested than I've been in a while. Even a good ASMR video doesn't help me sleep that deeply. Rolled on my back, the weight of a strong arm pins me to the bed. When I try to move it, Jack lets out a groan and pulls me closer to him.

I squeak in surprise, which only causes him to pull me closer until we're spooning.

"Good morning," he rasps behind me.

"Morning. Morning? Oh my God. It's morning!"

"That is usually what comes after night."

"Be serious," I say, turning in his arms and hitting him on the chest.

"Ouch," he whines. "Are you always this violent in the morning? You were docile as a kitten last night."

"Jack! Your brothers are going to know you spent the night in here." What will they think of us? Of me? I don't want them to think I came on tour to hook up with one of them. That wasn't my intention. What if they told Lainey? Shit. We need to talk to them; tell them what this is.

"And? They already know about us. You're freaking out for no reason."

"You're freaking out for no reason!"

Jack finally cracks an eye open at my outburst, a smirk on his too handsome face. Annoyed, I pull a hair on his chest. He yelps, catching my hand and biting it gently in retaliation.

"Stop panicking. I talked to them this morning and gave them the cliff notes version of us."

"And what is that?"

"That you're mine. And have been since the moment you stepped on this bus."

"Longer than that," I scoff before slamming my free hand over my mouth.

"What was that?"

Instead of answering, I shake my head. I am not diving into that right now. We've been together for twelve hours. He doesn't need to know I've been pining after him for years.

Unfortunately for me, Jack is not satisfied with my non-answer. Grabbing the hand over my mouth, he shifts with both hands in his and pins them above my head. "You're not getting off that easy, baby. What did you mean, 'longer than that?'"

"It's embarrassing," I cry.

"Even better. Tell me. I want to know everything, remember?"

"Fine. I may have had a crush on you for longer than just this tour."

"How long?"

I fight against his hold but the shift lines up our centers and positions him perfectly against me. I moan at the contact. His smirk deepens.

"Tell me," he singsongs, grinding into me again.

"Forever!" I blurt out.

"What?" he stills, eyes wide.

Fuck it. It's out there now. Might as well rip off the Band-Aid. "I've had a crush on you for as long as I can remember."

His cocky expression softens at my admission and he kissed me gently. His lips meld against mine sweetly until my mouth opens for him and his tongue slips inside. Before things get carried away, I break the kiss.

"Will your brothers tell Lainey?" I ask back to the matter at hand.

Jack huffs in frustration but answers anyway. "No, they'll be discreet. We can tell her together."

"What if we didn't?" I propose. "Not yet anyway. She hasn't been at her new job long. I don't want to stress her out thinking I was waiting for the chance to get you alone and make my move."

"Does she know you've had it bad for me your entire friendship?" he teases, but the phrasing makes me tense.

"It sounds bad when I put it that way," he admits. "But you know what I mean. I won't say I'm not concerned about her reaction, but she knows you and she knows me. She loves us. At the end of the day, she'll be happy for us. I think."

"I hope so."

Jack reaches down with his free hand and pulls my lip from between my teeth.

"If you want to wait for a bit, we can. I know what we are. I don't mind holding off."

"Really?"

"Really. There is something way more pressing I need to deal with anyway," he states, grinding his hips back into me.

"What's that?" I pant.

"I've been missing out on enjoying this sweet pussy for years, apparently. I need to make up for lost time." With that declaration, we stay in bed until the bus rolls into Louisville.

IF I WOULD HAVE KNOWN dating would be this much fun, I might have considered the idea sooner. But maybe it's just dating Jack that I enjoy. The man has the power to make the most mundane things fun.

I didn't realize how lonely I was without Lainey until he filled my time. Every night we have done something together, whether it is a Marvel movie marathon with Bryce, battling it out in Mario Kart with Grayson and Declan, or sneaking into a minor league baseball game, he always has something up his sleeve. The last one was my favorite. Partially because it was the first 'date' we got to go on and also because the Mighty Muskrats had riveting between-inning entertainment.

The real treat of that night was when Jack rewrote the words to "Take Me Out to the Ball Game" to be about all the dirty things he wanted to do to me when we got home. He really put those Grammy-award winning writing and tongue skills to use. Every time he quietly hums the tune I can't help but get wet. I don't know if he ruined baseball for me or made it ten times better.

Eliza was less than pleased by our attendance of the game, but Jack didn't care so neither did I. The guys' publicist is not my biggest fan. From what I can gather she was hoping to set Jack up in a PR relationship but he turned her down. Even though was well before we got together, it hasn't stopped her from throwing shade my way.

"Ellie," she cooly greets me when I run into grabbing lunch today. "Are you enjoying Richmond?"

Aside from attending the game deep in the suburbs last night, I haven't seen much of the city. As much fun as Jack and I can have at night, she keeps them busy during the day with press junkets and meetings, leaving me to my own devices. With my bestie gone and the roadies afraid to talk to me after the Donny incident, I don't have many people to explore with when Jack is busy.

"It has been nice. How about you?"

"It's not the most glamorous stop on the tour, but it is fine. Tour can be grueling. I'm thinking of sending an assistant on Declan's EP tour instead of going myself. I'm not meant for life on the road. I'm sure it's no problem for you."

I didn't know Declan was going on a solo tour. I know the guy's mentioned separate projects but I didn't realize it might be their own music. Now that I think about it, they have all been tight lipped about their plans.

It may have been subtle, but I caught the dig at the end of her statement. I have no doubt she knows who my father is and his history as a tour manager. He hasn't been a part of any huge scandals, but a lot can get swept under the rug when you have the right—or maybe wrong—team around you.

"It has been fun. It's nice to see parts of the country I've never visited before," I say instead of giving her the satisfaction of seeing that her comment got to me, mainly because it didn't. My dad is much more concerned with how I reflect on him than vice versa. He has been blessedly quiet the last few days, but I'm sure that won't last.

The two of us fix our plates in silence. It's always funny to me how people can look at the same spread and make completely different meals. Today we are served a taco bar or sorts. I've made nachos with chicken and black beans while Eliza has created the saddest taco salad I've ever seen.

"I'd love to stay and chat, but I have to take a call with my team back in Nashville."

"It never slows down, huh?"

"No," she hums, scanning me appraisingly before making her final dig. "How I miss the days when I had no responsibilities. I envy your ability to not care about all the time ticking by."

Her words hit center mass. Did she have a target right to my biggest insecurities? Reminding me that not only have I not made any progress getting my life together but also my time with Jack is dwindling. We haven't discussed what happens when the tour is over. We've barely been dating for a week. It would be premature to get too future focused.

Knowing that doesn't make me feel any better about the uncertainty, though. This relationship is another thing on the list of things I can't control. Jack has made it clear this is more than a fuck buddy situation. In fact, when I asked that, he threatened to spank my ass if I degraded our relationship again. But the gap between fuck buddy and longterm relationship is wide.

Sitting down with my nachos, I try not to sink too deeply into sad thoughts. Future Ellie can handle those problems. That girl's life sucks. Scrolling through my phone to distract myself, I don't notice a plate land beside me until someone rumbles, "Hey."

Gasping, I clutch my chest as my heart rate skyrockets.

"Sorry," Trent says when I turn his direction.

"It's okay. I haven't worked out much since joining the tour. It's probably good to get my pulse thumping." Not that Jack is doing a bad job of helping me get my cardio in.

"How's it going?" I ask awkwardly. I haven't had contact with Trent since Declan kicked Donny to the curb. I don't know if that was intentional on his part of if the Ryder's warned him away. It's bullshit that I fell a little bad I got his friend in trouble. It's not my fault but the guilt is there nonetheless. You would think I'd hit my quota with hiding my relationship from Lainey, but evidently not.

"It's good. They reshuffled our assignments. I help unload the band equipment now."

"Do you enjoy that?"

"It's pretty cool. Watching Grayson put his drum kit together reminds me of when my brother and I played K'NEX as kids."

"What are K'NEX?"

He shows me a picture to jog my memory. I remember my brother playing with those back in the day, too. It never appealed to me but it would keep him busy and quiet for hours. Having watched Grayson fiddle with his drums, I can agree with Trent's assessment. He gets in the zone, making imperceptibly tiny tweaks.

"Um, so listen," Trent stammers, looking everywhere but at me. I can sense his immense discomfort and am curious to see where this is going.

"I wanted to apologize for what Donny did. I knew he was a douche canoe but I had no idea he would try to force himself on anyone."

"Don't worry about it. It is neither of our faults that Donny is an ass."

"I know. I just don't want you to think I agree with anything he said or did. I heard some of his ranting when he was packing up his stuff and it was vile shit."

Yikes. I don't want to know what bullshit he was spewing. As much as I've tried to put him out of my mind, I am relieved to hear Trent wasn't down with his way of thinking. I thought he was a nice guy and it is good to see that instinct was right.

We spend several minutes chatting while we finish our meals. I can tell he still has something on his chest so before I leave, I give him an expectant expression.

Trent runs his hand over his barely there scruff before swallowing hard. "Do you think Lainey will come back at any point before the tour is over?"

His question surprises me and I am barely able to hold back my laugh. The only thing forcing me to keep it together is the hopeful look in his eyes. Not wanting to extinguish it, I tell him there is always a chance.

23

THE NEXT WEEK and a half are full of stolen moments between shows and sleeping together on the bus every night. Grayson and Declan have been surprisingly cool with our relationship. Once they realized I was serious about Ellie and she wasn't a passing fad, they were full on board.

Aside from one very Declan warning to tell Lainey before the press does, they've let us exist in peace. Ellie wants more time to 'get to know one another' before telling my sister. I don't need to know anything else about her to be sure she's it for me, but my girl likes to have all her ducks in a row. I'll let her have her way for now.

Keeping our relationship under wraps is surprisingly easy. As long as we avoid PDA out in the open no one suspects anything. She was staying on the bus with us already, meaning we don't have to explain anything to anyone.

I've made a habit of throwing my hat into the crowd at the

end of each show to ensure Ellie brings me a new one before the next. It's my new favorite pre-show routine. I get time with her, and I know she at least eats something since she always steals my chips.

We are on our way to Atlanta today. Not only is it a holiday weekend, but we don't have a Tuesday night show this week which means we don't play again until Friday. Declan and Grayson are heading home to Nashville to meet with various people on their side projects. I'm taking Ellie away to a friend's vacation house. It's located in a small town in Florida and sits on a private beach. No one will bother us for three blessed days until we have to report to the Tallahassee show.

I'm pulling out all the stops for this trip. Not only is the house gorgeous and secluded, I'm even borrowing another friend's private plane to take us to and from the area. Ellie says it's 'rock star shit' but at least this way the likelihood of getting caught by the paps is low.

Considering we are laying in bed, as we barrel down the highway, I would say my girl should be used to 'rock star shit' by now. Glancing up, I notice we are driving through an expanse of foothills. Allowing my eyes to adjust, I see wildflowers everywhere.

Sliding out of the bed, I run to the front. "Stop the bus!"

Bryce and Grayson stare at me from their spots in the lounge. "What?"

"Stop the bus! I need to get off."

"Why?"

"Does it matter? Just stop it."

Bryce walks to the front of the bus to make sure the driver heard my plea. A few moments later, the bus safely stops on the side of the road and I run down the stairs. Trailing behind me, Gray shakes his head once he realizes what I'm doing.

I ignore his laughter as I hop over the guardrail and trudge into the field. Scrutinizing the field in front of me, I walk over to a patch of Iris grabbing a few straight from the ground. Beside them I spot some pretty pink blooms. I round out the bouquet with some flowers I believe my mother called Black Eyed Susans and what I think are daisies.

Bounding back onto the bus, I take my collection over to the sink and get busy trimming the ends after thanking our driver for stopping. When they're all a uniform height, I grab the most vase-like cup I can find and arrange the flowers inside. I don't know if it is any good, but when I am happy with them, I turn to head back into the bedroom when I see brothers watching me in amusement.

"What?"

"You are whipped, man," Grayson observes.

"I'm not whipped. I'm considerate and thoughtful AF."

"Technically, I think it's only whipped if she tells him to do it," Bryce adds, helpful for once.

"Jealousy isn't a good color on you," I direct to Gray. His response is to shoot me the bird. .

"Speaking of being a great boyfriend, are my recordings ready yet?" I ask Bryce.

"I finished them up yesterday. I'll upload them to a cloud folder as soon as we have strong wifi again. They're too large to send over the hotspot."

"Sweet. Thanks, bro."

BASED on the text Ellie sent, she should be here with my hat of the night any minute. While I wait, my mind drifts to our trip and to the fact that my brothers have these big plans after the tour. I still have nothing. I wonder if I can make being a boyfriend my plan? It's not as if I have a ton of experience with it. I haven't been in an actual relationship in almost a decade. Something tells me that isn't what Eliza had in mind when she told me to 'get a hobby' at our last meeting.

A knock on my door pulls me from my thoughts as Ellie slips in. I told her she doesn't need to knock but apparently propriety dictates she does. Propriety is about be thrown about the window because Ellie is dressed like a wet dream in flowy skirt, a tour tee, and the cowboy boots she wore dancing last month. She hasn't worn them since and I forgot how spectacularly they show off her legs.

"Hey, Rock Star," she teases.

"Hey there yourself, sexy. You wear all this for me?"

"Maybe . . . "

"You better have. Fuck, Ellie, I swear these boots were made specifically to tempt me. I've been dying to know how they feel wrapped around me since the first time I saw you in them."

"That could be arranged." This vixen. As if I'm not screwing her six ways to Sunday every night. Grayson and Declan both conveniently bought noise canceling headphones two days after we made things official.

I hear the sound of the door locking before she saunters over to the snack basket. I think she's going to grab her chips, but instead, she pulls out one of the mini bottles of whiskey. I eye her curiously because in the few times I've seen her drinks it's always been tequila, vodka, or some other clear drink. Not beer and never whiskey.

Treasure secured, she stands between my spread legs, staring down at me with her pretty doe eyes gleaming mischief and lust, lip pulled between her teeth. Her expression turns into a pout, it takes great effort not to fall over myself to fix it. I suspect she has a plan and I don't want to interfere.

"I can't straddle you when you're manspreading."

"My apologies." I sit up taller and press my legs closer, allowing her to perch on my thighs. "Better?"

She nods as she settles on top of me. After opening the whiskey, one of her hands reaches to toy with the hair at the nape of my neck. I watch enraptured as she tips her face up and pours the whiskey into her mouth.

Instead of swallowing as I expect, she uses her hold on my hair to tilt my head back and press her mouth against mine. When my lips open, rich, smokey flavor mixed with something distinctly her floods my tastebuds.

Holy hell. This is the hottest thing that has ever happened to me. I don't know if Ellie was specifically trying to get fucked with that move, but that's what is about to happen.

"Please tell me you're wet."

"I've been soaked since you left me this morning," she confesses, chest heaving from our kiss.

Standing abruptly, I hike her up my body so I can reach my joggers. I shuck them down my legs and bunch her skirt up to her waist. I'm pleasantly surprised when I notice she skipped panties. Trying to get fucked indeed. One swipe through her center tells me she isn't lying about being soaked for me. And thank God she is because after everything that has happened, I don't have the patience to wait. I'll worship her tonight. Right now, I need to fuck her.

Sitting back down on the couch, I position her entrance on the tip of my cock. "Show me that those boots aren't for show. Ride me, cowgirl."

Needing no further prompting from me, she slides down my shaft as we let out twin groans. While she adjusts to the way I fill her, I remove her shirt.

"So deep," she moans, swiveling her hips in a way that has her hands tightening on my shoulders.

Rubbing her nipples through her lace bralette, I pull down the cups as soon as they pebble and latch on to one, sucking it into my mouth, teeth grazing the sensitive bud. The action makes her rhythm falter, but she recovers quickly as I soothe the sting with my tongue. I switch to the other nipple and deliver the same treatment.

When her tempo falters a second time, I slide my hands to her waist to lift and lower her on my cock. My hips thrust up to meet her. If she thought I was deep before, I'm even more so now.

"Fuck. Oh my God. Jack. I'm going to come."

I moan at the prospect of her tight cunt strangling my cock. I'm close, too. Needing to get her there faster, I snake one hand in between us and rub her clit. The motion causes her walls to flutter around me in the telltale sign of her impending orgasm.

"That's it. That's my girl. Come on this cock, baby. Finish what you started." Her body shudders against mine as her pleasure crests. With a few more stuttered thrusts, heat races down my spine and my own release takes over.

Collapsing against me, Ellies sucks in a ragged breath. "That was unexpected."

I bark out a laugh at her candor. "Not sure what you expected, Wildflower, but anytime you combine you and whiskey, you're asking to get fucked. Where did that come from, anyway?"

"Read it in a cowboy book." She shrugs.

"Oh yeah? Read anything else interesting?"

"Wouldn't you like to know."

"Desperately," I admit, half joking.

"Maybe I'll show you at the beach house. Do the beds at this place have sturdy headboards?"

This woman is going to kill me.

"THREE DAYS WASN'T ENOUGH," I whine from my spot on the bed as I watch Ellie pack her bag. "I need more beach time." Really what I need is more Ellie in a bikini time but beach sounds less horny.

"We're spending the morning at the beach before your fancy private plane takes us to Tallahassee. If you don't report on time Eliza will blame me and I don't need that smoke."

"I'll take full responsibility," I croon, grabbing her around the waist and pulling her into bed with me. Our mini getaway is over too soon, but it was a perfect escape. Seeing Ellie able to completely relax thanks to something I planned made me realize why she enjoys planning and organizing. Knowing I am responsible for her bright eyes and constant smile does something for me in a major way.

We spend most of our free time together on tour, but we are rarely alone except at night or when I can sneak away with her on off days. Being alone in this house, I felt even more connected to her. I got a glimpse of both adult Ellie and the wild girl I used to know. The college stories of the shenanigans she got into with her girls that would have given Declan a coronary, I found delightful. I can't wait to taunt Lainey with the dirt I have on her.

First, I'll have to explain where I got it, but that will come in time. Despite having ample opportunity, we didn't talk about Lainey or the future during our vacation. I'm torn between wanting to bring it up or live for the moment. Thankfully, Ellie makes the decision for me—kind of.

"It's funny you bring up Eliza." Ellie sinks deeper into my lap, tucking her head underneath my chin while I run my fingertips down her back.

"You brought her up," I point out.

"Semantics." I would normally push her on that, but she is back to fiddling her fingers, a tick she hasn't done since we got here. Whatever she wants to say must be making her nervous.

"She said something interesting to me the other day. Is Declan releasing a solo album after the tour?"

"Yeah," I answer easily. I thought she knew that but now that I think about it, she isn't usually in the room for those conversations. "He is releasing an EP. He plans to go on a mini tour to select cities across the country to promote it."

"Why aren't y'all doing it together?"

"The sound is more soulful than our normal music. It's a passion project for him and since Gray had the opportunity to judge *Singing Sensation,* we thought now was a good time for him to explore that style."

"Hold up!" she exclaims pushing out of my hold and resting on her knees in front of me. "Grayson is going to be a judge on *Singing Sensation*?! Does Lainey know?"

"Ye—"

"Of course she doesn't know. She would never keep that a secret, especially from us. How could you not tell me?"

"Sorry?"

"You should be. This is huge."

"I'm lost here, sweetheart."

"You don't know? Does Grayson not know?"

"Not know what?" I have no clue why Ellie is amped up. The show is popular, but it's been around long enough that it isn't a huge deal. There are several shows with the same format on different networks.

"You know how the girls and I watch a show together every week?"

I nod because I do. She's staring at me expectantly when it clicks. "That show is *Singing Sensation*?"

"Yes!"

"Why?"

"Aside from the fact that they are creating America's next superstar?" she asks, parroting the show's tagline.

My lips tip at her enthusiasm for the show. She's cute when

she blabbers about things she is passionate about. "Aside from that."

"We've watched every episode together. It started freshman year when our periods all synced and we needed a comfort show. There was a marathon and before we knew it, four years had passed and we were superfans."

"Grayson is going to get a kick out of this," I say mostly to myself.

"Do you think he'll be able to give us the inside scoop?"

The way her eyes shine with excitement makes me wish I was the one judging the show. If that didn't mean I'd have to spend a few months away from her in LA, I'd be petitioning for a spot now.

"I think the NDA is pretty tight, but I'm sure he could leak a few small things to you ladies. If he knew Lainey was a fan of the show, I'm sure he would have told her he was going to be on it. Technically, he isn't confirmed as a judge yet, but rumors have been circulating for a while."

Her excitement turns pensive and I know a question I don't want to answer is coming. Bracing myself, I wait for her to vocalize it.

"Declan is releasing an EP. Grayson is going to be on *Singing Sensation*. What are you planning to do? I'm sure it's going to be great if that is what they have in store."

Her faith in me is a knife to the gut. Despite Eliza's hounding, I am no closer to a decision than I was before the tour kicked back off. The pressure to choose something impressive is even greater now that I have Ellie. She is such a high achiever, I don't want to disappoint her.

"I have something in the works," I lie. I do have some feelers out, but nothing concrete has been decided. "I don't want to jinx it, though. As soon as it is set in stone, you will be the first to know. I want to impress you with it all figured out. I guess you're rubbing off on me."

I don't know if she can tell I am being dishonest or wants to push harder for details, but her expression is guarded. With less than twenty-four hours before we go back to reality, there is no room for that.

Standing from the bed, I scoop her off her feet and into my arms.

"What are you doing?" she laughs as I toss her over my shoulder.

"You seem a little parched. I think we could use a dip."

"Don't you dare!" she gasps. Unfortunately for her, I dare. Running through the open patio door I jump straight into the pool with Ellie in my grasp.

24

Ellie

AFTER AN AMAZING FEW days away from the real world with Jack, reality came back with a vengeance. I tried not to let Jack's evasiveness on the last night get to me, but my gut told me something was off. I would have pried deeper into his future plans if the comparison to me hadn't made me feel like a fraud.

As if he can sense my vulnerability, my dad chooses today to resurface. The irony that I took an escape trip from my escape tour, is not lost on me and it wasn't lost on my father, either.

1:15 PM

DAD

How goes the job hunting? I saw your pictures from the beach. I didn't realize the tour stopped there.

It's okay. I've had a couple of call backs but nothing concreted yet.

It didn't, but we had a few days off, so I decided to take a quick detour.

Isn't this entire tour a detour? I have a friend at a company in New York that needs a buying assistant. I set up an interview for you in two weeks.

What do they buy?

DAD

Clothes of some kind. Kids, I think. I'll forward you the listing as soon as I have it.

Thanks, Dad.

He thumbs up my last message. I appreciate that he wants me to get a job, but I wish he would discuss things with me before setting up interviews. Kids' fashion is not my area of expertise nor interest. I also didn't want to relocate. New York would put me closer to my grandmother and cousins, but further from Jack and the girls.

Did you talk to the boys about my offer?

I don't know how to respond to that question. On the one hand, I don't want to lie. On the other hand, I have no intentions of talking to the guys. They are happy with their current setup. They aren't going to rock the boat to hire my dad, who I suspect they don't even like. Plus, they're about to take a hiatus. That fact isn't public knowledge, though. I give him a version of that truth that is hopefully enough to put him off asking me again.

They aren't planning to make any changes right now.

Stressed after the exchange, I decide to do what soothes me most: organize. Thinking about the tour ending and the expiration date of my career hiatus and relationship bubble has me antsy. I need to channel this energy into something productive. Heading into the arena, I spot Shonda doing inventory. Perfect.

"Hey, Boss Lady," I greet.

"Hey. You're early."

"Yeah, I had an annoying conversation with my dad and needed to busy myself to forget about it."

"You came to the right place. You can start inventorying the small items."

Doing as she says, we work in companionable silence. The monotony of the task only distracts my mind for so long. Soon, I'm back to obsessing over my next move.

"You're brooding," a voice says beside me and I glance up to see Shonda studying me. "Want to talk about it?"

Figuring why the hell not, I dump all my career uncertainty on to my temporary boss who nods in all the right places and seems to think over my dilemma. "How did you know what you wanted to do?" I ask finally.

"Honestly, I kind of fell into it. Similarly to you, I wanted time to figure out where I wanted my life to go. My sister knew a guy who worked on tours and he got me a job as an assistant. One tour led to another and eventually, I landed a job doing merch and it clicked."

"You're saying I need to try on a bunch of hats before I find the right one?"

She laughs at the analogy since we are inventorying the hats. "Just because it worked for me doesn't mean it will work for you. You already have way more of a direction than I did. I can tell you have an eye for clothing and your organizational skills are incredible. I'm sure you can do anything you put your mind to."

"And I should put my mind to . . . ?"

"Nice try. Only you can make that decision. Think about your favorite parts of the things you've done. What are they?"

"I love picking out clothes. I love the satisfaction of helping people feel confident through their clothing. I even enjoy the marketing side of things."

"Have you thought about opening your own store?"

"Isn't that expensive?"

"If only you knew some fancy rich boys with money they could invest," she jokes. She's not wrong. I mean, she's wrong about the Ryders. I would never ask them for money, but I do have some connections that could lend startup capital—assuming I had a plan.

"It doesn't have to be all that expensive. You can start small with an online only store and expand. A friend of mine owns a store in Nashville. I'm sure she'd be happy to discuss the ins and outs of it with you."

"Really? That would be amazing."

"Happy to help. You can repay my kindness by untangling all the lanyards. Trent packed them wrong and now they're a jumbled mess."

"On it!" Owning a store isn't something I ever consider, but it does combine a lot of the aspects of the industry that I enjoy. Can I picture myself clocking in every day and helping women shop? Maybe. It's definitely worth exploring, but I am still going to explore other options.

AFTER TALKING, Shonda, I am more at ease. I'm excited to tell Jack about the conversation, but he isn't on the bus when I get there. As I step off and round the corner, I run into Eliza.

"Hey! Have you seen Jack?"

Barely glancing my way, she answers. "The brothers doing an interview with Paris from Backroad Radio. She is going to be around for the rest of the tour."

Ick. That is not exciting news. Last time I saw her, she was fawning all over Jack. With our relationship being so new, it makes me apprehensive. I know we haven't made any long-term plans, but at least for now, he said he was mine. We didn't specifically say that meant exclusive, but I can't imagine he meant anything else. Instead of stressing about it on the bus, I decide to find the guys and watch things for myself.

When I finally find them, they are in a large office upstairs. The three are seated in director chairs while the reporter from my first night on the tour sets up. Unlike last time, there is no cameraman, only Paris and her phone. Spotting me first, Grayson calls me over.

"Paris, I don't know if you met Ellie last time. She is our little sister's best friend and is working for us on this tour." I give her a quick wave and glance over at Jack to see if he plans to add our relationship to the explanation. When he doesn't, part of me is disappointed. I know we don't want it getting out before we tell Lainey, but I hate that this woman will be hanging around thinking he is on the market.

"Isn't that adorable," she coos as if I am eleven and not a few years younger than her. Ignoring the weird energy she is giving off, I turn on my brightest smile.

"Hi, it's nice to meet you. I love your concert outfit content. It helped me figure out what to pack for the tour."

"A fan, how sweet. I'm sure you boys get this often, but it gives me warm fuzzies every time."

Turning her attention back to me, she continues. "We'll have to grab lunch while I am here so you can give me all the dirty deets on what it's like traveling with these guys."

The guys tense when she laughs, but they know I'd never give away information about them. At least, I hope they know.

"Won't you get that yourself?" I ask sweetly. "Eliza said you'll be joining us for the rest of the tour."

"I will, but I'll be staying at hotels and flying to each stop. The bus life is not for me. This badge won't get me everywhere." She points to the VIP lanyard hanging around her neck that says 'Media.' I give her a commiserative expression, but I am secretly glad she won't have free rein the way she would with an all-access pass.

Which reminds me that I need to grab mine. It doesn't matter much during the day since everyone knows me, but as we get closer to showtime, I need to put mine on so no volunteers try to kick me out.

"We were about to start the interview if you want to hang around," Declan states. Thinking about it momentarily and deciding that I do want to watch the interview, I plop down on the couch behind Paris.

After fiddling with her tripod, she presses a few buttons and goes to stand behind the guys.

"Hey, hey Backroad Radio XM fans. I am here with the infamous Ryder Brothers. We're talking about their plans for the last few stops of the US tour and get the inside scoop on what's next for them."

She asks them a few mundane questions about their favorite stops on the tour places, they've eaten, fans they've met, and any funny stories they have from traveling together. Once they have all answered a few, she begins to discuss what is next for them.

"Rumor has it that the three of you plan to take a break once this tour is over. Is there any truth to that?"

Declan takes on the question. "That's right, Paris. We all have side projects we want to focus on. Our plan is to wait a bit to record the next album to give us time to dive into those projects."

"Any hints on what they will be? Rumors are swirling that

one or all of you will be judges on everyone's favorite singing competition show."

"We aren't ready to reveal what our exact plans are yet," Grayson answers. "But we hope our fans will enjoy us taking on these new challenges."

I'm happy to see I'm not the only one who gets evasive answers, even if the other person is a nosy reporter.

"Do any of these new challenges include new women in your life? Sources say that you, Jack, were spotted at a private beach in Florida earlier this month with a mystery woman."

Jack's eyes widen slightly before he schools his features. "All our plans are professional in nature."

"Are you saying there is no new woman in your life?" Paris presses.

"You'll be the first to know if anyone new comes into my life," he replies, putting emphasis on *new*. I catch the meaning but I fear Paris interprets it differently since her eyes take on a predatory gleam.

"You heard it here first, folks," she says to the camera. "Be sure to follow my account CountryGirlParis to see if the love bug bites our favorite mustached musician."

The guys are out of their seats as soon as the live stream ends. They all attempt to make a break for it before she gets her claws into Jack. Literally. Her neon pink nails are wrapped around his forearm.

"Jackie," she coos in a baby voice. "Eliza said you would give me the grand tour of the tour. The dressing room, backstage, and maybe even your bus."

"We keep our bus to family only," Declan interjects. I wonder if he will offer to give the tour instead of Jack, but he makes a quick exit. Chicken.

Jack glances between me and Paris as if he isn't sure what to do but resigned himself to being her guide and they leave shortly after.

Once they're gone, Grayson bumps his shoulder against mine. "You okay, Ellie Bellie? He'd never be interested in that viper." I smile at his attempt to reassure me. I haven't explicitly talked to the guys about me and Jack, but they know about us and we don't hide our connection in front of them.

"I know," I reply. "I just hate that we can't tell her Jack is taken. And she reminds me of a woman my dad dated shortly after he and Mom divorced. The vibes are bad all around."

"I get that, but you've got nothing to worry about. He's so into you it's disgusting."

Laying my head on his shoulder, I take a deep inhale. "Thanks. I'll deny it if you tell anyone I said it, but you are totally the pretty one."

"Hell yeah!" He hoots. "Come on, let's go grab some food and see if we can melt Paris with the force."

"You're such a nerd. Don't make me take back my pretty comment."

"Hey, you got the reference. What does that say about you?" he quips. "Last one to catering has to tell Bryce we ran out of jalapeño chips."

"Did we?"

When Grayson nods gravely, I race out of the room, knowing Bryce is as serious about his chips as I am about mine.

Chatting with Gray and Bryce takes my mind off Jack being alone with the obviously besotted reporter. That doesn't stop the jealousy from bubbling up when I see them laughing across the room. I try to remember that I have every reason to trust Jack and just because she wants him doesn't mean she can have him.

Shortly after he is done eating, Grayson gets looped into Paris orbit, leaving me with Bryce. We sit there in awkward silence for a few moments before I think of something to break the tension.

"I don't think I had the chance to say 'thank you' for what

you did that day with Donny. I don't know what would have happened if you didn't show up."

"Don't sweat it. If I'd known the full breadth of what was happening, I would have laid him out for you."

I can't help but smile at that. Bryce was four years younger than Lainey and I. It's hard to think of him now as a grown man, but he is definitely coming into his own. Like Declan, he is on the shorter end of the brothers but he makes up for it with muscle tone. Since he wasn't on a hit TV show as a kid, he went to traditional high school where he was a star soccer player and wrestler. I have no doubt he could've 'laid Donny out' if he wanted to.

It's been a while since I have had time to chat with Bryce one-on-one. We talk about what he has been up to since he graduated. Like his brothers, he prefers music over school, choosing to become an apprentice at a record label over college. He also told me he has been DJing on the side for extra money. He's considering trying to make a go at it professionally, but he's worried he'll only get booked because of his name.

"Why don't you do it anonymously?" I suggest.

"What do you mean?"

"Some of the biggest DJs are guys whose faces we never see. Whether they wear a mask or block out the DJ booth, they are killing it without revealing their true identity."

"Damn, that's not a bad idea. What would my name be?"

"I know how to stop while I'm ahead. That's up to you. I bet Lainey would have some good input, though."

"Thanks, Ellie. You've given me a lot to think about."

"No problem, lil Ryder. Oh! What about that? You could wear a flaming skull mask."

"That's an option," he states, but his tone tells me not a good one. Fair enough. Finishing our meal, we chat until we both need to get to our prospective stations.

25

Jack

"I KNOW I suggested getting in a fake relationship to occupy your time after the tour," Eliza drones, "but I thought we all decided against it. As much as the fans will eat up a childhood friends to lovers storyline, I had some other candidates in mind who could have boosted your image more."

I prickle at her insinuation that I would get with Ellie for PR purposes, but before I can jump down her throat, Declan chimes in. "His image is fine and his relationship status is none of our business."

"It's none of our business as long as it doesn't cause bad press," she corrects.

"Which it hasn't and won't."

"We'll see," she snips. "How does this factor into your post-tour plans?"

"What do you mean?" I ask.

"I mean, what is Ellie's plan? Is she going to mooch off her rich boyfriend or start working? And if so, where? Doing what?"

"Hey! Ellie is not a mooch," Grayson defends. "She graduated with her master's degree and accepted a job *we* offered her. She didn't ask for it."

"And she plans to do what with that degree? Does she have a position lined up? We'd want any company she works at to align with your values and sponsorship deals."

Everyone turns expectantly to me. Shit. Am I supposed to know that? Ellie spends a lot of time stressing about her future. I do my best to distract her from those worries when we're together. I know she has been applying for jobs, but she hasn't mentioned any interviews.

"I don't know," I hedge, much to Eliza's disapproval. "Her career decisions are hers alone, but I will ask her about them."

"If she is going to work a traditional job, you can't use her as the reason you don't have any other projects going on. Have you thought at all about what you will do to fill your time?"

"I've got some irons on the fire," I lie the same way I did to Ellie when she asked. I can't toss Eliza in the pool or orgasm her as a distraction from my non-answer, though. Thankfully, she doesn't push.

"See that you do," she states, pinning me with a hard glare. "I need an answer by the end of the tour."

"Aye, aye, Captain." Seeing as Eliza runs a tight ship, it's a fitting title. I don't always love her brusque approach, but it gets results. I know it irks Declan more, rubbing against his more dominant personality. There was a time where I thought the two of them would end up hate fucking each other. But they're both too bossy to let go of the reins enough to enjoy it.

When I think about it, I'm not the only Ryder who hasn't had a relationship in recent years. Grayson has dated some, but hasn't had a major relationship since our TV show went off the air. He and Selena—a guest star on our show—were previously together. Long distance turned out to be too much for them when her career tied her to LA.

I've never seen Declan with a girl for more than a few dates, and most of those have been arranged by Eliza. I wouldn't be surprised if he had a secret weekend lover, Christian Grey-style. He invested in Club Hedone, a sex club in Nashville a few years ago, so it isn't far-fetched that he's into some kinky shit. I've never asked since it is none of my business. We may be brothers and friends, but there are some lines even I don't want to cross.

Tuning back into the conversation, I listen to Eliza detail our obligations for the next few days.

"Does that mean our afternoon is free?" I ask hopefully. Ellie has seemed particularly stressed over the past few days, and I would love to do something fun together. I tried to ask her about what was on her mind, but she waved me off. I know she spent time yesterday helping Shonda inventory all the merch. I'd be worried that was the issue, but organizing relaxes her.

"After this meeting, you are free until a radio interview tomorrow, yes," she answers. I decide to leave before she can ask for details she doesn't want. Better to ask for forgiveness and all that.

"Sweet. See ya!" I say before jumping up from my seat and leaving the meeting. If they call after me, I don't hear it.

When I get back to the bus, I find my girl in the lounge surrounded by colored pens and her notebook. Uh oh. She only brings out the G-2s when she is getting serious.

"Whatcha doing, baby?" I ask, settling in the chair across from her. I know better than to mess with the system she has in place.

"Making a list," she replies absentmindedly.

Seeing how deep she is into a notebook I know she has only had for a few weeks, my eyes widen. "I think you've made more lists on this tour than I've made in my entire life."

Her cheeks turn that shade of pink I love so much. "I like

making lists. It helps me plan things out and make sense of them."

I nod my head knowingly as she moves the notebook off her lap and spreads out her legs. Taking the vacancy, I lay my head on her thighs. As if on instinct, she runs her hands through my hair and scratches my scalp. It feels so good, I almost forget the conversation I wanted to have.

"How many of those lists come to fruition?" I ask.

"What do you mean?"

"You're always making and remaking lists. How many of them do you put into action?" When she stares at me, stunned, I continue, "I think the process helps calm your brain, but you're afraid of the execution."

"I'm not afraid . . . " she challenges. "It does calm me, though. Getting the words out of my head makes it easier to relax and focus on other things."

"Things such as screwing your handsome boyfriend?"

"I meant more like sleeping, but sure, we'll go with that," she teases.

"Speaking of." I pull out my phone and forward her an email I've been holding onto for weeks. "Check your inbox."

She eyes me curiously, but does as I ask. "What's this?"

"Click on it."

When she does, the small living area is filled with the sound of my voice.

What's up, baby? You wanted to see what I was doing? C'mere. Come lay beside me. I'm working on a new song. You want to hear it? It has a ways to go, but I have the chorus melody down.

Guitar music filters through for a few beats before my voice takes over again.

Thank you. I thought it had promise. You look sleepy. Oh, you were going to take a nap? Want me to join you? I am in the zone, but I don't mind stopping for you. Are you sure? How about you nap here beside me? I can work on the song and you can snuggle up next to me. Of course, I don't mind. Yeah, I'll wake you up in a bit. You know I love having you near. Want me to play you a lullaby?

Okay, okay. I'll get back to work. Sweet dreams, Wildflower.

My voice cuts out until the sounds of writing and strumming are all that remain. When I peer up from her lap, Ellie is staring down at me, tears in her eyes.

"You made me boyfriend ASMR?"

I nod anxiously. It seemed like a good idea at the time, but I'm second guessing it now. People have told me my voice is calming, but maybe I did it wrong.

"I thought you deserved your own personal recordings, not something generic, but if it's too weird, you don't have to listen to it."

"I love it."

"Yeah?"

"Yeah. When you put your mind to something, it's amazing what you can accomplish. I can't wait to see what you do next."

Leaning down, she kisses me gently on the lips. I try to deepen it, but it's difficult upside down. Spiderman made this look way easier.

"As much as I would love to keep this going, we have plans."

"We do?"

"Yep. I have the afternoon off. You and I are going to play hooky. Can you be ready in fifteen?"

"What are we doing?"

"That's for me to know and you to find out. Now kiss me again and go get dressed. Comfy but appropriate for public."

I sit up, allowing her to move off the couch. She nips at my lips before running to the back of the bus, giggling when I tried to keep her pulled close.

"Temptress! I'll get you back for that." While she gets changed, I consider her earlier statement that I can accomplish a lot when I put my mind to something. I know she meant being her boyfriend, since I've expressed insecurities about not having been one in a long time. But I wonder if that's true in other areas of my life. All I need is something as worthy as loving Ellie to put my mind to in order to figure it out.

Shit, love? It hasn't been long, but I can't think of another word that describes how I feel about Ellie. She's been a part of my life for almost as long as I can remember. The transition from sister's best friend to love was easier than it should have been. Hopefully, if I keep being the boyfriend she deserves, she'll feel the same way soon.

In the back of my mind, something is screaming at me that until Lainey knows about us, none of this is as real as I want it to be. I shut that part up. We'll deal with that when we have to. I don't want guilt tainting the day I have planned.

26

Ellie

CHANGING out of my lounge set, Jack's words play through my head. *Am I afraid?* I know I'm cautious, but maybe that caution has been holding me back. He's not the first to suggest I spend less time planning and more time doing. My mom has harped on that for years, but I've ignored her criticism since if she'd done more planning, her life wouldn't have been as chaotic.

Once I'm dressed, I clip back my hair and do my five-minute makeup routine: tinted moisturizer, blush, eye shadow pencil as liner, mascara, and lip tint. Once complete, I meet Jack back in the front of the bus.

"Ready?" he asks. When I nod, he leads us out of the bus and through the arena parking lot. I'm surprised when we get to an SUV and a lanky kid hops out, handing Jack the keys.

"No security?"

"They're going to follow behind us, but we shouldn't need them for what I have planned."

"If it's going into a hotel to screw all afternoon, you're wasting your money. We could have done that on the bus."

"No smart ass. We're doing actual things, but there shouldn't be many people around."

It takes about twenty minutes for us to get to what I've gleaned is the first of a few stops. "The SCRO Hall of Fame?"

"What's more Charlotte than stock car racing? I thought it fitting that we come to the Stock Car Racing Organization Museum. Plus, it was the easiest to get into short notice since G&K reps a few drivers."

"Fair," I conceded. "What are we going to do, though? Do they even have exhibits?"

A mischievous grin overtakes Jack's features. "You'll see."

After walking through a few exhibits about SCRO drivers past and the different race tracks, we end up in a room that resembles a garage and is filled with race cars. "Bring me here to have a mustache beauty pageant?" I tease, pointing to all the pictures on the wall.

"His stache is good," a voice says, "but it's no match for some of the mechanics and team members in the back."

Peering up, I spot a man standing between two cars. He is in his late thirties with rich brown hair that has of grey salted at his temples.

"Cohen Daniels, it's nice to meet you, man. You were my dad's favorite driver back when you were on the circuit." Jack greets. "This is my girlfriend, Ellie."

"I appreciate that. I'm a fan of yours as well. I gotta say when Molly called and asked if we could open the museum for a few hours, I didn't expect you. I figured musicians tried to stay as far away from vehicles as they could when living on a bus."

"We normally do, but my girl and I could use a thrill and since my contract forbids skydiving, white water rafting, and basically anything fun, this was the next best option."

Cohen nods in agreement. "Then let's make this count."

"What exactly are we 'making count'? Jack has kept me in the dark about this whole thing."

"Racing."

"Racing," I echo. Can they hear the panic in my voice? I am a decent driver, but nowhere near good enough to drive a race car.

"Simulated racing," Jack amends, running his hand up and down my arm in a soothing motion. "It will feel like a real race, but our cars will remain firmly parked in the garage."

"In that case, get ready to eat my dust."

"Big talk from a girl who never beat me at Mario Kart."

"That's because you cheat!"

"You can't prove that." He's right that I can't prove it, but I know it in my soul. All Ryders cheat at Mario Kart, it's in their DNA. I'm fairly confident he can't cheat at a SCRO simulator, though.

"Should we make this interesting?" he asks.

"What did you have in mind?"

"If you win, I'll buy you as many books as you want at the indie bookstore we're visiting later." I perk up at the suggestion. If he said jewelry store, I might be worried about spending his money, but Jack can more than afford to drop a few hundred bucks on books. My favorite author recently came out with limited edition covers I have been dying to get my hands on. Hopefully the store will have them.

"And if you win?" This is where things could get dicey. I have no clue what he'd want as a prize.

"If I win, no making lists for a week."

I suck in a breath. "No lists?"

"No lists. No pro-con lists, no to-do lists, hell, no groceries lists. Think you can handle it?"

"Why?" I ask, curious about his choice. I assumed he would pick something dirty, but this request is throwing me for a loop.

"Because I think you can get too hung up on accomplishments and checking things off that you miss out on the journey."

Damn, that is sweet. How can I say no? Pretending to think it over, I dramatically tap my chin before sticking out my hand for him to shake.

"You're on, Rock Star." His smile is so genuine I'll almost feel bad when kicking his ass wipes it off his handsome face.

Jack shakes my hand then pulls me in for a quick, dirty kiss.

"Alright, Cohen, tell us how this works. I have a bet to win."

"YOU DON'T HAVE to be so pleased with yourself," Jack grumbles as we leave Booked & Basic, the cutest romance bookshop.

"Don't be a sore loser. Besides, I remember you loving the results from the last book I read."

His eyes heat as he recalls that moment in his dressing room a few weeks ago when I took a page out of my favorite cowboy romance. Maybe if he's a good boy, I'll find something in one of the books to try out.

"Where to next?" I ask as we load my purchases into the trunk.

"First, we're going to grab a snack, and then I have another surprise on my sleeve."

"You mean up your sleeve?" I question.

"Nope."

Before I can ask anymore, he is opening the passenger door for me and shutting me inside. It's a quick drive to our next stop, an adorable twenty-four-hour bakery. They specialize in French pastries but have a wide selection. I choose some macaroons and an iced lavender latte while Jack gets a quiche and macchiato.

"You have to try this," I tell him after taking a sip of my latte.

Jack opens his mouth and watches me expectantly. It takes a moment for me to register his callback to our earlier conversation.

"I am not kissing latte into your mouth," I chide.

"That's a shame." He makes a show of pouting before he grabs my cup and takes a long sip. I can't hold back the giggle when whip cream gets stuck in his mustache.

I know I said I wouldn't feed him my latte, but that doesn't mean I can't enjoy some sweetness off him. Leaning forward, I kiss him firmly before licking off the excess cream.

"Good?" I ask when I sit back in my seat.

"Fucking fantastic. If we didn't have another appointment to keep, I would steal that whipped cream, haul your ass into the back of that rental car, and show you how good."

Dirty boy. I know I started it but sheesh. The only consolation to my dampening panties is the bulge I spot straining against his jeans. When he catches my gaze, he licks his lips and mouths, 'later.'

"Speaking of later, I am planning to visit my grandmother when we are in Boston and was wondering if you might want to go with me?" I propose hesitantly. "She's one of my favorite people and she is all but demanding I stop by and see her. She says she wants to 'tell me something important before she croaks.'"

"Is she sick?"

"No, just dramatic."

When Jack notches his finger below my chin, I realize I'm not meeting his gaze. "I'd love to meet your grandmother."

"Yeah?"

"Yeah. If she's anything like you, we'll get on great."

"She's nothing like me, but she'll love you."

A weight lifts off my chest with Jack's answer. I didn't realize how much I wanted him to meet Grammy O until I asked.

As we throw out our trash, Jack leads us away from where we parked past a row of shops. "Where are we going?"

"Our next stop is down the street. I was able to snag an appointment with an amazing tattoo artist. He's the one who recommended the bakery."

"You're getting another tattoo?"

"Yes and no. Technically he will be adding ink to my body, but it will be within my existing sleeve. I get something for every tour and haven't found the time until now."

Walking into a shop a few doors down, I'm surprised by how clean it is. I don't know why I expected it to be grimy, but it isn't. Once we check in, the receptionist shows us to a private station in the corner where we meet the owner of the shop, Michael.

"Hey man," Jack says, giving the man a bro hug. "Thank you for fitting me in."

"The pleasure is all mine," Michael replies. "It's an honor to have my ink on your body. I'm a huge fan."

"You're too kind."

"I saw the ideas your team sent over. Let me show you what I've drawn up." While Jack and Michael chat, I check out some of the designs on the wall and pictures of past work. Zeroing in on a poster of delicate 'flash tats,' I trace my finger or a small clover.

"See anything you like?" a woman covered in colorful tattoos asks.

"Oh, no. I mean, yes. This work is fantastic, but I'm not here to get anything. My boyfriend is over there with Michael. I was browsing, I guess."

"If you are interested, my next appointment is running late.

It wouldn't take long to put that clover on you if you want it small, which based on your virgin skin, I imagine you do."

Worrying my lip, I shift my gaze between the design and her. Noticing my indecision, she asks, "Any particular reason you wanna clover?"

"My family is Irish. I thought it might be a good nod to my heritage. Plus, you can never have too much good luck on your hands right?"

"Absolutely. It would be killer on your wrist, behind your ear, or on your ankle."

Jack comes over and joins the conversation right as I am on the verge of turning her down. "Are you thinking about getting a tattoo, baby?"

"Maybe. Do you think it's a bad idea?"

"I think it's an awesome idea!"

"Can I pull it off?"

"You can put off anything you want," he replies with a kiss to my temple. "I'm gonna be here for a while. You might as well make use of the time to get something for yourself."

"Are you sure?"

"Of course. Do you want me to hold your hand?" He's joking, but I know if I asked him to, he would.

"No, you need to get started on your tattoo. I'll come back here when it's done."

"Sounds good, Wildflower. Holler if you need me."

While Amika, as I learned my tattoo artist is named, preps her station, I text the girls in our group chat.

3:42 PM

I'm doing a thing.

MACY

What is it?

ALEXIS

???

Instead of answering I send a picture of the set up in front of me with the tattoo gun and walls covered in past work.

ALEXIS

Oh my God you're getting a tattoo!

Do you think that's crazy?

MACY

It's a little out of character but if you want to go for it.

What are you getting?

A small clover on the inside of my wrist.

ALEXIS

I love that. That's such a good place for a dainty tattoo.

Hopefully you don't touch the bug and get addicted. Next time we see you, you'll be covered head to toe.

I don't think that's a risk.

ALEXIS

Send us a picture when you're done

LAINEY

OMG!!!!

absjhdbksjalncjfksdvz

MACY

I think you broke Lainey.

Before I get the chance to respond, Amika is ready with the stencil. I can hear the sound of my phone buzzing as she places the tiny clover outline on my list.

Once the stencil is placed, I'm surprised by how quick the process is. True to her word it only takes about fifteen minutes for Amika to ink the small design on my skin. It's about the size of a dime, but I love it. Not enough that I think I'm gonna be covered as Alexis jokes, but I am excited to be able to say that I now have a tattoo.

I send the girls a picture before opening up my solo chat with Lainey.

LAINEY

You're getting a tattoo without me??

I knew I should have peer pressured you harder in New Orleans.

Let's catch up soon.

Yes, please. Let me know when your boss gives you a second to breathe.

Guilt sits heavy in my gut at her words. Not that I got a tattoo without her, but that I am keeping such a big secret from her. If she wasn't so swamped with her fellowship, I'd feel terrible for not talking to her as much. Thankfully, she has been too busy to notice.

I doubt that will be this century, but I will. How goes the job search?

Seeing as I am at a tattoo parlor on a random week day, it is safe to say I am still unemployed.

I don't think it counts as unemployed if you aren't trying to find a job. Plus you technically have one!

I am trying!

Not very hard if you are "at a tattoo parlor on a random week day.

Her last text catches me totally off guard. Take care of her brothers? Does she know about me and Jack? There is no way, right? Except for today, we've been beyond careful about being seen together. Dread pools in my stomach as I attempt to reason with myself. Lainey isn't one to beat around the bush. If she knew, she wouldn't pretend she didn't.

As soon as Amika wraps my wrist, I return to the room where Michael is working on Jack. A spot on his pec is already covered in plastic. I'm about to ask about it when I'm distracted by Jack asking about my own tattoo. Since it's wrapped, I show him the pictures I took.

Settling in, I watch as details are adding to Jack's existing sleeve, while he points out what the other elements in it represent. For his tour, one of the things he is adding is a ball cap, representing all the different hats he's worn on the stage. He shoots a wink my way when he notices me clocking the newly added mini bottle of whiskey.

An hour later, Michael wipes down Jack's arm and puts wrapping over the rest of the tattoo. While I can take off my wrapping in twenty-four hours, Jack has to wait a few days if he can. Wardrobe will have fun styling around that.

"Thanks, man," he tells Michael. "I'm excited with how this

all turned out. I'll be sure to tag you on socials when I debut the new ink."

"It was a pleasure. Be sure to stop by next time you're in town and I'll hook you up again. You all set, Ellie?"

"Yep," I answer with a smile, flashing in my wrist.

Jack and I grab takeout from a local hotspot before bringing it back to the bus to enjoy dinner with his brothers. The rest of the night is spent with the guys playing games and me reading one of my new books before Jack and I fall into bed.

It's been a while since I've had a day this amazing. It should fill me with contentment, but instead my anxious brain wonders how long this can last. The tour is already halfway over and I'm worried about what the end means for Jack and I.

This time to focus on each other has been amazing, but what does our relationship look like back in Nashville? I have no idea what Jack's plans are or even where I'll be working. The interview my dad set up for me with that company in New York still looms over my head. As much as I want to blow it off, I'm already pushing him off on the tour issue. My people pleasing heart can only handle so much.

I feel guilty that I haven't mentioned the interview to Jack, but I reason that there's nothing to tell yet. No use causing him to worry about it, too, until something comes to fruition. I don't want to jinx what we have now by talking too far in the future. And I definitely don't want to add my father trying to take advantage of our relationship to the mix.

I know he said he's in this. But when the reality of limited PTO, long hours, and hard days hits, is he going to stick around when he could be hopping on private jets at the drop of a hat? He is content now when everything is sunshine and roses but if my childhood taught me anything it's that it's hard for 'normal life' to compete with the glamours of the music industry.

27

TODAY IS one of our more exciting press events of the tour. Declan, Grayson, and I are playing a few songs for the kids at UPMC Children's Hospital of Pittsburgh and then sticking around to chat. Considering the issues facing these children, I was surprised how many of them knew the words to our songs.

After our performance, Declan takes a tour with the hospital staff while Grayson goes to visit the ICU. I hang around the area they set us up in to say goodbye to the kids as their parents and nurses take them back to their rooms. As people clear out, I notice a little girl sitting alone at one of the tables. With no other adults around, I check on her.

"Is this seat taken?" With widened eyes, she shakes her head, allowing me to sit down beside.

"I'm Jack."

"I'm Johanna." She appears to be around ten years old with

wild brown hair and big blue eyes. She reminds of a mix between Lainey and Ellie at that age.

"Did you enjoy the show?"

"It was pretty good."

"Only pretty good?"

"It would have been cooler if Grayson had his drums instead of the keyboard." Because of the limited space, we played an acoustic show as a trio. Dec and I on guitar and Gray on the keys.

"You're right, drums would have been cooler. Do you play any instruments?"

"I had a harmonica for a while, but my mom said it was keeping my little brother up and she made me stop."

"That stinks. Sometimes moms can be lame." She smiles at that.

"She traded me a Switch for it. There is a game on there that lets me play the drums which are way cooler than a harmonica."

"Sounds like an upgrade to me."

"Yeah and it doesn't keep my brother awake. He sleeps a lot when he's sick."

"I'm sorry to hear that. Did he come to the show?"

"He's not allowed to leave his room 'cause of all the tubes. I usually sit with him but Mom said I could come down for your concert, but I would have stayed upstairs if I knew about the drums." Damn. This kid is harsh. I love it.

"Do you know how to play real drums?" I ask.

"Not yet, but Mom said she'll get me lessons when I'm older and Kevin isn't in the hospital anymore. She might even send me to a summer camp where they'll teach me since we don't know anyone who has drums. Have you ever been to summer camp?"

"I have not. I spent my summers on my grandparents' farm."

"Did they have horses?"

"They did."

Johanna pauses for a moment as if to consider the merits of my childhood before nodding her head. "Horses are cooler than drums."

This kid. When I peer up, I realize the space has cleared out and aside from staff members walking around, it is only the two of us.

"Is your mom meeting you down here?"

She glances around as if noticing the same thing. "She said she would come get me, but if the doctor stopped by, it could be awhile. I'm not supposed to take the elevator alone."

"How about I take you back to your mom and brother?"

"Okay," she agrees, jumping out of her seat.

Letting her lead the way, we hop on the elevator and take it to the cardiac ICU. When we arrive, I see an older version of Johanna talking to none other than Grayson. He waves as we approach.

"There you are!" the woman says. "I was about to come down and grab you. Thank you for bringing her up here. I'm Nadia, her mother."

"This is Jack," she tells her mother who gives me an appreciative and tired smile.

"Johanna, this is my brother Grayson. Grayson, this is Johanna. She thinks drums are cooler than the keys."

Crouching down to her eye level, he addresses the spirited girl. "Me too."

My chest almost bursts at the toothy grin she gives him. Until The sensation is wiped away by laughter caused by monologue on how the drums are cool, but that horses are cooler. As Grayson and Johanna debate the merits of both, I talk to her mom.

"That is some kid you got there."

"She's a firecracker. I wasn't half as easy to deal with at her age and I hadn't been through nearly as much."

"She said her brother is sick?"

"Kevin and his dad were in an accident when he was two. He's had several surgeries to repair the damage but his heart sometimes has trouble keeping up." That's heavy. I was blessed growing up to not only have two parents but also four healthy siblings. I was the one in and out of the ER the most for my daredevil ways.

"She is a great big sister, though," Nadia comments.

"I bet she is. She reminds me of my sister, Lainey. She told me all about the summer camp where she is going to learn to play the drums."

"She's my little musician. Her school doesn't have much of a music program and professional lessons are expensive where we live. Sleepaway camp will give her the chance to learn how to play and give her a break from all the craziness here."

Nadia and I talk for a while longer about the families struggles while Johanna schools Grayson on Switch drumming game. The buzz of our phones lets us know it's time to head downstairs to get to the venue for soundcheck.

"I know we just met," I say to Nadia, "But I would love to sponsor Johanna's time at camp and pay for lessons throughout the school year. She deserves them."

"I want to turn you down. But one thing I've learned throughout this journey is to not rob my kids of opportunities because of my own pride. Thank you," she replies, eyes glistening. Getting her information, I tell her my team will be in touch to get everything squared away.

On the ride back to the arena, I think about how fulfilling that interaction was. Hearing about their struggles tugged at my heartstrings. The knowledge that little spitfire will be jamming away on her beloved drums, gives me a sense of satisfaction I've rarely had outside of music. I know how much being able to channel my emotions into my performance helps me. I would love to ensure other kids have that same opportunity.

If I could do something like this as my side project I would in a heartbeat. I don't think finding kids to give music lessons to is what Eliza had in mind, but maybe she will know of something I can get involved in. I bet my list making queen could find me several local charities to support that involve kids and music.

After sending an email to my finance manager with Nadia's info, I filter through the emails waiting for me in my inbox. One that piques my interest is from a distillery in Boston. They know about my love of whiskey and want to discuss a potential partnership. I don't know if it will go anywhere, but I agree to the meeting next week.

MY POSITIVE ATTITUDE is struck down later in the day when I get a text from Lainey.

2:13 PM

RYDER PRINCESS

Hey loser. You taking care of my girl?

I haven't spoken to Lainey in a few days and that's her opener? Does she know about me and Ellie? Is this her way of offering her approval? That would be nice. Declan has been back on my case about telling her. I want to, but Ellie hasn't mentioned it again and with things going good between us, I don't want to rock the boat.

Of course. I feed her, water her, and take her for walks twice a day.

You make her sound like a pet. That your kink?

If she's joking around, she doesn't know. She is protective over Ellie. There is no way she wouldn't be reading me the riot act at the very least to tell me not to hurt her friend. Everyone seems to be afraid I'm going to hurt Ellie, but none of them realize that of the two of us, I am the most likely to get hurt.

Once Ellie realizes how unambitious I am, she'll kick me to the curb for someone with more drive. It makes a man *almost* wish she was into me for the money and the fame because I could at least keep her enticed. I am more hopeful than normal about my ability to keep Ellie interested. Visiting the children's hospital has gears turning in my head that could lead to something fulfilling and worthy of my time and attention.

Lainey and I are close, but we aren't divulge-my-problems-to-her close. For no reason other than wanting our baby sister to always look up to us and save her from unnecessary stress, the guys and I try to keep that shit between us. We never wanted Lainey to have to face the darker sides of our life after stealing away pieces of her childhood already.

It's part of why I keep it light with her. And why hiding my relationship feels wrong. The good things were always what I could share with her and for now, I am keeping the best thing that has ever happened to me under wraps. Not wanting to slip up, deflection is the name of the game.

> Nah. I leave the kinky shit to Declan. Although, I wouldn't be opposed to wearing a leash for the right woman.

> That is more information than I ever wanted to know.

> You're welcome. Can't wait to see you when we get to LA!

> Back at you, Jackie. I miss you guys more than I expected.

Us, too. Laines.

28

Ellie

"WHAT ARE WE DOING HERE?" I ask when Jack drags me over to the park beside the arena in Cleveland. I helped Shonda unload the trailer this morning while the guys were at the hospital meaning we both have a free afternoon.

"Pickleball."

"Pickleball?"

"Yeah. It's the fastest growing sport in America?" he replies, staring at me as if I live under a rock.

"Is it really?"

"I don't know but it sounds right."

"You're ridiculous."

"Yeah but you like me, anyway. Now come on, let's play!" He puts down the bag I didn't realize he was carrying and pulls out two pickleball paddles and a ball. After briefly explaining the rules we give it a go. A few games later and one instructional video I come to a few conclusions.

The first is that the reason no one else is out here on this gorgeous summer day is because it is way too hot. The second is that while he may have the body of an athlete, my boyfriend is terrible at this game.

When he dragged me out here earlier and turned his ball cap backwards, I was ready to do anything the man wanted. What is it about a man in a backwards hat that is so damn appealing? It should be illegal for one outfit tweak to make a girl weak in the knees. I suspect the move was intentional since wearing it forward would have been more practical. At least I would suspect that if he was actually good at this game and trying to get a leg up.

"Jack," I state calmly as the ball bounces past him once again.

"Yeah?" he replies, wiping his brow. The only perk to the heat is the sight of Jack in a backward baseball cap. It doesn't do much to hold back his hair, but it does a lot of my libido.

"I mean this in the nicest way possible, but you suck."

He barks out a laugh as if he didn't expect me to comment on his abysmal pickleball skills, but voices his agreement. "I know."

"You know?"

"I know."

"If you know you're bad then why are we doing this?" I question.

He shrugs in response. "I enjoy it."

"You enjoy it even though you're bad at it?"

"Yep."

"Shouldn't you have brought someone out here who knows what they're doing to help you get better? You could easily afford an instructor."

"I don't need an instructor," he laughs. "I'm not trying to go to the Pickleball Championships. I do this for fun, not to compete."

"Winning *is* fun."

"Yes, my little overachiever, it is. But if I only did things I could win at, I would miss out on a lot, don't you think?"

I think my brain may have short-circuited because I have no response to that. My entire life has been focused on achievements and checking boxes. The idea of doing something I don't know if I would excel at or not is unfathomable.

As if a lightbulb went off, I now see my entire collegiate life much more clearly. I *am* afraid to fail. I won't even try out a career because I am scared it won't pan out. What's the worst that could happen, I have to get another job?

Jack must sense the epiphany I am undergoing because he lets me stand there in my thoughts for a while. Breaking the silence, he says, "There was another reason I wanted to try out pickleball with you."

"What reason was that?"

"I had to come up with something to see if you were as sexy as I imagined in that lilac skort."

Peering down at my legs, I scan over the purple garment Jack met me with after his trip to the hospital.

"What's the verdict?"

"Way hotter than I could have dreamed. If you let me take you back to the bus, I'll show you how much."

A heady thrill runs through me at the prospect. "Lead the way."

WHEN WE GET BACK to the bus we take turns showering before Jack meets me in the bedroom. Grayson and Declan are somewhere entertaining Paris, leaving us alone on the bus. I don't know how Jack managed to miss the outing, but I'm glad he did.

I'm finishing up my braid when Jack enters the room. With wet hair and a towel around his waist, I am having déjà vu to my first night on the tour. Through the mirror, I notice the expansion of his sleeve. It now extends from his shoulder over his entire left pec.

Standing up to examine it more closely, I notice Jack holding his breath. Tracking my fingers along the new designs, I bring my eyes up to his. "Wildflowers?"

The left side of Jack's chest is covered in a field of wildflowers.

"Why?" I ask.

The question elicits a soft grin as he runs the callus pad of his thumb across my cheek bone. "Because I wanted a representation of what's in my heart over my heart."

The confession almost guts me. It isn't my name, but it might as well be for the claim it represents. This man inked me to his body and I find my reaction is joy. And lust.

Watching me cautiously, I realize Jack must have expected me to get emotional. I'm not a big crier, though. And this did not make me sad. It made me happy and horny. Deciding to show him my appreciation instead of telling him since I can't seem to get any words out, I tug on the knot of his towel until it flutters to the ground.

Following it down, I grip the base of his cock and stare up at him from my knees.

"Baby, you don't have to—that's not why I—holy shit." I cut off his denial by licking the tip of his cock and swirling my tongue around it. I know I don't *have* to suck his cock, but damn if I don't want to.

Once I've gotten him wet with my tongue, I slowly envelop him with my mouth. Taking as much of him as I can, I use my hand to twist his exposed shaft in time with my bobs. When he lets out a guttural groan, a thrill runs through me and I take him even deeper.

Pulling back when I gag, I use the saliva to coat him before sucking him back into my mouth. I jolt when Jack slams his hands onto the mirror behind me, but when he doesn't move further, I continue my efforts. Between his curses and praises, my own need increases. If he keeps it up, I'm going to need the hand fondling his balls to rub between my legs.

As if he can sense my desire, Jack pulls back dick sliding out of my mouth. When I try to chase it, he stops me. "No more of that. I want to come in your pussy, not down your throat."

Pulling me up to stand, he turns me toward the bed. "Get on all fours and stick that sexy ass out for me, baby. It's my turn to play."

29

WATCHING ELLIE GET INTO POSITION, I take a few moments to collect myself. That girl is a vixen with her tongue. It took all my willpower to stop myself from filling her mouth with my cum. I wouldn't say I had a specific reaction I expected when she saw my new tattoo, but dropping to her knees wasn't in my top three guesses.

I've never gotten a tattoo for anyone else before unless you count the brand from my grandparents' ranch. I've always thought it was cliché, but then I had the idea for wildflowers and saw what Michael had sketched out, I couldn't resist. I thought Ellie would have seen it while it was getting done, but since she opted to get her own tattoo, I was able to surprise her with the finished product. And I'm glad I did, since it got us here.

Moving behind her, I brush my palms against her pale skin from her neck down to her ass. Usually when we have sex, we

200

are both worked up, frantic, and trying to be quiet. Not today. Today I am going to take my time and show her how good I can make her feel. Prove to her that I can be in tune with all her needs and not get overwhelmed by desire.

Reaching between her legs, I find her wet for me. She's always so wet and ready to go when we are together.

"You're soaked already. Is all this for me?"

"Yes," she moans as I tap my fingers on her clit, causing a shiver to run down her spine. "I need you."

"You'll have me."

Leaning forward, I kiss between her shoulder blades before slowly pushing inside her. Once I am fully seated, I pull out and slide in again. Maintaining a slow pace, I revel in the sensation of gliding in and out of her hot core.

Wiggling below me, Ellie tries to speed me up by meeting my thrusts. Instead of allowing her to dictate the pace, I give her ass a soft smack. The pinkening of her skin almost has me changing my mind and bucking into her, but I hold on to my resolve. "Stay still."

It doesn't take long until Ellie is pleading for me to go faster, but I don't.

"You don't need it fast, baby. You need it deep, just like this. Enjoy the buildup. Feel the pressure coursing through your body, begging to be released."

"I am begging," she whines. If I wasn't straining so hard, I would laugh. My chest is moistened with sweat from restraining myself. I'm sure the grip on her hips will leave bruises, but she doesn't appear to mind.

"Do you feel it? Do you feel how close your orgasm is?"

"Yes. Yes. Please make me come, Jack. Please." Her sweet pleas are music to my ears. I will never get tired of making this strong girl come undone for me or the way her body fits me perfectly.

"That's it, good girl. You're gripping my cock so tight. It

won't be long until I fill up this sweet little pussy." And it won't be. She's already gripping me like a vise. The second she comes around me, I will be done for. My dirty words driver her closer as I continue to pump into her.

Reaching below us, I maintain my pace, but bring my hand to her soaked center. Rubbing languid circles, I pinch her clit at the same moment my cock drags against her front wall. With that movement, she shatters around me. Two thrusts later, I do the same.

After we both shower again and Ellie falls asleep soundly on my chest. As I run my hands through her soft hair, I think about how lucky I am that the girl next door is giving me a chance to prove I can be the man she needs.

WHEN I WAKE up the next morning, Ellie is still fast asleep. It's rare for her to sleep longer than me. I let her slumber while I wrangle up breakfast. When I get to the kitchen, I see Declan and Grayson in front of a tablet, talking to a familiar face.

"Jack!" Lainey yells from the screen. Peering behind me to ensure she couldn't see that I came from the bedroom and not a bunk, I, too, crowd the screen.

"Is that the elusive Lainey Ryder?" I ask. "I heard she moved to LA and forgot about all the little people."

"Come off it. It hasn't been that long and we both know you are plenty busy." For a moment, I panic, thinking she knows about me and Ellie, but when she asks Grayson if we're taking care of her friend, I relax. I'm also slightly offended since I told her yesterday that I was.

I don't know why I'm worried she'll find out. No one on tour outside of my brothers and Eliza knows. The few times we've been in public, we kept things PG. No pictures have gotten out of us being overly friendly. Paris mentioned me and a mystery woman in Florida, but from what I can gather, there are no photos circulating.

As Lainey catches us up on all things LA, the knot of guilt I shove deep down grows in my stomach. I'm no longer worried about her reaction to me dating Ellie. I keep telling myself she will be happy to make Ellie an official part of the family. Lainey can only hold a grudge against her favorite brother for so long, especially once she sees how good Ellie and I are together.

My inner turmoil comes from the fear that she will feel betrayed that we didn't tell her sooner. As her brother, I am supposed to protector her from situations like this, not cause them.

After Declan plays her a song from her latest EP and Grayson talks about them living together when he comes to LA after the tour, Ellie wanders into the room.

"There's my bestie," Lainey shouts through the phone.

"You don't have to yell, Laines. She can hear you fine," Declan chastises. Even over video call he's a bossy bitch.

"Good morning!" Ellie greets. "Are you up early or still awake?"

"It's 7 a.m. in LA. No way is she still awake," Gray answers for her.

The knowing expression on Ellie's face and grimace on Lainey's tells me he's wrong. Grabbing my mug of coffee, I snicker to myself. Not wanting to admit the truth out loud, Lainey changes the subject.

"Did you read that book I lent you, El?"

"What book?" Grayson asks. "It must be dirty since Ellie is red as a tomato."

Glancing up, I see he is right, My girl is blushing hard.

"Don't worry about it," she rushes out. Lainey doesn't heed her request though.

"It was this cowboy romance I saw recommended on Cami Graham's show. Who would have thought you could recommend smut on Daytime TV. That whiskey scene had me . . ." Lainey finishes the sentence by fanning herself and I choke on my coffee when I realize what book she is referring to.

Bryce pats me on the back as I try to regain my composure. Stricken Ellie has been replaced by barely contained laughter Ellie. That brat. I have to go through life knowing the sexiest experience of my life came from a book my sister recommended.

The girls chat for a few minutes about plans they have when Lainey gets back to Nashville. Lainey's fellowship is only for a few months and she doesn't know if it will be extended into a job offer. Eager for privacy, Ellie asks if she can take the tablet into her bedroom. Since calls with Lainey are rare these days, they want to add in Alexis and Macy while they have the chance.

After my brothers and I say goodbye to Ellie, the dread over my future sets back in again. Not only do I not know my own plan. I haven't checked in with Ellie to see what her next move is. I know she is applying for jobs, but I haven't seen her interview or heard her mention any leads. I want her to be able to talk to me about those kinds of things.

I'm one to talk since I'm not sharing my ideas, either. I've got my meeting with Kennedy Distillers in a few days and hopefully that will lead to something to focus on during our hiatus. I can't come to the girl with a goal tracking journal with a half-baked plan. I need something more substantial if I'm going to show her I'm the type of man who can take care of her not only physically, but also that understands her values.

While the girls chat, my brothers suck me into another Mario Kart battle. By the time Ellie comes out, she's showered and gotten ready for the day. I can't read how she is feeling and I hate it. She should be happy after girl talk, but something in her expression reflects an undercurrent of anxiety that I don't know how to ease.

Pulling Ellie into my lap, I continue to own Bryce at the game. I relish in her fresh, floral scent as my lips find her temple. I can't help the elation that washes over me as she melts into my chest. There is time to talk later. For now, I'll enjoy the feeling of her relaxed in my arms.

30

Ellie

WHILE CALLS with the girls are usually a balm to my soul. But this one left me more stressed than relaxed. That isn't entirely fair. Most of the stress is from the job interview I have tomorrow with my dad's contact in New York.

I mentioned the interview to the girls and while they were supportive, I could tell they were freaking out at the prospect of me moving. They said they'd support me no matter what, but leaving Nashville is not ideal.

With Lainey on the call, I couldn't get into the deeper reason for wanting to stay since we haven't told her yet. It's been a while since Jack mentioned telling her and I wonder if he, too, thinks we should wait until things settle after the tour.

I would hate to jeopardize my relationship with Lainey over something that doesn't last once we hit the Davidson County limits. I don't believe Jack intends to end things when we get home, but I can't picture a world where we stay together. Both his brothers are taking on adventures. I know he will, too.

Best case scenario, whatever secret project he's cooking up will keep him in town. At least that way, we have a chance. Going from seeing him all day every day to having to plan date nights is going to be hard, for me but even more for him. Jack is a shockingly clingy boyfriend. I don't hate it, but it will be harder to satisfy when I am putting in forty-plus hour weeks.

How long will he be okay with me falling asleep in the middle of the movie or canceling dates due to a work even?. There are so many variables when it comes to jobs in fashion, I can't begin to know what specific obstacles we'll face. He says he's invested, but he's a man used to living on easy street.

It's not that he doesn't work hard. He does. But most of his success thus far has been one long ride. He doesn't have that hustle mentality. I'm not sure he'll understand it. How many declined invitations will it take before he stops asking? How long until he decides he'd rather have someone who can fit more easily into his life instead of the other way around.

With the growing pit in my stomach, I shift my focus on the positive moments ahead of me. Tomorrow I get to see my grandmother in person for the first time in a few years and get one of those famous Grammy O hugs.

Growing up in Tennessee, I haven't been able to see her as much as I would have like. Thankfully, she didn't let the distance factor into our relationship, even with all her other grandchildren much closer. Visits to see her each summer are some of my most treasured memories.

Aisling O'Leary and her husband, Finneas, came to the US shortly after getting married and shunned by their families. It was a whole Romeo and Juliet situation without all the dying. They settled in Boston, where they had five children, all of who stayed in the Northeast except for my father. He jokes that having children is the thing that made his mother love him again. She has neither confirmed nor denied this statement like the badass she is.

I'm excited to see Grammy O, but I am low-key nervous of what chaos she and Jack will cook up. I am also anxious to hear whatever news she has for me. She is normally direct. It is out of character that she wouldn't tell me during our last phone call. I asked , but he didn't know either.

By the time Jack comes to bed later, I am round so tight, I'm afraid I might snap.

"I come bearing tater tots," singsongs.

"I'm not hungry," I grouse.

"Unfortunately, the answer we were searching for is, 'Thank you, my magnificent boyfriend whose mustache makes Tom Selleck's look like a schoolboy.'"

"Sorry, babe. Tom has you beat. Yours is better than Burt Reynolds, though. Oh my gosh. Is *our* Burt named after *the* Burt?"

"That is a distinct possibility. We'll have to ask him tomorrow," he replies, sitting down beside me and placing a plate of tots and chicken in my lap.

"I'm really not hungry."

"Eat a few for me, please. You haven't had anything since lunch."

"Fineeeee."

"That's my girl," he says with a kiss to the temple. "I will be sure to reward your efforts."

"Do you want to tell me why you're stressed? I thought you'd be happy after talking to your friends. Is something wrong?"

"With them?" He nods.

"No." As I dip my tater tots into the sauce, I think about how to answer his question. I haven't told him about the interview tomorrow and I don't want to. Instead, I go with the easy answer: Lainey. Jack nods in understanding, running his hand up and down my back as he listens.

Once I've finished eating, he takes my plate into the kitchen. "You're still tense," he observes.

"I know. I can't turn it off."

"I might have a way," he suggests.

"I'm all ears." The timber of his chuckle sounds alarm bells in my head, but it's too late. Jack lifts up the bottom of the comforter and crawls up the bed until his face rests between my thighs. As he nips my sensitive skin, I lift the cover.

"What are you doing? Get out of there."

Pinning me with a stern gaze, he shakes his head. "I didn't interrupt your meal. Don't interrupt mine."

Two orgasms later, I am much more relaxed and fall into a peaceful sleep.

31

Ellie

CHECKING THE CLOCK ONCE AGAIN, I pace the front of the bus, waiting for Jack. He is normally punctual, but he was acting shifty this morning. I didn't call him out on it because I was being shifty, too.

The call with my dad's friend in New York went fine. He runs an athletic uniform company that services little leagues and schools throughout the eastern US. It has absolutely nothing to do with my career trajectory, but at least that makes turning it down easy. I knew there was no reason to worry Jack over it. Though now, he is worrying me.

I needed to leave five minutes ago in order to get to my grandmother's on time. When I hear the bus door open, I turn toward the entrance. My heart sinks when Eliza comes up the stairs instead of Jack.

Wrinkling her nose, she greets me. "Is Jack not back from his meeting yet?"

"No, and I need to leave. Do you know where he is? My calls are going straight to voicemail and none of my texts show as delivered. He's okay, right?"

"I'm sure he is fine. Security would have notified me otherwise," she answers dismissively. "He isn't on a sanctioned media stop, so I can only go off his calendar. All it says is 'Kennedy.' Do you know who that might be?"

My stomach twists. Jack has never once mentioned a girl named Kennedy. Oblivious or uncaring about my internal strife, Eliza theorizes out loud. "The only Kennedy I know is his ex. I believe she is leading a seminar at Yale Drama school. Maybe she made the trip up?"

Great. Not only is Jack blowing me off, but it's for his gorgeous ex who is teaching at an Ivy League school.

"I don't have time for this," I grumble. "If you see Jack, tell him I left. Or don't, since we don't tell each other where we're going anymore."

Eliza gives me a dismissive wave of her hand and I stomp down the stairs, ordering a rideshare as I walk to the front of the arena. It takes longer than I'd like, but it gives me time to collect myself and push out all the negative emotions. I'm not going to let this ruin what should be an amazing visit with my grandmother.

THE FIRST THING my grandmother does when I get to her house is pull me into a tight hug and tell me how skinny I've gotten. I've gained weight during the tour since Jack is constantly feeding me and the general lack of healthy options, but I let her think what she wants.

I'm glad I didn't warn her beforehand that Jack was coming.

I'd hate to see the disappointment in her eyes. Instead, I let her fuss over me.

Ushering me into her kitchen, she pulls out ingredients from her fridge and makes us both lunch. While she preps the ingredients, we chat about Dad, Finn, and what all my cousins are up to. Most of my cousins are older than me. They all either have families, PhDs, or joined the Priesthood.

Once she's made way more food than the two of us can eat, she sits at the table and we enjoy our meals. Grammy gives me all the gossip about her Mahjong group. She tries to explain the rules of the game to me, but it all goes over my head. We settle into stories of my dad as a kid instead.

Hearing what a sweet, but mischievous boy he was, I wonder when it all changed. I remember when I was super young what a fun dad he was. But somewhere along the way he grew jaded and overly concerned with other people's opinions. Maybe he was always that way and I was too young to notice, but part of me mourns the relationship we could have had.

"What was so important that you needed to tell me in person and not over the phone?" That question has burned in my mind ever since she demanded I come for a visit. I would have come regardless, but her insistence was suspicious.

"Can't a grandmother coax her granddaughter to see her with vague statements and declarations?"

"She can, but then she has to deliver."

"Fair enough. I have an announcement," she states primly, wiping at the corners of her mouth with her napkin. The woman loves a dramatic pause.

"A real announcement or a 'the Pope spoke to me in a dream' announcement?" I ask.

"He did speak to me in a dream!"

"Of course he did."

She glares at my obvious pacification, but continues on regardless. "On to business. Before your grandfather passed,

God rest his soul, we decided to set aside money for each of our grandchildren to help start their new lives. Some of your cousins have used it to buy homes, some for weddings, some for traveling the world. Now that you've graduated, it is the right time to bestow this gift on you. I'm sure you will use it to do great things and make us all proud."

"Grandma," I choke. "You don't have to give me anything."

"Pish posh," she waves me off. "You're entering a new phase of your life. If Finnegan and I can make that any easier, we are thrilled to help."

"I don't know what to say."

"You don't need to say anything, lovey. I know whatever you do with it will make me and your grandfather proud."

Getting up from my seat, I launch myself at her and swallow the small woman up in a hug until she pushes me off. I know she and Grandpa lived frugally. The fact that they would share what they had with me is heartwarming.

"Alright, enough of the gushy stuff. I'm not getting any younger and the Pope told me we should have cake," she says with a wink. Lifting up the lid of her cake plate, she reveals my favorite cookies.

After tucking the check in my purse and devouring a cookie, I spend the rest of the afternoon reconnecting with grandmother. I turn off my phone to avoid directions and stay longer than intended. Since Jack didn't come, I have no need to be back at the venue for soundcheck. As long as I get to my post at the merch booth by the time doors open I am good.

On the car ride back to the arena, curiosity wins out and I pull out the check. My jaw drops when I see how much Grammy O gave me. Fifty thousand dollars. The same woman who used Cool Whip tubs as Tupperware gave me fifty thousand dollars. This has to be a mistake. Except in the memo line it says, 'This is not a mistake.'

My mind stutters, trying to process this. I would have

guessed it was five thousand dollars, *at most*. To be ten times that is mind blowing. I have fourteen cousins. Does that mean she has been sitting on eight hundred thousand dollars since my grandfather passed?

What am I supposed to do with fifty thousand dollars? I don't even have a job lined up yet. Fifty grand is far and away more supplemental income than I need to live on until I find a job.

My previous conversation with Shonda pops into my mind. I could use this money to open a shop. The idea has grown on me ever since she planted that seed. I'll have to take her up on her offer to chat with her friend after the tour. This money opens a lot of doors for me in terms of career options. I can't wait to tell . . . Jack.

Jack, who was potentially with his ex. Jack, who even if he wasn't missed out on meeting my grandmother for some shady and unknown reason. I hope he has a good explanation when I see him later because the thoughts my mind is conjuring up are not kind.

GETTING BACK DURING SOUNDCHECK, I quickly changed in the bus before staying out of sight for as long as I could. It helped that my dad decided to give me a call. Since I am getting ready and no one else will be on the bus, I put him on speaker.

"Hello?" I answer.

"Hi, Ellie. How are you?"

"I'm good, Dad. How about you?"

"I'm well. I just got off the phone with your grandmother." Geez, Grammy O doesn't waste time. I've barely left her place an hour, and she's already told Dad all about it. The visit was wonderful, but his tone conveys disapproval.

"That's nice. I loved spending time with her. I need to make a point to come to Boston more often."

He grunts in agreement, I think, but it's hard to tell. "Is there anything you want to tell me?"

Shit. Did my grandmother tell him about the money? I didn't get the vibe she was going to, but she's a wildcard. Better play it safe in case she didn't.

"No?"

"How did your interview go?" Right. Of course, that's what he wants to discuss.

"It was fine. I'm not sure it's the best fit, but it is always good to make a connection. Even if the position made sense, I'm looking to move to New York right now."

"It makes sense you want to stick close now that you have a celebrity boyfriend. It'd be hard to keep his interest from hundreds of miles away."

"I-what?" Is he referencing what I think he is?

"It's a small industry, Elenor. Did you think I wouldn't find out about you and the Ryder boy?" The insistence of my dad calling grown men boys is grating. But right now I'm more concerned he knows about me and Jack. We've been super careful about who we share our relationship with. Only the inner circle knows.

"Where did you hear that?"

"Does it matter?" he sneers.

"I'd like to know who is talking about me, yes."

"The son of a friend worked on the tour and said he was kicked off for talking to you. That's controlling, don't you think?"

Fucking Donny. I knew he wouldn't keep his mouth shut. I'm surprised anyone believed him though.

"I hadn't heard those rumors," I reply cautiously.

"Most people don't believe him since that would be out of character for them, but I remember how you always had a crush on him. I told you that a tour was no place for you. Now you've got yourself wrapped up with a musician."

"You realize that your entire career is built on tours and musicians, right?"

"We aren't talking about me. We're talking about the mess you've gotten yourself in. Not to mention you haven't even leveraged your new found relationship to get your dad an in. Johnny Ryder cut me out when the boys were younger. He never liked me for some reason. Now that you're dating one of them, it only makes sense I join the team."

That doesn't make sense to me at all. There is no connection between who I date and where my father works. In fact, this is the first time he's ever even inquired about my love life. Not that I may even have a relationship with Jack after what went down today, though.

"The tour is almost over. They wouldn't bring on a new manager this late."

"You don't know how these things work. They could bring me on for a trial run of a few shows before hiring me on to help in the future."

"Dad, I can't deal with this right now. I'm going to be late for work. We can talk about this later."

"After everything I've done for you, it's the least you can do."

"Okay. I'll talk to them. Bye."

Hanging up, I throw my brush across the bedroom and scream in frustration. When I go to pick it back up, I swear I see movement, but when I listen, I don't hear anyone else on the bus. Between my dad and Jack, my head is pounding. It doesn't help that the similarities between the two are stark today.

When Jack's texts started rolling in, it took everything in me not to reply. I've heard the pretty words my dad said to my mom every time he got caught in a compromising position and I wasn't interested. He didn't even deny that he was with Kennedy. I guess kudos on the honesty, but he only seemed remorseful to miss lunch, not the reason behind his absence.

It's times like these I wish I had anywhere else to hide for the night. Unfortunately, the only thing that will stand between me and Jack is a flimsy door lock. I have a suspicion he isn't going to let hardware stop him.

I'm confused about everything that went down today. My gut is telling me that Jack isn't a cheater and there must be another explanation, but I can't for the life of me think of one. This is the type of issue I would normally talk over with Lainey, but, of course, I can't.

By the time I got to the merch booth, I knew it was only a matter of minutes until the gates opened. That would allow me plenty of time to stew in my anger over the day. Jack tried his best to get me to talk, but time wasn't on his side and he had to disappear behind the security checkpoint to avoid being overrun by fans.

Listening to the familiar sound of the Ryder's set, I attempt to focus on happier thoughts, like what I'm going to do with the money from my grandmother. My attention is much better spent on my next move than wondering what is happening with Jack and me.

As the brothers play their final song, there is a lull in activity at the booth. Seizing the opportunity, I get Shonda's attention.

"What's up?" she asks, saddling up beside me.

"Do you think your friend would still be interested in chatting with me about opening a store?"

Her cocky smile tells me she knew we would eventually have this conversation. "She would for sure. In fact, she is expecting your call."

"How can she be expecting something I decided on today?"

"Call it a hunch. Are you good? You've seemed distracted tonight."

"I'm fine. Personal stuff and stressing about where I'll work after the tour."

She nods her head knowingly. "I'll text you her number so you can give her a call when you have downtime. For now, let's get ready for the post-show rush."

32

WHEN I GET KENNEDY DISTILLERS, I am met by brother-sister duo, Paul and Kat, who run the place. They took it over from their parents a couple of years ago and have been working to reinvigorate the brand ever since. I am interested in learning more about their process and what it is they want from me.

"Jack, thank you for coming," Paul says in greeting. "Welcome to Kennedy."

"Paul, Kat, thank you for inviting me. I can't wait to see how the sausage is made."

"Let's not waste any time, then," Kat replies. "I know you have a tight schedule today since you play tonight."

"We'll try not to give you too many samples so you can put on a good show," Paul jokes. "This tour will be fairly informal. If you have any questions, ask away. We love talking about the product and history."

"Y'all have been around for over a hundred years, right?"

"One hundred and thirty," Kat answers. "The Kennedy family has a long legacy of making whiskey in Boston, but some of the original recipes date back to our time in Ireland. The building we are in right now has been used as our family's distillery since 1933 when prohibition was lifted and we could make it on the up and up again."

"And before then?"

"Here, there, everywhere they didn't get caught and a few places they did."

The siblings go on to tell me about the evolution of their brand, process, and how their product is made today.

The tour concludes in the rickhouse, where we sample their different offerings and they answer all my burning questions. Wanting to support the brand, I pull out my phone to post on social media, but it won't go through.

"Service is terrible down here," Kat notes. "Adding Wi-Fi is next on our list for modernizing the building. Renovations have taken a backseat while we've been focused on the brand."

"This has all been fascinating, but I am not sure what it is I am here for. Don't get me wrong, I've enjoyed the hell out of this tour and tasting, but I figure you uninvited me for a reason?"

Sharing a loaded glance with his sister, Paul takes the lead on answering me. "Our father ran the business alongside his father for twenty years and then twenty years on his own after that. As much as he created a great product and held true to the brand, marketing and innovation weren't his forte."

"Paul and I spent years in school learning the finer details of business and then more years under Dad's tutelage," Kat supplies. "One thing we both agree on is that while Kennedy's is a favorite among the country club elite, we aren't reaching many others. There are millions of whiskey drinkers who don't even consider us when making a purchase and we want to change that."

"And that is where I come in?"

"That's where you come in." Pulling out her tablet, Kat shows me a mockup of an updated Kennedy's design that features my name.

Paul explains the meaning. "We want to partner with public figures that have a genuine love of whiskey. We want more than simply a spokesperson. We want to work with you to create a signature recipe that encapsulates the essence of you and your favorite elements. You'd have a say on the ingredient ratio, barrel type, age, design, and more. Together we would create a truly unique drink to co-brand-slash-market it."

Damn. That is a cool idea and an amazing opportunity. I have always had a passion for whiskey, but outside of drinking and collecting, I didn't know how I could get involved in the industry. This would be a great foot in the door and give me the chance to be a part of a cool project.

As Kat and Paul name other celebrities they've invited to be a part of their collaboration line, I can't help but wish Ellie was here. I'd love to hear her thoughts on all this. Since I wasn't sure what they wanted, I didn't bring her with me. Plus, she had a video call before . . . oh, shit.

Today was lunch with Ellie's grandmother. That is what she had going on this afternoon. Checking my phone again, I see it is well past the time we needed to leave. I scramble to text her, but remember there is no reception down here. And based on what time it is, we have been down here longer than planned.

"Thank you both for thinking about me for this opportunity and I am going to consider it seriously. Send all the details to my management team and we'll review it. Unfortunately, I forgot there was somewhere I needed to be and I am already running late."

Paul and Kat appear slightly startled by my sudden need to leave, but they agree to send the details to G&K and show me the exit. Hoping in the SUV, my driver guns it back to the arena.

On the way, my phone is flooded with missed calls and texts from Ellie. They start off calm, asking when I'll be back and turn more concerned the longer she goes unanswered. The last one informs me she is leaving without me. I can't tell from the tone if she's mad, sad, or homicidal. Whatever way she is feeling, I deserve it.

The messages I send her go unread. When we make it back to the arena, I sprint onto the bus, but she isn't there. I search for her all over until Trent tells me she hasn't made it back yet. I order him to come and find me as soon as she is here. I hate that I am having to rely on this fucker to get information on my girl, but with soundcheck in fifteen minutes, I don't have any other options.

AFTER THE LONGEST soundcheck of my entire career, I open my phone to a picture from an unknown number. Context clues tell me it is from Trent since it is an image of Ellie at the merch booth. I double check that she hasn't responded to my texts but see nothing. She's big mad.

Making my way to the booth, I don't have long until I need to get with wardrobe. The opening band kicks off at 7 p.m. and the doors to the arena will open an hour before that. I can't be out and about when that occurs.

As I slowly approach, her eyes shift in my direction before returning to the t-shirts she is aggressively folding. With volunteers milling around, I don't want to make a scene and draw attention to myself. We are still keeping our relationship under wraps until we have the chance to tell our friends and family, especially Lainey.

"Baby," I coax quietly when I am within earshot. The rise of her shoulders tells me that she heard me, but that she is ignoring me.

"Ellie, sweetheart. Look at me. I'm so sorry. I completely forgot about our plans today and my morning meeting ran long, but that is no excuse for missing lunch."

Her angry glare lands on my face and the hurt beneath the surface is enough to gut me. I can tell from the sheen of her baby blues that she is holding back tears.

"The meeting that was so important you didn't tell me about it and had your phone off during it?" she questions.

"I didn't have my phone off. Reception was terrible there," I defend.

"I thought something terrible happened to you!" she whisper-shouts, aware of the surrounding audience. "It wasn't until Eliza told me you were with Kennedy and that security said you were okay that I even knew you weren't on the side of a ditch somewhere."

Something about the way he says 'Kennedy' sounds wrong to my ears, but I don't have the luxury of time to analyze why. In the wings, my security team is motioning me to get back into the restricted area as the venue is about to flood with fans.

"Come to the dressing room. We can talk about this. Let me make it up to you."

"You can't 'make this up to me' in the dressing room, Jack. Besides, I have to work and, unlike you, my commitments mean something."

"Ouch." I rear back. I've never seen Ellie this angry, not with me or anyone else.

"I have a job to do. Why don't you go do yours?"

Security is on me now, and I know my time is up. "We'll talk after the show," I grit before running back behind the barrier as I hear the first, "Oh my God, is that Jack Ryder?"

I don't know how I'm going to get through this show with our problems unresolved, but it seems I don't have a choice.

DESPITE MY FOUL MOOD, the show goes off without a hitch. Declan sends me a few worried glances throughout the set, but I shrug him off. In addition to my nerves being raw due to the fight with Ellie, this is also the first show in recent memory I performed without a hat. I held out hope that Ellie would stop in and bring me one but by the time we went on stage, it was too late. It was surprisingly vulnerable performing with nothing on my head.

Gathering in the green room, the last thing I want to do is a meet and greet. I collapse onto the couch, pulling out my phone to exactly what I expected, no missed texts from Ellie. Fuck.

Hanging my head in my hands, I miss Eliza entering the room. "Boys, we need to talk."

"Now is not a great time," I mutter, not able to deal with her negativity right now.

"It can't wait. I got some information about someone trying to manipulate you on the tour and I think it needs to be addressed ASAP."

"Who is that?" Declan asks with a hard tone.

"Ellie."

"No way!" I shoot up, pissed at the insinuation.

"I know you two have something going on, Jack, but I heard it with my own ears."

Grayson wears a skeptical expression to rival mine, but Declan's face is blank. "What did you hear exactly?"

"I was on your bus earlier trying to find something a brand sent you that needed to be featured on social. While I was there, I overheard Ellie on the phone with her father. They were discussing a plan to get him installed as the tour manager."

"Ellie hates her dad," I say. "No way would you be helping him get a spot on the tour. Plus, she loves Tim."

"It doesn't make any sense," Gray adds. "The tour is literally almost over."

"I'm telling you that's exactly what she said. He asked her to talk to you guys about replacing becoming the tour manager and she said she would. I don't know why you're surprised. It's not as if she plans to stick around Nashville much longer if she's offered that job in New York."

"What job in New York? She's not interviewing in New York."

Eliza sends a pitying glance my way. "It sounds like she already did with a friend of her father's. Maybe that's why she agreed to help him. A job for a job."

I sink back down onto the couch totally dismayed. I can't believe Ellie would do that. I know not having a position lined up was making her anxious, but I didn't think she'd cash in on her connection with us to get ahead.

"I don't know what the two of you talk about, but I would be careful what you say around her moving forward. I'd hate to think she's giving her dad some sort of insider information."

"Thank you for letting us know, Eliza," Declan says. "We'll talk it over and figure out what to do. How long till we have to be at the meet and greet?"

"I need you there in twenty minutes." Before heading out the door she adds, "I know it's not my place but I think it would be better for all of you if she wasn't here anymore. You shouldn't have to watch your back on your own bus. Let me know if you want me to arrange a flight back home for her."

"This is bullshit!" I yell throwing my bottle of water across the room as soon as the door closes.

"I don't know what to think," Grayson replies, sounding dejected.

Observing us both Declan takes a seat, clearly mulling something over. "As much as Eliza can be a snake, it's in her best interest to look out for us. I don't think she would lie about this. There has to be at least some truth to it. Jack, why don't you go talk to Ellie and see what she has to say. I'm sure it's probably a misunderstanding."

"No way was our Ellie Bellie trying to pull one over on us. Fifteen years is way too long of a con," Grayson agrees in her defense. I hope he's right. I don't know what I'll do if she's been lying to us—to me—this whole time.

My mind is reeling from Eliza's accusations. Nothing makes sense. Not Ellie helping her dad, not Ellie interviewing for a job in New York. I know we hadn't explicitly talked about what would happen next, but I thought we were both under the assumption that we would be in the same city. Does Lainey know about this? She's going to be crushed if it turns out to be true.

"I'm gonna go wait for her on the bus. Give us some time, yeah?"

"You got it," Declan says. "We'll cover for you at the meet and greet. Let us know what you find out ."

As I walk back to the bus to wait for Ellie, my mind replays everything that happened not just today but the last few weeks. Being able to call her mine has seemed like a dream. Now I'm worried it is turning into a nightmare. The idea that any part of this has been fake is soul crushing. I thought I'd gotten smarter about who to trust.

Thanks to our disagreement earlier, the situation is even more intense. We're both going to enter this conversation with emotions high. I pace the length of the bus trying to get a grip on mine. Checking the time, I'm annoyed at how long Ellie is taking to get back. I know it's a reaction to my misstep this morning, but it's pissing me off. I'm about to search for her when I hear the door click open and she emerges up the stairs.

33

Ellie

I SPEND LONGER than normal helping Shonda and Trent pack up the remaining merch. I restack hats until I am shooed away from the booth, which is pretty rude in my opinion, but I'm sure my boss could tell I was stalling.

Taking the long way back to the bus, I wonder if I can somehow trick Jack into getting off to look for me so that I can sneak on. As I walk past the catering area, I hear an unwelcome but familiar voice.

"I've gotta say, for being country stars, these Ryder Brothers are pretty dull. Don't get me wrong, the 'daddy vibes' coming off Declan are strong, but the man is a vault. I haven't had to work this hard to get laid on a tour like ever," Paris complains into her phone.

"It's not even about getting hot gossip or bragging rights. At this point, a woman simply has needs." She pauses as if to listen to whoever is on the other line.

"I tried that. I even wore my lucky top and no bites. Grayson hasn't glanced my way the entire tour and while Jack has been a consummate flirt, even he has shied away from my advances."

Jack has some standards, I guess. Not knowing what happened is killing me. Waiting for Paris to turn her back so I can sneak past, she says something that catches my interest. "Eliza was wrong about this tour."

What did Eliza say to her about it? Did she lead her to believe she could get with one of the guys? That doesn't sound like something a PR manager would want, but who knows what game she is playing. I've never been able to get a good read on the woman.

Risking being seen eavesdropping, I dart past the open door and make it outside to the parking lot. Steeling myself for round two, I get on the bus.

As anticipated, Jack is waiting for me in the lounge, elbows resting on his knees. When his face tilts up at the sound of my arrival, he looks more haggard than I have ever seen him. He has the audacity to seem annoyed at how late I was getting here.

"Took you long enough," he murmurs.

"I think if we're keeping score of who waited for whom the longest today, I'll win."

It's a petty thing to say, but I'm feeling petty. I expect the comment to cause Jack to look a little chagrin, but aside from the slight tick of his jaw, nothing happens.

"Do you have anything you want to tell me?" Why do men keep asking me that today?

"About what?"

"About a phone call someone overheard earlier."

I overheard Paris's call like five minutes ago. How did he already hear about it? And what does it have to do with me? He can't be mad that I haven't mentioned it. I've barely gotten back.

"Um, I heard Paris talking about some plan she and Eliza had—"

"Don't try to sully her name right now," he scoffs.

"Paris?"

Taking off his signature ball cap, he runs his hands through his hair, pulling at the ends in frustration. "No, Eliza. After what she overheard earlier, I get why you would try to discredit her, but I'm surprised you'd stoop that low."

"What are you talking about? The only time I saw Eliza today was when I was searching for you, and she told me that you were with Kennedy."

"I wasn't *with* Kennedy, I was *at* Kennedy's." Seeing the confusion on my face, he continues. "Kennedy's is a distillery in Boston. I was meeting with the owners about a potential collaboration opportunity."

Relief washes over me, the missing pieces of the puzzle clicking into place. I almost feel silly for not putting them together myself, but I can't help the instinct that Eliza purposefully misled me. If it was a business thing, shouldn't she have known?

"Why didn't you tell me?" A little communication could have saved us so much trouble.

"I'm not the only one keeping secrets," he clips.

"What are you talking about?"

"The phone call you had with your dad earlier. Eliza overheard you two talking."

"Oh." I cringe. "Having to talk to my dad is bad enough but other people hearing our dysfunction is embarrassing. I still don't understand what there is for him to be this upset about, though."

"Were you ever going to tell me about the job in New York?"

"I-no."

"At least you're honest," he mutters.

"There is no job in New York. I was only interviewing to humor my father. I had no intention of taking it."

"The same father you promised to get hired on this tour. Is

that why you agreed to come in the first place? I know you were reluctant. Did your dad convince you to come so he could be brought on later as our tour manager?"

"I never said that."

"No? You didn't tell him you'd talk to us?"

Okay, I did say that, but I didn't mean it. "I did, but he's been harping on me to do it for weeks and I haven't. I wouldn't have wanted him on tour. It would have cramped our style."

"Cramped our style? What does that mean?"

"Just that my dad being here would have complicated our relationship. He was afraid I'd come on the tour and have a fling with a musician. And he wasn't wrong. Lainey was barely gone less than two weeks before you and I were hooking up."

Jack barks out a humorless laugh. His eyes are swimming with hurt when I meet them. "Is that all this is to you, Ellie? A hookup? A fling? A way to pass time before you get on with your real life in New York or wherever the hell else you've interviewed?"

His words sting, but they aren't completely wrong. I have been thinking of this as a fling. Not because that is what I want, but because I thought it would be foolish to want more. "Is that what you want?"

"Us to be a fling?" I nod, voice clogged with emotion.

"If that's what you think, then you aren't as smart as I thought you were."

His condescending tone riles my already frayed nerves. Moments ago, I thought he may have cheated on me. Now I'm the bad guy? For something I didn't even do? The emotional whiplash is too much and I snap.

"What should I have thought, Jack? We've never once talked about the future. We've been living in the now. Neither of us knows what the hell we're doing after the tour is over. We haven't even told your sister about us. I went into this assuming it had an expiration date. I didn't want to get my hopes up. I can't bounce back like I'm sixteen anymore."

His eyes harden. I don't think I've ever seen them so cold. "An expiration date," he repeats, nodding to himself as if he's decided.

"You're right, Ellie. We did have an expiration date. And it came early. I think it's best if you leave the tour. I'll have Eliza book you a ticket home for tomorrow."

With that declaration, he leaves the bus, slamming the door on his way out. I stand there frozen. What just happened? It feels like I've been sucker punched when my brain finally catches up. Screw waiting for Eliza to get me a ticket. I can't spend another night on this bus.

Running into the bedroom, I make quick work of packing up my shit. If Jack wants me gone, then I'm gone. As much as they care about me, I don't think his brothers would fight him on this. And I wouldn't want them to. I have no desire to be somewhere I'm not wanted.

I consider getting a car to take me straight to the airport, but it's late and there won't be any flights tonight. Thank God this happened in a city where I have family. I text Shana, the cousin I'm closest to, asking if I could crash at her place. By the time I've gathered everything important, she responds telling me her guest bedroom is ready and waiting.

34

HEARING Ellie say she thought we had an expiration date hurt more than knowing she was using us to get her dad a job. Ryan O'Leary is a jackass of the highest order. Not only did he cheat on his wife and essentially abandon his kids, he is also a slimeball. There is a reason our dad declined all his offers to help us in the past and we continued to do so.

I didn't think he'd stoop as low as to use his daughter to get an in. I have a hard time believing Ellie planned to take advantage of her connections to us since the beginning. But I do wonder if a plan came to fruition once Lainey left. It never crossed my mind that maybe Ellie should have gone home, too, probably because I was trying not to fall into her bed.

I don't want to believe I got played again, but when Eliza came to us with what she heard, I was crushed. Declan and Grayson were both skeptical, but agreed to let me talk to her first.

I thought maybe Eliza heard wrong, or that she was venting after being mad at me for missing our meetup with her grandmother. Never in a million years did I expect it to all be true. And that Ellie thought I was cheating on her to boot. If it wasn't clear we were not on the same page, that would have been a dead giveaway.

There isn't a universe in which I would have ever cheated on Ellie. She was my dream girl. The girl I thought could finally make an honest man out of me. I didn't tell her about the meeting, but that's because I wanted to get my shit together and have a plan first. I couldn't go to the woman whose to-do list has to-do lists when a half-baked idea.

I'm teeming with emotions when I storm out of the bus. I spend an hour walking around trying to calm down. It's past midnight at this point and everyone is either out partying in the city or asleep. I consider going to a bar, but even I know that isn't advisable. I settle for pacing the parking lot until the sun peeks out of the horizon. Only then do I return to the bus.

When I get there, I find Grayson asleep in the lounge as if he was waiting up for me. My entrance rouses him as he slowly blinks awake.

"Where the fuck have you been?" he asks when his brain fog lifts.

"Out."

"Out? We called you over a dozen times. Declan wanted to send out a search party for you two, but I convinced him to let you have some space."

"I was walking around to clear my head. Wait, what do you mean 'two'?"

Grayson shoots as stern an expression as he can with pillow marks on his face. "When we got back earlier, both you and Ellie were missing. Since her shit was all gone, we figured you took her to the airport or something. I thought Dec was going to blow a gasket at the idea of her spending the night at Logan."

Ellie's stuff is gone? I told her we'd book her a flight out tomorrow. I didn't mean she had to leave tonight. As angry as I am, worry stirs in my gut, wondering where she could be and if she is safe.

I pull out my phone to check, noting all the missed calls from my brothers. Before I can call her, Gray stops me. "We talked to her."

"You did? Where is she?"

"She went to crash with a cousin. Said she'd figure out her own way home, despite our insistence she let us take care of it."

"That's good," I say, blowing out a breath.

"What happened, dude? I knew you were going to talk to her, but things seemed to have escalated."

"We broke up," I say in defeat.

"Fuck." Grayson slumps back in his seat. "Are you sure?"

"Considering I told her to go home, and that we hit our expiration date, I'd say I'm pretty sure."

"You kicked her out?"

I nod, holding up my hand to stop him from diving deeper. "I can't do this right now. I'm exhausted and walked like 50,000 steps last night. I need to get some sleep, then I'll tell you all the story, at least the parts she didn't."

"She didn't tell us shit except that she was safe at her cousin's and not to worry about her. You know Lainey is going to freak out about this."

I didn't even think about Lainey in this mess. This is exactly what I was trying to avoid by staying away from Ellie in the first place. Why didn't I listen to my gut? If I thought telling her we dated was bad, telling her we broke up will be worse. This is going to be hardest on her out of all of us, and she wasn't even involved. I'm the worst fucking brother in the world.

Not having the emotional capacity to deal with anything else, I nod my agreement and then crash in my bunk. I avoid peeking into Ellie's room. Even though I told her to leave, I don't think I can bear to see the room I've spent the last several nights empty. It would be way too close an analogy to how hollow my heart feels.

35

Ellie

AFTER SPENDING a tearful night at my cousin's house, I got the first flight to Nashville I could. I hoped getting back to my apartment would make me feel better, but it made everything worse. The space is filled with reminders of Lainey and I.

My best friend is going to be devastated when she finds out about everything that went down. I know she won't believe the lies Eliza was peddling about me trying to help my dad. I told her on day one what he was trying to pull. She knows I would never help him get a job with Ryders or where I would have to be around him more than necessary.

She is going to be pissed about me dating her brother and keeping it from her. As strong as our bond is, I worry I threw away fifteen years of friendship over a four-week fling. Will she forgive me for lying to her and keeping my crush a secret for all these years?

With nothing else to do, I bury myself in my slightly musty

bed and vow to sleep for three days straight. I need to air out the house, but I don't have it in me right now. I'm pretty sure I've cried more in the last twenty-four hours than I have in the last twenty-four years combined. It's exhausting. Add in a restless night in my cousin's guest room and worry over my friendship, and I pass out in minutes.

Before I let sleep take me, I text Declan to let him know I made it back home, something he insisted on when he found out I left. He and Grayson seemed freaked out when I was gone last night. I thought Jack would have filled them in, but he was still MIA. They clearly have some bad information, but I'll let them figure it out or not on their own. Eliza may be playing them, but that is not my problem. They invited a snake into their midst. Maybe I'll try to warn them later, but I have my own wounds to lick for now.

HOURS, days, or weeks later, I am woken up by a persistent buzzing sound. Scrambling for the phone, I answer it without checking my caller ID, too dazed to think of the multitude of people I don't want to talk to right now. Thankfully, it is none of them.

"Hi, is this Ellie?"

"It is," I reply hesitantly. Pulling the phone away, I notice I don't have this number saved in my phone.

"Oh wonderful! This is Shonda's friend Misty. She gave me your number and said you were interested in learning more about owning a store. I've had my place in Hillsboro for twenty-five years. Would you like to grab coffee this week?"

More guilt washes over me at the mention of my, now former, boss. I texted her when I got to the airport that I left the tour. I didn't offer up many details, but apologized for leaving her in the lurch. She graciously thanked me for all I did to help her over the past few months and told me not to be a stranger. I'd completely forgotten about her friend after everything that went down. She must have given her a call now that I am back home.

"I would love that. I am getting caught up on things, but I should be free the day after tomorrow if that works for you." I honestly have no idea what day it is, that's how hard I slept, but a two-day buffer sounds doable to pull myself together.

"That works wonderfully. There is a place right by my store where we can meet. I don't usually open until ten. Does nine work for you?"

"That sounds great!"

When she tells me the location, it jogs a memory in my mind. Misty! She owned the shop I stopped into after I had lunch with Macy and was still on the fence about the tour. That seems a lifetime ago, but in reality wasn't that long ago.

"This is going to sound strange," I hedge, "but I think I was in your store a while back. I bought a fringe skirt to take on tour with me."

"Oh my goodness! I wondered if this was you. Fate has a way of working out. Now I'm even more excited to get together."

"Me, too. I'll see you in a couple."

Once we get off the phone, I check to see that it is noon the day after I made it back from Boston. I note a missed call from my mom, a 'liked message,' from Declan, and a barrage of texts from a group with Macy and Alexis.

As I try to scroll through the messages, another pops into the chat.

12:02 PM

MACY

It's been long enough, El. We are officially declaring a state of emergency. If you don't respond in the next hour, Alexis is coming over and I will be by after work.

How do you know where I am?

ALEXIS

Did you forget we all share locations?

Yes . . .

MACY

Are you going to tell us why you're home early? Did something happen?

ALEXIS

Aiden is ready and waiting to kick Ryder ass.

I can't help but laugh at that prospect. He may be from New Zealand originally, but Aiden is the biggest country fan out of us all.

He loves them.

ALEXIS

Yeah, but he loves me more. And you are an extension of me.

He doesn't need to beat them up, it's complicated.

MACY

Sounds like we're coming over after work. That gives you five hours to get yourself together.

ALEXIS

I'll bring Chinese!

By the time the girls get there, I've managed to shower and air out the apartment. Since Lainey and I were both expecting to be gone for months, there is thankfully no rotting food or messes I need to take care of.

As we dig into the takeout Alexis brought, I tell them everything. I rehash everything we discussed before the 'self-care' incident all the way through Jack telling me to leave. By the time I finished, they're both staring at me in stunned silence.

"Wow. That is a lot," Macy remarks. "I can't believe you went through most of that alone. I get why you couldn't tell us, but my God girl!"

Aside from the first week without Lainey, I haven't kept them updated on everything with me and Jack. I know they said they were cool with it, but I didn't want to put them in the position of having to lie to her. And I *really* didn't want her to feel betrayed by all three of us. It did suck not being able to share.

Telling the story of our relationship from start to finish gave me a new perspective on it. When you're living only for the day, you miss so much that you can see in the bird's-eye view. Not to mention, I still saw him through this lens of 'unattainable celebrity,' which wasn't fair to him or us.

Jack was right when he said I wasn't as smart as I thought I was. His care for me was evident throughout the weeks we were together, even if I was too scared to see it. The man stopped the bus to pick me flowers. He inked me on his body for Chrissake. How much clearer could he be? Seeing it now doesn't change the fact that everything got screwed up. And the fact he hasn't reached out since I left speaks volumes.

"I don't know where to go from here," I confess. "He was so mad last time we talked. I know it's due to misconceptions, but at this point, I don't know how to change his mind. Even if we take the Eliza allegations away, my expiration date comment and lack of faith in him is still there."

Macy and Alexis share a look before responding. "I think there is only one thing you can do. You gotta talk to Lainey. If anyone knows how to deal with Jack Ryder and the intricacies of their life, it's her."

I know she's right, but I am dreading it. I have no idea how Lainey will react. All I can hope is that she understands where I was coming from and sees that we at least tried to protect her.

Macy and Alexis leave after we catch up on our show. The mood is more somber than usual, as we were missing our fourth musketeer. It was nice to be around my friends again after ten weeks surrounded by men, though. Knowing there is no time like the present, I decide to shoot Lainey a text. It's not as late on the West Coast, but part of me is hoping she is in for the next. My luck is shit, though, because two minutes after sending, my phone lights up with an incoming call. Here goes nothing.

36

DESPITE SLEEPING through the entire drive to New Jersey, I am in a foul mood. After I give my brothers the cliff notes version of my fight with Ellie, I swiftly ban all mention of her. Declan tells us she made it home safely. Now that I no longer have that worry in the back of my mind, I focus on the shows we have left.

After tonight's show, we fly to LA and have a few days off before closing out the tour there. It's bittersweet that the tour is over, but we are excited that we'll get to see Lainey. The rest of the guys are, I am low-key dreading it.

Like yesterday, I funneled all my frustration over everything that went down with Ellie into my performance. Despite a ball cap being my signature, I opted to wear my Stetson the past two nights. Choosing a tour hat reminds me too much of Ellie and our pre-show hangouts.

Exiting the stage, sweat soaks through my shirt as I head into my dressing room. Opting to cool off instead of regroup, I

242

go straight into the shower. The cold water feels amazing as it slides down my skin. Tipping my head back under the stream, I focus on the sensation.

From this position, the only thing I can hear is the water rushing past my ears, causing me to miss the sound of someone else entering the bathroom. It isn't until a warm body slides against mine that I realize I am not alone.

For a fleeting moment, I think it might be Ellie. That she came back to me even though we don't have anything straightened out. The breasts against my back are much larger than Ellie's and the lips that land between my shoulders are lower than where hers would have set.

With only a few seconds to get the jump on whoever joined me, I turn away quickly, pushing off them and reaching for my towel. I manage to hop out of the shower, water still running while they try to stay upright from my escape.

The woman squeals as she gets a face full of cold water. "What the hell are you doing?" she sputters.

"What the hell am *I* doing? What the hell are you doing?! Who is in there?" I should go get security right away, but considering she is naked in the shower and much smaller than me, I don't think she poses much of a physical threat.

Pulling back the curtain, I find a shivering Paris in the spot I vacated. Despite her body trembling from the cold, she poses her body seductively.

"Aww, you don't seem too happy to see me," she faux pouts.

"What the hell are you doing, Paris! You aren't allowed to be back here and you sure as shit aren't authorized to get in my shower."

"Come on, Jack. I was only trying to help you unwind. You've been so grumpy the last few days, I thought you could use a pick me up."

"You are insane, woman. This is far beyond acceptable journalist behavior. I'm getting security to remove you immediately. You are banned from all future Ryder events."

"You can't do that!" she whines. All her attempted seduction is gone as she stomps her foot. Whatever dramatic effect she hoped for was quelled by the splash.

"I just did. You have two minutes to get dressed, otherwise Martin will throw you out in what you have on."

I exit the bathroom at the same time Eliza walks in. "Everything okay? I thought I heard yelling?"

"Everything is not okay. Your little reporter protégé bust in on me in the shower and tried to join."

Eliza's eyes widen in shock. "She did what?"

"How did she even get back here?" I question, knowing I don't need to repeat myself.

A cool mask shutters over my publicist's face when she says, "She said she wanted to do a post-show live. One of the interns was supposed to be escorting her. I'll get to the bottom of this."

"You know we don't do anything after the show for thirty minutes to come down from the adrenaline high."

"I know, but I thought just this once—"

"You thought wrong," Declan interrupts. He, Grayson, Bryce, and Martin joining us.

"Martin, can you please escort the woman in my shower out of the venue and revoke her access? Permanently."

"Let's not be hasty," Eliza remarks. "Backroad Radio is a huge outlet for us."

"They have other journalists. And even if they didn't, I don't want her anywhere near me. She's lucky I'm not pressing charges for assault."

Appearing as if she's going to make excuses for Paris, Grayson breaks in. "If this was a male reporter who got into the shower naked with a female client, would you be siding with the journalist?"

"No, no. You're right," she agrees. "I knew she was flirty, but that is the name of the game for these media personalities. She crossed the line today. I will make sure she never covers another event you're at again if she even keeps her job."

"Thank you," I reply as Martin drags a shouting Paris out of the room. She says something about Eliza who accompanies the pair to ensure no other media see the spectacle.

"You okay, bro?" Grayson asks as a scowling Declan locks the door behind them.

"Yeah, I'm fine. She didn't touch me, but it was a shock."

"I bet," Bryce whistles. "As much as I love DJing, I don't know if I want to make it big if it means attracting crazies."

"It's a balancing act," Grayson notes solemnly. To my knowledge, none of us have had to deal with anything that extreme, but we have our fair share of overzealous fans.

"Didn't you say Ellie was trying to blame something on Paris the other night? Could she have heard her planning this?" my older brother asks.

"Maybe? I didn't ask because I assumed she was trying to cover her ass and thought she was making it up to discredit Eliza." Part of me wants to hold on to that small kernel of hope that Ellie didn't play me the way I thought. The rest of me wants to keep our walls up high.

"What did Eliza overhear?" Bryce questions.

He wasn't around when she told us about Ellie's conversation with her dad. As much as I don't want to rehash it, I relay it to him, his brow knitting in confusion.

"That's what Eliza said she overheard?"

"Yeah," I reply resignedly, but Declan must see something in Bryce's expression because he probes him further. "Why?"

"I overheard that phone call, too, and Eliza left out some parts."

"What do you mean you overheard it?"

"I was in my bunk playing around with some beats when my earbuds died. As the noise canceling cut off, I realized Ellie was on the phone and I didn't want to crawl out and have her think I was eavesdropping the entire time."

"So you stayed and eavesdropped the rest of the time?" Grayson surmises.

"What else was I supposed to do?"

"Did you see Eliza there?"

"No, but my curtains were closed."

"What did you hear that was different?"

"Her dad was pressuring her to get him on the tour, but she said no. She only agreed to mention it to y'all after he badgered her about it and based on her tone, I don't think she was going to."

Declan and Grayson appear a mix of relieved and conflicted. If I had to guess, they are glad we cleared that up but now are upset she's gone and we didn't—I didn't—give her the chance to apologize. We were so quick to assume the worst and not remember we've known this girl since before anyone knew, let alone cared, about our name.

"What about the job?" I ask. As much as it was the being used thing for me, I was also hurt that she was planning a future without me. Her expiration date comment has been haunting me since the moment it left her lips.

"She said she never planned to take it and wanted to stay in Nashville. That's when he brought up you and the job."

"He brought me up?"

"Yeah, he knows you two are dating, and he was not happy about it."

What the hell? I've never been anything but nice and professional toward him.

"Don't feel bad," he says when he notices my annoyed expression. "He doesn't seem to have a high opinion of musicians in general."

"His whole job is supporting musicians," Grayson gripes.

"That's what Ellie said! Anyway, it seems as if Eliza didn't give you the full convo. Maybe she didn't hear it all? Unless she was hiding in one of your bunks, I was closer to the bathroom than she was."

"Thanks, man." I say, patting him on the back. "That is all good to know."

37

I SPEND the entire flight to LA replaying the fight with Ellie in my mind and comparing Bryce's version of the phone call to Eliza's. How could I not give her a chance to explain? Especially after screwing up the visit with her grandmother so royally. I never even found out what the big news was.

I have no idea how I am going to face my sister after everything that went down. The two of us are normally pretty close, but I have felt the distance lately. I don't know if Ellie told her what happened or if those rumors her dad mentioned reached her. I guess we'll find out when she comes to the show tonight.

As always, Lainey gets there early and insists on zhuzhing up the outfits wardrobe selected. After changing Grayson's t-shirt and forcing a leather bracelet on Declan, she makes her way to me. It's hard to tell by her demeanor if she knows anything. Lainey has the best poker face of us all. She had to get around not only two parents but also three big brothers.

Without a word, she pulls a hat out from behind her back. I eye it dubiously.

"Relax, there isn't a fake spider in it," she chides. Clue number one she may have talked to Ellie: the fake spider ASMR incident.

"That'd be a dumb prank," I say, trying to play off the comment.

"Wouldn't it?" is her only reply. Touché, Laines.

"I take it you want me back in a ball cap?"

"I don't, the people do." Placing it on my head, she nods in approval and then eyes the basket of snacks on my dressing table. "There are lots of voodoo chips in there. That's curious." Is it hot in here? I am sweating.

"Lainey! Leave him alone. We know you talked to Ellie," Declan chastises.

"You know nothing!"

"If you hadn't talked to her, you'd be up our ass asking where she was. And if you thought it was any reason other than the truth, you would have demanded she come back."

"You are such a fun-sucker, Declan," she whines.

"Hasn't the man been through enough? We can't have him passing out before the show," Grayson coos to pacify her. I don't know why he is trying to make her feel better. I am the one on the verge of a stroke.

"Fine," she says, flopping down on our couch after grabbing a bag of said chips.

"Fine? You don't have more to say about that?" I ask cautiously.

"About what? You dating my bestie behind my back or you accusing her of being a backstabbing wench?"

"You called her a wench?" Grayson asks.

"No, I did not."

"Tomayto, tomahto," Lainey replies. "Which one do you want my thoughts on?"

"Both?" I reply in answer to her question. Even I can hear the uncertainty in my voice. I shouldn't be afraid of my little sister, but I am.

"Am I mad you dated my best friend? No. She may have thought she hid it well, but I've known she had a crush on you forever. She forgets I know all of her tells. It didn't bother me back then because she never acted on it and you were oblivious, not to mention too old for us."

"And now?"

"And now I think you guys would be a perfect couple if you would get your heads out of your asses."

Grayson snickers beside me, earning him a glare from Lainey. "I could start on your failures in love if you would prefer?"

"No, thank you," he replies, ducking his head.

"Even with my head out of my ass, I think it's too late," I admit.

"Maybe it is." She shrugs.

"Is it?" It's one thing to think it—it's another thing to know it. I'd be focused on Lainey's reaction being negative. I hadn't considered what I'd do if she was okay with us dating. Now that I know she is, I can't help but wonder if it's a moot point.

"I'm not getting in the middle of this. You two are both grown adults. You're capable of deciding what you want all on your own. Would I love to have Ellie as a sister? Of course. But if that isn't in the cards for you two, then I will make my peace."

"And your thoughts on the 'wench' part?" I recall the latter part of her question.

"Oh that." Unexpectedly, Lainey pinches my nipple and twists hard.

"Ouch! Damn it, that hurt."

"It was supposed to," she deadpans. "How could you ever think Ellie would be using you or this family? She has practically been a Ryder for fifteen years."

"I don't know. Emotions were high already from her being

mad at me and then Eliza filled my head with nonsense. I let things get away from me.”

“You think?”

“What do I do now?” I ask solemnly. I’ve never wanted to give someone a second chance before. Technically, this is still her first chance but regardless, I have no idea how to get her back. I don’t know how she feels about me. She could hate me for all I know.

“Now you wait.”

“Wait? That’s your big advice?”

“I’m sorry. Did you not want my help? You know how Ellie is. She needs time to process and digest, make a pro-con list. No matter what, you won’t get anywhere over the phone. You may as well wait until you’re back in Nashville and can see her in person.”

That’s fair. I can’t think of anything I can do virtually that would fix the mess we made. We need to sit down and talk through things like adults. What does it say about my commitment that I’m throwing in the towel at the first sign of trouble?

AFTER TWO SOLD-OUT SHOWS, we finally make it back to Nashville. I want to go to Ellie’s immediately and sweep her off her feet. But after a long and stressful week, I know I will be better served after a good night’s sleep.

The first thing I do when I get back to my house is scream bloody murder. Standing in the middle of my kitchen is a silhouette. Flipping on the lights, I find it is a full size cut out of Lainey. When my heart stops racing, make my way over to it and find a note attached.

Making a mental note to text Lainey about the heart attack her cut out caused. I pull out my phone and go to the folder. Clicking on a file name, "The Apology," the knot in my chest loosens at the sound of Ellie's voice.

Hey, Rock Star. I'm so glad you're here. I've missed you. I know you might think I didn't based on how we left things, but you'd be wrong.

The time away has given me time to reflect and as easy as it would be to blame our disagreement on you for jumping to conclusions you should have known weren't true, that wouldn't be fair. I have as much culpability, if not more in what went down.

I should have been more forthcoming with you about a lot of things. I was enjoying our time together so much that I kept putting everything off to be the problem of future Ellie. As easy as that was in the moment, it has sucked now that I am future Ellie. I did us both a disservice by not facing my concerns with you head on and allowing you to do the same.

I care about you deeply. I always have, but now that I know you, really know you. I can safely say that my childhood crush has turned into a grown up love. I know we haven't said that word and it's too soon, but you've had my heart since I was ten years old. I think it's time you knew that.

I know this is a lot to take in. Take all the time you need. When you're ready, I would love to talk about how future Ellie and future Jack could share that future together.

This audio is everything I didn't know I needed. I was fully prepared to fall on my sword for the things that I had done. I wasn't prepared for her to do the same or to realize how much that means to me. We both had faults in our breakup. But hopefully together we can overcome our issues and move forward.

I've put off all my plans, but now it's time to set them into motion again so I can be the man Ellie deserves, a man she can be proud to call hers. I finally realize that doesn't mean having goals *to* get her to love me. She does that already. It means having goals *because* she loves me. She's my recharging station as much as I am hers. I need to give her the opportunity to support me the same way I want to support her.

38

Ellie

WORKING the register at Misty's store, I grumble for the millionth time how dumb of an idea it was to leave Jack an audio. He probably didn't even listen to it. Lainey swears if I stay patient, it will be worth it, but that's big talk coming from the least patient person I know.

Doing everything I can to not think about it, I agreed to work with Misty in her boutique. She offered to show me the day-to-day operation of running a store and is even willing to give me first right of refusal when she finally lets the place go. It's an opportunity I couldn't pass up.

My father was pissed to learn I was working as a glorified shopgirl but after everything that went down and what he said to me, I don't care. It's been a long time since he supported me, financially or otherwise. I think I was holding on to hope that he would one day be the dad I needed, but that ship sailed long ago. Until he can treat me with the respect I deserve, our contact will be minimal.

Deep in thought, I almost miss the bell chime above the door. "Hi welcome to—" I greet absentmindedly before peering up to see Jack. I freeze.

"Hi," he replies, open smile on his face. "Cool place."

"Um, thanks?"

"You wouldn't happen to have any recommendations, would you?" He came here for recommendations? This is weird, but I'll play along.

"Of course. Shopping for yourself or . . . ?" He smirks when he glances around to confirm we only sell women's clothing. If he's going to play, I'm going to play.

"Not for me. It's for a girl."

"I see. What can you tell me about her?"

"Hmm, well, she's on the taller side with these gorgeous long legs that perfectly wrap around my waist and shoulders. She has light blonde hair that reminds me of a woodland fairy with a sweet personality to match." I nod along as he describes me, pretending to browse our selection.

"What else?"

"She has an obsession with voodoo chips and has a tendency for violence if you wake her up too suddenly. She loves making lists, and being organized, and when I press my thumb into her clit just right." His smile morphs into a smirk at that before his eyes turn soft. "She's smart and kind. Patient as hell. She's the best thing I never knew I needed, but had all along."

I suck in a breath at that sentiment. He did always have me. I think no matter what happens, he'll always have a piece. Swallowing my emotion, I try to keep up with our pretense.

"You know, I don't think we have what she needs here."

"No?" he turns to me, gaze vulnerable and questioning.

"I think what she needs is you."

"I think I need her, too."

We both stand there, eyes locked on one another until his

impatience wins out. Scooping me up in his arms and he brings his mouth to mine. Kissing me softly, he whispers, "Fuck, I missed you, Wildflower."

"I missed you, too." As if my admission breaks his thread of control, he grips the back of my head with one hand and tilts my mouth back up to his, plunging his tongue inside.

"Did you like your present?" I ask, heaving for air when he finally pulls away.

"No. Cut out Lainey is creepy as hell," he replies. "And being able to hear your voice but not actually having you was pure torture. I want you in my house. In my bed. On my couch. Everywhere. My world was bleak without you in it. Don't make me go through that again."

"Don't make me leave."

"Never," he whispers as a vow. "I'm sorry for not giving you the benefit of the doubt. For not giving you the chance to explain. For not making sure you knew in no uncertain terms that what we had was forever."

"I want that, too."

"Good. Because now that I know you love me, I'm never letting go."

"You're going to have to if any customers come in." I laugh.

"Can't I just buy the store? Then I could do whatever I want."

"You could but you'll have to beat me to it."

Leaning back until we are eye to eye, he gives me a curious expression. "It seems we have a lot to discuss."

"I'd say so."

"Alright, future Ellie. Lay it on me." And I do.

39

TODAY IS one of my favorites of the year: Opening Day. And we are spending it at the ballpark. I've always said that if I didn't go into music, I would have wanted to try to play ball. Not that I had a ton of talent, but I wasn't bad. With the right coaching and training, who knows what I could have been.

It's been eight months since Ellie and I fixed our issues. I'm excited to enjoy my third favorite pastime with her—the first two being performing on stage and between her thighs. While I could easily afford suite tickets, even my money wouldn't have gotten us in the friends and family suite. My girl has connections.

Macy works in the sports division of the same agency that reps us. She wasn't able to make today's game, so she gave them to Ellie. She doesn't even realize what a treat she's in for. My mind is already reeling with plans to fuck her in her new Nashville Songbirds jersey. But for now, we are celebrating.

Today, Ellie officially got the keys to her new storefront. She spent some time shadowing Misty before they reached a deal for Ellie to take over the mortgage. I wanted to buy it outright for her, but she insisted on doing this 'the right way.'

The money her grandmother gifted her, along with a business loan and some investor funds are going to pay for a renovation of the space. A friend from college is starring in a renovation show that focuses on small businesses in Nashville and Ellie's boutique will be one of the featured businesses.

"Cheers, baby. Happy closing day," I tell her with a kiss to the temple.

"Thank you," she beams. "I'm not the only one with something to celebrate. Don't you get your first cast of whiskey this week?"

After releasing a limited edition whiskey with the Kennedys, I decided I wanted to create a brand of my own. They were gracious enough to show me the ropes and with their help and some investors, Wildflower Whiskey was born. My distillery is located here in Nashville and each barrel is lined with flowers before it is sealed infuses a slightly floral taste into it. The idea came to me listening to Ellie order her favorite, lavender latte. It took a few months to get the recipes right, but that's why I hired the best master distiller I could find.

When I pitched the concept and the name to Ellie, she cried. Then she dove headfirst into helping me figure out everything I needed to do to get started. My little planner has become an expert on Tennessee liquor laws.

As we settle into our seats, I hear a gasp from in front of me. When I glance forward, a tiny brunette is staring at me.

"Um, hi?" I wave at her awkwardly.

"You're Jack Ryder." I nod because yes, I am. I wasn't expecting to run into a fan here since everyone is related or close to an MLB player, but I guess they enjoy music, too.

"I'm Carina," she says as if I should know her. Shit. Should I?

Noticing my panic, she waves it off. "I'm Robby Becker's girl-friend. Wife now, technically. But I was his girlfriend kind of, when you guys recorded that video for me."

"Oh, yeah!" I say as the connection comes back to me. A couple of years ago, the pitcher for the Songbirds asked us to record a video playing a song for his girlfriend's birthday. She worked at a nonprofit and he was sponsoring a lunch program in her honor.

"How is nonprofit life?" I ask. Ever since I volunteered at that hospital in Pittsburgh, I've been searching for something locally I could get involved in.

"It's great. When I moved here, Robby and I founded our own that focuses on helping kids who face food insecurity with healthy meals and sports programs. We're expanding to offer an art camp this summer since there are so many great artists here."

"Have you considered adding music? Not all kids are athleti-cally gifted," Ellie chimes in from beside me. "Jack here has the body of an athlete, but I didn't grow into my limbs until senior year."

"You were cute when you were gangly," I coo, earning me a glare with no heat behind it.

"We'd thought about it," Carina replies. "But I wouldn't even know where to start. The sports are Robby's thing. Do you know anyone I could talk to that might want to help sponsor a music camp? I'm all about offering anything the kids would be interested in."

"You know, I just might," I say as the wheels turn in my head.

THE SONGBIRDS PULL out a win for their season opener and thanks to Macy's hookup, we are able to congratulate the guys after the game. The Beckers invite us to join them at their post-game celebration, but I think it will be wild enough with professional baseball players. No need to add a country singer to the mix. Selfishly, I want to get my girl home and make some of the dirty thoughts filtering through my brain come true.

When we get back to my place, I'm on Ellie the second we close the door. Lifting her up to press her back against it, I wrap her thighs around me as I take her lips in a crushing kiss. It's sloppy, passionate, and gives her a preview on exactly how I plan for the rest of the night to go.

"I have a surprise for you," I whisper against her mouth. Carrying her over to my kitchen island, I place her down before disappearing to the bar I have set up in the living room.

"What's that?" she asks, eyeing the bottle I come back with.

"It's the first of many Wildflower Whiskey bottles. This one is infused with roses."

"And you want a repeat of me kissing it into your mouth?"

"Not quite," I answer setting it down beside her. I slowly push the jersey off her shoulders while my fingers lift her tank top, thankful she went braless today. Moving to her jeans next, I direct her to lift her hips so I can pull them, along with her panties off.

"Nothing has ever looked as delicious in my kitchen as you do," I tell her.

"That would be a bigger compliment if you cooked."

"Sassy," I comment, tweaking her nipple. She jolts in surprise.

"What is the plan then?"

"I want to see how much better this will taste off your sweet skin."

Before she can ask for an explanation, I crack open the bottle and pour a little onto her collar bones. The amber liquid drips down her chest and I meet it at her on her breast with my tongue. She moans appreciatively as I suck the pink peak into my mouth.

Moving one hand down to knead her thigh, I use the other to tug her ponytail and expose more of her neck to me. Kissing until I reach her ear, I nip at her lobe. "Lay back, baby."

She obeys without argument, even when I pull her legs to dangle off the quartz surface. Once I have her how I want her, I drip more whiskey on her body. Sipping it out of her belly button, I lift my head to watch her reaction to the cool liquor hitting her clit. When a throaty cry leaves her lips, I descend on the sensitive bud, circling it with my tongue.

Her hands move into my hair and the vibration of my moan has her pulling tighter. "This is the best thing I have ever tasted."

"Jack, please."

"That's it, baby," I coo. Taking a sip into my mouth, I press my lips against her without swallowing. She shudders as the whiskey floods her center and I lick up all I can, letting the rest drip onto the counter.

My cock is straining against my jeans but I don't dare touch it for fear I would come on contact. Needing her to get there, I increase the pressure of my tongue flicking across her clit. After a few moments, her thighs tremble and her orgasm washes over her. Licking her through the aftershocks, I stand when she lets out a soft sigh.

"I'm not done with you yet, sweetheart." Standing I pull off my shirt. Overcome by my need to be inside her, I unbutton my pants and push them and my boxers down below my ass. They fall to my ankles but I don't move to remove them completely. With her spread out below me on the counter, I have enough range of motion.

Ellie spreads her legs wider, inviting me in as she stares up at me, lip pulled between her teeth. "Ready for me?"

"So ready." Her reply fades into a moan as a rub the tip of my cock against her overstimulated bundle of nerves.

"No teasing."

"No chance of that," I say before I slam inside her. When my thighs hit hers, I fold her legs over my arms and lean forward. The shift in angle allows me to get even deeper and hit that spot I know makes her see stars.

My speed is punishing, having driven myself wild tasting her. "Fuck, Ellie. You feel so good. I'll never get enough of this pussy."

Sliding back into her, I almost stutter in my rhythm as she clenches around me. My hold on her legs keeping her in place, I thrust harder into her until her soft whimpers turn into incoherent cries.

"There it is. You're so close." Desperate for her to get there, I say the phrase that I know will tip her over the edge. "Be a good girl and come for me, Ellie."

As if I flipped a switch, her wet heat grips my cock as she writhes below me. He back bows against the counter, pushing her tits in the air. Hearing my name cross her lips as she orgasms while seeing the marks from my tongue on her skin, forces me over the edge with her.

"Holy fuck," I pant when I finally catch my breath. "You are perfection."

"That was all you, Rock Star."

Nuzzling into her neck, I take in the scent of her rose shampoo mixed with the rose whiskey on her skin. "Let's get cleaned up."

"The lily flavor comes in next week," I comment as I carry her up the stairs.

"At this rate, I think you're going to keep coming up with infusions to taste them off me," she giggles.

"My favorite flavor will always be you, Wildflower. And I have a lifetime to enjoy it."

EPILOGUE

Ellie

RUNNING AROUND MY BOUTIQUE, I stop in my tracks as the bell above the door rings. It's too early for someone to be here for the grand opening. At least someone who isn't my bestie. Sticking my head out the back, I see Cassidy, my newest employee.

"Hi, Ellie," she says, a smile plastered on her face. "It's amazing in here."

Stopping to take in the space, I realize that it does. Raven, a friend from college who helped me design the store as part of her HRN show, *Music City Revitalized*. The show doesn't air until September, but our involvement has already been used in teaser content.

I can't believe this day is finally here. It's been a labor of love the past year to get here. Between buying the space and renovating to choosing items to stock, it's been a whirlwind. I couldn't have done it without Jack by my side. Between reminding me to eat lunch to forcing me to take days off when the stress was too much, he's been my rock.

I'm so proud of everything he's accomplished, too. Not only is Wildflower Whiskey critically acclaimed, it's also a consumer favorite. On top of that, his conversation to Carina Becker at the Songbirds game we attended last year turned fruitful. The Becker Foundation hosted their first music camp this summer. Grayson and Declan were both busy with their side projects, but Jack wrangled several up-and-coming artists to help and served as the official spokesperson.

It was such a success that they'll be adding music as an option to their after-school programs this summer. Not only are more kids going to get music training but retired and aspiring musicians will get the chance to earn money and practice their craft.

"You seem lost in thought, baby," Jack croons from beside me. "Thinking about me?"

"Always," I half joke.

"Are you ready for tonight?"

"I think so. It's a soft opening, only family and friends. That shouldn't be too bad." Jack stills my hand from running over the tattoo I got on my wrist after getting back together. I figured since he inked me on his skin. I could do the same. I love the symbolism of the clover on one hand representing my past and the Jack of Hearts on the other representing my future.

My family and friends have been supportive of the store since day one. All the girls can't wait to abuse their friends and family discount. Mom has told every woman at her country club about it. Even Dad was excited about the idea. It took him longer to warm up to the idea of me and Jack but once he realized he got as much say in my love life as I did his, he came around. Our relationship has gotten better since then.

"You say that now. You're going to have to put a cap on how

much my mom can buy or she'll buy up everything before the public grand opening this weekend."

I laugh knowing he's right even though my store is geared toward a younger demographic. She'd buy me out if she could. Mama C's reaction was the opposite of my father's. She might be more excited about Jack and I being together than Jack and I. When we told her we were dating, I worried she'd dehydrate from crying.

As excited as I am for everyone to see the finished store, I am most excited to have all my favorite people back together. Declan can't make it as he is touring his solo EP, but Grayson and his girlfriend plan to be here. And Lainey is flying out, too. She's been living it up with her fancy stylist job in LA for the past year. Not only is she coming back for the first time since Christmas, but she also promised a major surprise.

"I know there will be food circulating the party, but I think we should grab a quick bite now. You'll be too busy talking with everyone to enjoy any of the food," Jack says, wrapping his arms around my waist from behind. My stomach grumbles at the mention of food and I sense his silent laughter against my back.

"Alright, feed me."

"Careful what you wish for, Wildflower."

Jack

WEARING A PINK TULLE DRESS, Ellie is as fairy-like as ever as she floats around her store chatting with our friends and family.

I'm so fucking proud of my girl. I still remember the dated

shell this build was when I found her here a year ago. Not only is the space totally transformed, but she is, too. She still loves to make a list and plan things to death, but now she puts those plans into action. I've learned to harness that list making power for good by having her create a naughty and a nice bucket list that we can use to check things off. It's hard to decide which one is my favorite.

I can't help the smile that stretches across my face as I watch her embrace her friends. Lainey hasn't arrived yet, but I know they're all excited to be reunited. As much time and energy as I spent worrying about how my relationship with Ellie would affect Lainey, nothing has changed. They were basically sisters before. If anything they should be thanking me for making it official.

Not yet, but soon. The ring I got Ellie is sitting heavy in my safe. Grayson tried to convince me to propose tonight, but I didn't want anything to overshadow her night. She worked way too hard to make this dream a reality for me to steal her thunder with a proposal.

We have a vacation planned in the fall once Grayson's show wraps and Declan has a break in his schedule. I can't think of a better time to propose than surrounded by family. I've been secretly talking to her brother to see if he can arrange leave to surprise her and, of course, Macy and Alexis. I've long accepted those four are a packaged deal after the third *Singing Sensation* watch party that took over my living room.

"Everything looks awesome," Brady Miller says as he and several other players from the Songbirds approach.

"I'm excited to see what Carina comes home with," Robby Becker admits. "Based on what I have seen so far, it will all be killer."

"Ellie has a good eye," I reply. "She'll pick something that will knock your socks off."

"Let's hope more than just our socks."

I shake my head. I've never seen men who are bigger of simps for their women, except for me, maybe. I can't say I blame them. All our women are incredible.

"If you'll excuse me boys, I need to extract the woman of the hour from my mother. She has a speech to make."

Making my way across the room, I pull Ellie away from my mom. After a speech thanking everyone for being here, she opens the register and everyone shops.

"No Lainey yet?" I question.

"Her flight was delayed," she murmurs, leaning into me. "She should be here any minute."

"What's the register limit? Lainey is going to have a field day with these selections."

"Don't I know it. She already has women lined up for the pieces she helped me choose." Ellie turns in my arms until we're face to face. I kiss her gently on the lips, granting me one of her beautiful smiles.

"Any idea what her surprise is?"

"No id—oh fuck," I mutter right as my sister walks in with NBA star Xavier Dillon on her arm. The man himself isn't even the biggest surprise. It's the giant rock on her finger that has both mine and Ellie's eyes widening in surprise. The air in the room stands still as everyone stares at the guest joining the fray. Out of nowhere, I hear my oldest brother mutter beside me, "Things are about to get interesting."

THANK you for taking the time to ARC Broken Chords. This version of the story was uploaded before final proofing. If you see any errors, feel free to send them to the author, but keep in mind a final round of edits is underway!

I sincerely hope you enjoyed this story. It was my first non-sports romance. I can't wait to bring you more. Declan's book is the next in the series and will be coming in 2025. You can preorder it today.

Be sure to subscribe to my newsletter to read about Ellie and Jack sneaking away to the Mighty Muskrats game and to hear Jack's dirty rendition of "Take Me Out to the Ball Game."

ACKNOWLEDGMENTS

As my first non-sports romance, this book really took me for a ride.

Thank you to Bobbi Maclaren for helping transform my initial draft into a viable story, EJL Editing undertaking my hot mess draft, and Truly Yours PR for managing my ARC campaign.

I also want to thank all the country artists who gave me the musical inspiration for my Ryders.

Extra special shout out to Maggie for reverse bullying me to get this book complete when my drive was low. You and Molly's are the best motivators around.

No acknowledgement would be complete without thanking the my amazing readers for continuing to support me and inspire me to keep writing. I couldn't do this without you!

ABOUT THE AUTHOR

Kat Summers is a millennial spicy, contemporary romance author living in Tennessee. Her books are filled with just enough angst to hurt your feelings, witty banter to make you laugh, and steamy, swoon-worthy men to make you blush. She creates stories with strong, sassy heroines who can hold their own but love being called a "good girl."

When she isn't writing, she can be found reading (duh) and spending time with her family and furbaby or gossiping over Mexican food. Fueled by Diet Dr Pepper and a dream, Kat is excited to bring the couples that live in her mind to the rest of the world. Follow her for sneak peeks of future projects.

Find her at @katsummerswrites on all the things.

katsummerswrites.com
facebook.com/katsummerswrites
instagram.com/katsummerswrites
tiktok.com/@katsummerswrites
https://amzn.to/43lCnWf
threads.net/@katsummerswrites
pinterest.com/katsummerswrites

ALSO BY KAT SUMMERS

Nashville Songbirds Series

Filled with sexy athletes and strong females leads, this sports romance series follows players of the Nashville Songbirds baseball team, the women they fall for, and a few friends along the way. Prepare for witty banter, heart and panty melting MMCs, and plenty of spice.

Backcheck Heart

Backcheck Heart is a grumpy x sunshine opposites attract sports romance with a protective MMC who wants nothing more than to prove to his girl she is worth the world. This hockey novella is full of sugar, spice, and no third act breakup.

Zealous Intentions

In order to land the biggest client of her career, workaholic Molly needs help from the flirty tattoo artist who has had his eye on her since they first met. Will this tatted cinnamon roll MMC get the girl? With a little fake dating and a whole lot of spice, he just might.